BLIND TO MIDNIGHT

BOOKS BY REED FARREL COLEMAN

THE NICK RYAN SERIES

Sleepless City

Blind to Midnight

ROBERT B. PARKER'S JESSE STONE SERIES

Blind Spot

The Devil Wins

Debt to Pay

The Hangman's Sonnet

Colorblind

The Bitterest Pill

THE GUS MURPHY SERIES

Where It Hurts

What You Break

THE GULLIVER DOWD MYSTERIES

Dirty Work

Valentino Pier

The Boardwalk

Love and Fear

THE MOE PRAGER SERIES

Walking the Perfect Square

Redemption Street

The James Deans

Soul Patch

Empty Ever After

Innocent Monster

Hurt Machine

Onion Street

The Hollow Girl

THE DYLAN KLEIN SERIES

Life Goes Sleeping

Little Easter

*They Don't Play
Stickball in Milwaukee*

THE JOE SERPE SERIES

Hose Monkey

The Fourth Victim

STANDALONE NOVELS

Tower (with Ken Bruen)

Bronx Requiem (with John Roe)

Gun Church

REED FARREL COLEMAN

BLIND TO MIDNIGHT

A NICK RYAN NOVEL

BLACK STONE PUBLISHING

Printed in the United States of America

First edition: 2024
ISBN 979-8-8748-2390-0
Fiction / Mystery & Detective / General

Version 1

Blackstone Publishing
31 Mistletoe Rd.
Ashland, OR 97520

www.BlackstonePublishing.com

For Darby Roselyn Martin

We do not create our destiny; we participate in its unfolding.

—DAVID RICHO

PROLOGUE

SEPTEMBER 11, 2001, 11:43 P.M.

He is the last man alive. Or at least, things would be less complicated if he were.

He is standing on the platform at the Smith and Ninth Street subway station. The tallest station in Brooklyn looms over the Gowanus Canal. The canal, so polluted with toxins and heavy metals that you don't have to be Jesus to walk on its waters. A writer once joked it was the only body of water that was 90 percent guns. Nobody is joking tonight. Nobody! Not about anything.

The lone man is waiting for the G train. He smells the acrid wind-blown smoke continuing to rise from where the World Trade Center stood. His blue Mets cap is squashed low on his forehead, his eyes fixed on the pebbled concrete under his running shoes. He hopes that by not looking up he might be invisible. It makes no rational sense. Today the world stopped making sense. Still, he can't help but peek at the place where the towers once stood. He quickly looks away. The pile smolders. Ash, shreds of paper, and carcinogenic dust still rise into the air, carried by the prevailing winds. A downy coating of gray snowflakes falls around him.

The city is eerily silent. The sirens that all day filled the air have gone quiet. He has never experienced the city so hushed. Even the tracks are mute. He wonders if any train will come. The only things he hears are in his head: his scrambled thoughts and the blood rushing in his ears.

He feels he is no longer alone. He forces himself to glance across the tracks to the Coney Island–bound platform. *No one.* He looks right. *No one.* Left . . . There, by the maw of the staircase where thousands spill out onto the platform each morning and get swallowed up each night, a light flickers. Then nothing. *Was the dancing shadow caused by falling debris?* He dismisses it as a measure of his unease but moves farther along the platform. Movement is good. Movement helps fight the anxiety.

He has to get to the Queens storage unit where he keeps what his American friend calls a bugout bag. He tried phoning car services. The lines rang and rang or were endlessly busy. He tried to hail a cab. He might as well have tried to will himself to fly. He got his bike out of the basement. Two flat tires. *Why today? Why me?* He has no answers. He eyes the buildings below in Gowanus, in Carroll Gardens. Everyone is in shock, hiding away in their apartments, watching the horrors over and over again, wrapping the walls around themselves like brick-and-mortar wombs. He thinks they're trying to wish the day away, to de-blade the box cutters, to un-crash the planes, to put the desperate jumpers back into their ergonomic desk chairs. All the wishing in the world cannot undo things already done. He knows this better than most.

The tracks clank. The sound of salvation. He breathes again, exhaling for what feels like the first time all day. He brushes the September snow off the shoulders of his jacket in anticipation of stepping onto the subway. He goes over the steps of his escape in his head: *Get to the storage unit in Astoria. Walk or hitch to LaGuardia.* There are no flights, but there is a car for him at the Nifty lot on Ditmars Boulevard. His only good fortune was in getting the reservation. From what he hears, people are snapping up every available rental car to get out of the city. Once he has the car, it's straight to New Hampshire to lie low until he can cross into Canada. He hasn't aroused suspicion because this is when he would normally go to work. No one is paying attention anyway. Even the woman in the token booth, her face as blank as a zombie's, waved him on.

"It's free. Just go through the exit door, mister. You be careful now."

He thought to ask her if any trains are running, but he didn't want to hear the wrong answer.

The tracks clank again. He looks up. His anxiety isn't playing tricks on him. A tall figure, half in shadows, is coming up the platform toward him. The man isn't running, but there is a determination in his stride. He girds himself, for he has no doubt the stranger is here to do him harm. Although he can't make out his face, he feels the stranger's stare burning through the night.

His shirt is wet. His sweat is sour, stinking of panic. *Where's the fucking train?* The tracks answer with silence. He is ready to run. He's been running his whole life. The striding man is closer now, maybe twenty yards away. *Nineteen, eighteen, seventeen, sixteen . . .*

The strider stops. "Yo, buddy," he calls out, lighting a cigarette. The man's white face glows red and yellow in the match flame. There's nothing particularly remarkable about it. The flame goes out. The man exhales smoke in a long, unhurried stream. "I know this is illegal, but hey, fuck it." He waves the cigarette around, the orange tip a flitting firefly. "If anything comes of this day, at least I can do this, right?"

"Right."

"The G running?"

"I am hoping so," he says, still ready to run.

"Lotta hoping going on today. Woman downstairs in the token booth, she didn't know neither. I guess we wait."

"Yes, as you say. We wait."

"You lose anyone today . . . at the Trade Center, I mean?"

"No." He is annoyed at Cigarette Man asking such a rude question but understands that people are frightened and frightened people like to talk. He's frightened too, but for reasons very much his own.

Cigarette Man is now silent.

Thank Christ the man has shut up. He almost crosses himself. Doesn't.

He notices something moving along the stone ballast between the tracks, bends over to look. A lone rat, its grimy fur agleam under the platform lights. As he leans forward something whines past his ear. *Fuck!* The bullet ricochets off the platform. His body reacts reflexively. He tucks his left shoulder, falls, thumping down hard. He's up, fighting to catch his wind. He runs across the tracks, zigzagging toward the Coney Island–bound platform. He hops over one third rail, then another. He turns back, sees a flash. This bullet ricochets off the track. The spark lights up the night like a tiny dying sun. He's nearly there. A third shot, a fourth shot misses. Just a few more steps . . .

"Don't shoot him, you fuckin' idiot!" A squat guy steps out of the shadows on the Coney Island–bound platform. He shakes his head in disgust. "How many times I gotta tell you?"

He doesn't recognize Squat Guy or Cigarette Man, but he knows why they are here. He runs down the track, trying to land his feet on the wooden ties. He has to keep moving. He calls to the men in broken English, "I am disappearing. Let me go. Tell him I will say nothing. I am swear to you on this." He had always told himself he would never beg for his life if it came to that, but here he is, panicked and begging. It's moot. They are here to kill him. To spare him would be to impose their own death sentences.

He's done pleading. Running as fast as he can, he turns his head left, then right to see where Cigarette Man and Squat Guy are. He is surprised because they're not keeping up. *Good!* He has almost cleared the end of the platform. Ahead of him, a curving, unbroken line of descending track. He will keep running until he has a big-enough lead on his pursuers. At that point, he'll figure something out. He always does. If he got out of Belgrade, Rome, and Pordenone, he is sure he can get out of this.

Encouraged because he is so easily outpacing the men sent here to end him, he stops checking on them. He feels something brush up against his foot. He looks down. The rat! Startled, he feels his right Nike slip off the edge of a railroad tie. His ankle twists. *Snap!* He stumbles forward, pain shooting through his lower leg. He staggers, fighting to keep his balance. It's no good. Gravity trumps adrenaline. Falling in slow motion, he throws his arms out in front of him to soften the impact, but he doesn't land. Strong arms catch him. *Another man!* Before he can scold himself for his lack of anticipation, his abdomen is on fire. A second fire is lit. A third fire. A fourth. Now all the fires blend into a single conflagration.

"Turn him over," he hears the third man say as consciousness ebbs away. "We don't want his blood here. Get him onto the platform."

He smells that Cigarette Man is helping carry him. He has many things to say, but his mouth will not work. He feels the platform concrete on the back of his neck, on the backs of his hands. He wonders why he doesn't see stars as he faces the sky. He wonders why on such a mild night, with a fire raging inside him, he feels so cold. Snow falls on his cheeks. He thinks, *It is not snow at all.*

ONE

Shea Flannery, the president of the laborers' union, sat across the table from the man he believed to be Marty Berg, the fixer for the largest real estate law firm in town: Wiley, Straw, Salzberg & Goldman. In the viper pit of New York City real estate, that was saying something. The new fuck-you-finger additions to the Manhattan skyline made money for everyone except those who needed it most. Nobody cared that few people would actually live in these buildings or that the funds to build them were as foul smelling as the brown crust at the bottom of a suburban cesspool. Like a swarm of flies, they all wanted their taste from the investments of Mexican drug cartels, Eastern European human traffickers, corrupt Russian oligarchs, Chinese fentanyl producers, and American arms dealers.

Flannery, a slender, charm-oozing man with a seductive smile, was the hungriest fly of all. He was as sharp as he was charming, as slippery as he was seductive. It was a well-known secret that the man had his hand in everybody else's pockets. No project, union or nonunion, got built in the city without his say-so. As clever as Flannery was, he hadn't a clue Marty Berg was really Nick Ryan Jr. In his way, Nick was every bit the fixer he pretended to be and then some.

"Prove Shea Flannery is dirty. However you do it, no matter what it takes, even if you have to supply the dirt."

Those were Nick's marching orders. It always came down to the same thing: his job was to clean up the messes of other people's making. And as successful as he was, only a few people would ever know. The irony being that Nick wouldn't ever know who those people were. There were no medals, no applause. None. Never! Only another call, another assignment, another mess to clean up. That was okay with him. While his bosses' concern was the kings, queens, and bishops of this sleepless city, Nick looked out for the pawns. Someone had to watch out for them. Nick Ryan's soul was for the little guy.

"What'll you have, Marty?" Flannery said, the corners of his smile flattening as he looked down at his cell. "Gotta have a drink after a meal like that."

"Double Macallan Twenty-Five, one ice cube."

The waitress said, "Very good, sir."

"Two." Flannery winked, patting the waitress's backside. "Now, run along, honey."

They were the last two patrons in L'Autobus, the Meatpacking District bistro in the shadow of the High Line, a place where waitresses said silly cinematic things like "Very good, sir" and "Would you like chipotle dust on your Wagyu tartare?" Exactly the kind of place where a law firm fixer would take a man like Shea Flannery. But Flannery was off his game tonight, tense and frayed around the edges. His laughs too loud. His backslaps too frequent. He was unnerved, constantly checking his cell. Cracks in his hail-fellow-well-met demeanor appearing each time a text came in or when he excused himself to listen to his voicemails.

The meal was a celebration of their deal. Nick had set up a numbered offshore bank account for Flannery into which two hundred thousand dollars had been wired, 15 percent of which had in turn been wired back into Marty Berg's own fake offshore account.

Flannery checked to see that the waitress was out of earshot. "Did you get that gift I sent over?"

Gift indeed! It was the oldest, most effective trick in the book. Make your partners dirty by kicking back a percentage to them. Dirty partners can't suddenly find religion, can't go to the cops without incriminating themselves. Nick felt warm inside because an avalanche of shit was about to come down on Flannery's head.

Nick's preference was to use Flannery as bait to go after bigger prey. His frustration both as an NYPD detective and as the city's shadow watchman was that those decisions were out of his hands. He'd heard it all before, the rationalizations of the rich and powerful about how going after big prey was an exercise in futility.

As Joe, Nick's handler, once said, "In crime and politics, big prey never goes extinct."

Nick couldn't argue the point. Drugs didn't stop flowing into the country when Pablo Escobar was killed or when El Chapo was captured. Same as it ever was. There were always candidates eager to fill the void. Money was honey. All you needed to take it was ambition, an abiding disregard for innocence, and a stomach for blood.

The waitress delivered their aged scotches, a single perfect sphere of ice in each glass. She nodded politely and disappeared.

"To us." Flannery raised his glass.

"To us."

Flannery sipped, letting the peaty flavor with grace notes of vanilla, sherry, and caramel wash over his tongue. His eyes looked down as his cell vibrated on the tabletop. Nick watched as the scotch turned to sawdust in his mouth.

Nick would never know precisely how his bosses would use Flannery. He was certain of one thing: Shea Flannery was not going to trial for his crimes. Leverage and favors were power. That's what it was all about. Nick would do as he was told, but he too had learned a little something about leverage and favors.

"Look, Shea," Nick said, putting his palm on Flannery's forearm, "I know this thing between us is about business, but I guess I kind of like you and I guess I know you a little bit. Tonight should be about us celebrating, but it's like you're not really here. It's like you're scared or something."

Flannery stonewalled. "I don't know what you're talking about.

C'mon, buddy, drink up. You're nobody's bagman anymore. Time to be the hammer and not the nail."

"And I appreciate that more than you know, Shea. Thing is, if I get caught taking a dime, it's my neck."

"Don't get caught, Marty. What's your point?"

"My point is we've been dealing with each other for months now. Only idiots and guys in prison totally trust their partners. I get that." Nick took his hand off Flannery's forearm and pointed his right index finger at him. "But you're scared about something. If it's going to blow back on me, I need to know. Remember this, the reason you're dealing with me at all is I'm a fixer, the best in this soulless fuckin' town."

Flannery rubbed his clean-shaven chin, brushed back the silver-gray hair at his temples. "Nothing. It's nothing, Marty. Relax."

As they drained their glasses, the manager came over. He thanked them for their patronage and offered to buy them a good-night round.

"No, no," Flannery demurred, raising his palms. "We've overstayed our welcome."

"Everything was great, thanks," Nick said, handing the manager Marty Berg's credit card. "Add thirty percent on for a tip and we'll get out of here."

———

They walked out into the night, turning up their coat collars against the freezing rain. The streetlights reflected off the thin sheet of ice forming on the pavement and storefront overhangs.

"You want a lift, Shea?"

"I'm good." Flannery stepped off the sidewalk, waving his hand at the yellow cab coming up the side street. Its tires *th-dump th-dump th-dumped* over the uneven cobblestones. Shea turned back. "My luck seems to be holding, getting a cab in this weather. What are the odds?"

Nick stood stone-still—silent, waiting.

As the yellow Camry eased to a stop, Flannery grabbed the cab's back door handle. The rear passenger door wouldn't open no matter how hard he tugged. "Unlock the fucking door!" he shouted, banging on the window, his wedding band clinking against the foggy glass. The rear window sucked down into the door. "Goddamn it, asshole, open the fucking . . ." He went silent as he looked up and saw the muzzle of a big revolver aimed at his head.

Nick tackled Flannery. They thumped down on the icy cobblestones. There was a flash and a loud explosion. The stench of urine was strong in the frigid air as Flannery wet himself. Nick shielded Flannery's body with his own. The second shot ripped through the metal skin of the cab's back door. The bullet whizzed just above them, ricocheting off the sidewalk.

Nick whispered, "When I count to three, you crawl under the car parked ahead of us."

"Whatever you say."

"Ready? One, two, three . . ."

Nick rolled. Flannery crawled. The driver floored the cab. The Camry's front wheels skidded on the ice-slick cobblestones.

Nick came up shooting. The cab's back window spiderwebbed, crumbling to pieces. The Toyota didn't get fifty yards before rolling to a stop against the rear bumper of a parked cargo van. Its horn droned a solitary note echoing through the empty streets. Nick approached the Camry, gun raised. Trailing behind him, Flannery slipped on the pavement.

The heavyset cabbie was hunched over the wheel, blood oozing from his mouth onto his graying red beard. The back of his blue-and-white flannel shirt was a bloody mess. Nick pushed the big man back in his seat. The early morning was quiet once again.

"Dead?" a breathless Flannery asked.

"Very. Cab's stolen," Nick said, pointing at the license photo of a rough-looking Black man displayed on the dashboard.

"Fuck, Marty!" Flannery said, opening the back door. "The real driver's unconscious on the back floor. There's a crowbar next to him."

Nick came around to Flannery, gun still drawn. "Listen to me, Shea. You have to stop stonewalling me. I just saved your life and killed a man doing it. I can make this go away, but I need names. Who was texting you all night? What are you so scared of?"

"I don't know who. I swear."

"C'mon." Nick pulled Flannery by the wet coat sleeve. "We need to talk before the cops get here. We have to go. Now!"

"But this guy here that got whacked with the crowbar."

"Fuck that guy. We gotta go."

Flannery followed Nick under the High Line. They didn't stop until they got to the lobby of the Roxy Hotel. Nick guided Flannery straight to the elevators.

"I keep a room here. There's certain kinds of entertaining I arrange for our clients," he said as they rode the elevator up to eleven. "When the room isn't in use, I stay here sometimes."

————

Fifteen minutes later, they were sitting at a round Formica table. Their chairs were orange fabric and white plastic and looked like props from an episode of *The Jetsons*. Flannery was in a hotel robe, his hand-scrubbed pants drying in the bathroom.

"Okay, Shea, no more lying, no more stalling."

"Why do you carry a gun?"

"Sometimes I need to convince people with more than my charm and winning smile. The shortest distance between two points is sticking a gun barrel down someone's throat. You ask another question, I'll consider that stalling. Who's mad enough at you? Who do you have shit on who's scared enough to want to kill you?" Nick slid a pad and a pen across the tabletop. "I want to know their names and what you've got on them. Don't hold back. Understand?"

Flannery, ashen-faced, nodded.

————

An hour later, Nick slid Flannery's pages of notes into his suit jacket pocket.

"Call your wife and tell her you won't be home tonight. Don't scare her. Just make an excuse. She'll be safe. I'll have people watching your house. By tomorrow, this will all be cleared up like it never happened."

"You can do that?"

"Not if you keep talking," Nick said. "Just let me do what I do."

Flannery was incredulous. "No one knows better than me the behind-the-scenes shit that goes down in New York City, but this . . ."

Nick smiled. "This . . . this is nothing, Shea. Stay here tonight. I'll send someone to pick you up tomorrow after I've done my magic. Once you've spoken to your wife, shut your phone off. No, wait, I have a better idea. Call your wife now."

"Okay, whatever you say."

When Flannery got off the phone, Nick snatched the cell phone out of his hand. "It's safer this way. I'll lead whoever is after you on a wild-goose chase."

"Thanks, Marty. It's generous of you."

Nick was feeling generous. He had gotten both what his bosses wanted and what he wanted: leverage.

TWO

Nick looked at his watch, closing the GTO's door behind him. Even at this hour the traffic noise on Ocean Parkway would have masked the sound of a halftime marching band. There was no quiet in Brooklyn—ever. Most of the borough's residents were asleep. Not Lenny Feld. Nick looked across at the cemetery gates on the opposite side of the broad boulevard. They were even more foreboding in the freezing rain.

Nick stared briefly at the gilt Hebrew lettering on the red concrete facade of the brutalist-style synagogue. He walked around the side of the temple to the staircase to the basement door. He knocked. Waiting, he ran the tips of his fingers over the mezuzah affixed to the doorjamb. Though Nick was raised Catholic, he and God had abandoned each other long ago. His fascination with this symbol of the Jews' covenant with God had to do with Lenny. Lenny, who believed less in God than Nick did times ten over, yet chose to live in the basement of a synagogue. Nick figured Lenny had his reasons. That was good enough for him.

The door pulled back. There stood Lenny Feld in all his deformed glory: half-bald, his once-handsome face burned and scarred, wrecked finger stubs on one hand, a ragged stump for an ear, blind in one eye.

In 2007, Nick rescued Lenny from the fire that nearly killed them both. It bonded them forever.

"Come in," Feld said without joy.

Nick followed him down the cold, unadorned corridor. Lenny's Salvation Army wardrobe fit him more loosely than during his last visit. Lenny seemed to be shrinking away before Nick's eyes. They stepped into the windowless room that defined Lenny's universe.

"You okay?" Nick asked.

"That's always a relative question with me, isn't it?" Lenny turned, smiled. "Sit."

Nick didn't have to think too long on where to plant himself. Lenny's concrete bunker was a blend of monk's hovel and high-tech jungle. To one side: a cot, a tiny fridge, a metal folding chair, a hot plate, a duct-taped dresser. On the other side was a makeshift plywood platform on which sat three computer towers, monitors, laptops, a printer, police scanners, and equipment Nick was at a loss to figure out. It was nearly cold enough in the unheated basement to see your own breath, but the electronics warmed Lenny's room to a tolerable temperature. Nick sat on the folding chair.

"You didn't answer my question, Lenny."

"I did, just not to your satisfaction. Three thirty in the morning. This isn't a social call."

Nick handed over Shea Flannery's phone. "Whatever you were texting and emailing him tonight unnerved the shit out of him."

"I have my moments. Computers are amazing tools if you know how to use them. Of course, most people who think they're tech savvy haven't a clue. Really, though, I used a magic wand."

"You should do stand-up."

"You think? Quasimodo could be my stage name. Did that joke ring your bell?"

This comment worried Nick. Lenny wasn't generally a man possessed by self-pity.

"I need everything you can find on that phone—calls, texts, photos . . ."

Lenny shrugged. "I am familiar with the implications of the word *everything*. Is this for Detective Ryan or the shadowy Nick Ryan I'm not supposed to know about?"

"Does it matter?"

"You didn't answer my question, *boychick*."

Nick laughed. "I did, just not to your satisfaction."

"Maybe stand-up is *your* calling. A lot safer than this gig you've gotten for yourself. Time frame for the material I cull from the phone?"

"A few days."

"Who do you think you're dealing with, some Russian hacker? Give me an hour. You want to wait?" Lenny shuffled to his workbench. "Any progress on . . ."

Lenny didn't have to finish the question. Nick had heard it asked before. This was part of the bargain between them, an understanding that grew out of Nick's having saved Feld's life. Lenny, twice a PhD from MIT who held seven patents in the areas of chip design and digital data manipulation, would help Nick with his work if Nick would track down the arsonist who had burned down his house with his family in it.

Nick had to live with the uncomfortable truth that if he ever brought the person who murdered Lenny's family to justice, Lenny would end his own life. Lenny made it clear the only thing that kept him breathing was the hunt for his family's killer. Nick had stopped trying to talk him out of it. Difficult to convince a man so lonely and grief-stricken that he had a lot to live for.

He stood. "No, Lenny, nothing new. Sorry."

"But . . . you are . . . working on it?" Lenny had trouble catching his breath when he got emotional. The result of his lungs being scorched by superheated air. He used to joke with Nick that he was in worse shape on the inside than out. As if that were possible.

"I promised you I would and I am."

"It's hard to . . . hang on . . . sometimes." Lenny's voice cracked. "I wish . . . you'd never saved—"

Nick walked over to the workbench and put his hand on his friend's shoulder. "I know, but you have to stay alive. I need you. You know how much I would have to pay someone else to do for me what you do?"

"You don't have that much money. Nobody can do what I do. Good night, Nick."

"I know that too. I'll be by soon, pal."

Brooklyn was no quieter when Nick stepped back outside. Although the freezing rain had stopped, the night seemed bleaker than it had when he arrived.

THREE

Nick, Ace, and Mack sat in a booth, eating a late-morning breakfast at the Floridian Diner on Flatbush Avenue. Ace, the shaven-headed Black man, his face scarred by too many unblocked left hooks, was smashing his rye toast into the soft yellow yolks of his eggs. He was pretty perky for a man who only hours earlier played the unconscious cab driver on the back floor of the yellow cab. His perkiness was far less miraculous than the presence of the heavyset, bearded man seated next to him. Mack, the dead cab driver, looked with disdain at his plate of sausage, bacon, eggs, home fries, and white toast.

"I can't credit it. You'd think a man could get a proper fry-up in a Greek diner. They do a good job with every other type of ethnic food," he said, holding up a strip of well-done bacon. "Pathetic, what you people call bacon . . . Jesus wept. What do you say, Ryan?"

Nick was staring out the window at the traffic.

Ace snapped his fingers. "Ryan, the Irishman's talking to you."

"Sorry, Mack."

"I'm Lazarus, come from the dead. You'd think you might pay the resurrected some mind when discussing a proper breakfast."

Mack's early-morning performance as the man at the wheel of the cab wasn't his first time playing dead. A former "dirty tricks" operative in Northern Ireland for British intelligence, he had been forced to fake his death to avoid being assassinated.

As he had explained to Nick, "I was employed by one of those departments that had neither a name nor a number. Our cover was so deep not even the other services had a notion we existed. Gave Her Majesty's government plausible deniability. Christ, I love that feckin' phrase."

He'd also said that once it was clear the Good Friday Agreement would hold between the warring parties in Northern Ireland, people from his team began dying at an alarming rate. "If the shite we did to foment the Troubles in the North ever came to light, it would have been an embarrassment to the Crown. They had to rid themselves of us, as the line from the movie goes, with extreme prejudice. They didn't train me to be a fool, Ryan, so I faked killing me own self before they could exercise their prerogative."

Ace asked, "Did you get what you needed from Flannery?"

"And then some." Nick laughed. "Flannery was so freaked and grateful, he would've confessed to killing JFK."

"So," Mack said, "it was worth me using up the third of my nine lives?"

"Speaking of nine lives, Mack. You came a little too close with that second shot. It didn't miss my head by much."

Mack shrugged. "You wanted authenticity. Am I to blame that Ace's bloody hand cannon could blow a hole through cement?"

Nick didn't tell them about getting Flannery's cell. Neither of them knew about the phone or about Lenny Feld. Nick trusted both men, but only to a point.

Mack's intelligence background made him as dangerous as he was useful. He had killed for the Brits and to save his own neck. Nick didn't doubt that if Mack saw another opportunity to be free of his past, he would take it no matter who he had to sacrifice.

Ace's bosses were Nick's bosses. Ace had once had Nick's job. Only Ace didn't have the stomach for it, and by his own admission, he lacked the nuance. Because he had walked in Nick's shoes, they were simpatico. Still, Nick could never be certain Ace's loyalties weren't divided.

Nick pointed to Ace. "You get rid of the cab?"

"Cab company in Long Island City. Already broken down for parts."

Nick turned to Mack. "What happened when the cops showed?"

Mack roared, slapping the table. "Ah, the look on them fookers' faces. Grand. There wasn't anything for them to see. Ace had already driven off. I'd thrown a coat over my bloody shirt and watched from across the way."

"That wasn't the question, Irish."

"True, but I supposed you'd enjoy the details. They questioned the restaurant manager and the waitress, a *bhean álainn*, that one. There was a lot of gesturing toward where I'd let the cab come to rest. They pointed out where you and Flannery had gone beneath the High Line. When they began knocking on doors to the lofts above the shuttered establishments, I left. Didn't see much point in lingering. You know, Ryan, those wee squibs, there's a lot of liquid in them bastards. Ruined me best flannel."

That was another part of Nick's wariness about Mack. It was impossible to know where the performance ended and the real Mack began.

"Okay," Nick said, taking two twenties out of his wallet. "Here you go. That'll also cover the cost of your shirt."

"Much obliged, Ryan."

Nick slid out of the booth.

Ace's expression soured. "You off to see the man?"

"Later." He looked at his watch. "I have something more important to do first."

FOUR

A chill wind blew off the East River, whipping up mounds of fallen leaves into swirling eddies. The sun was telling autumn lies, bright and fierce, but barely warm enough to disappear the ice from last night's storm. The sky was a deep, cloudless blue, a 9/11 sky. No New Yorker who had lived through that day could gaze into such a sky without a sense of mourning. Nick's uncle Kenny, the only Ryan in three generations not to wear an NYPD uniform, was the one member of the family to die at Ground Zero. It was his death that set off a series of events that had, all these years later, led Nick here.

John Jay Park was too empty to suit Nick. In spring and summer, with all the activity, with so many kids, parents, and nannies, no one stood out. On those days, Nick blended into the scenery. With older kids back in school, and the cooler weather, he had to keep his distance.

Nick found a bench far from the play area from which to watch the little girl in the puffy blue coat and fake-fur hat. He smiled a brokenhearted smile as the blue-coated girl chased a boy around the green bars of the outdoor gym. The wind blew the little girl's long and untamed dirty-blond hair. Nick was too far away to see her crystalline blue irises, but he knew they glistened. She had her father's eyes and hair. Nick's eyes and hair.

Becky usually came to the park with her au pair. Odile deGail was a twenty-three-year-old college-educated woman from Toulouse, France. Nick had come to know a lot about Odile deGail. He made it his business to find out all there was to know about anyone with access to Becky Carlyle. He had watched Odile with Becky many times. She was alert and attentive, and unlike many of the older nannies who used time in the park to socialize, Odile didn't let anything distract her from focusing on Becky.

Today, Becky was with her mom. Shana Carlyle was a tall, long-limbed woman, graceful as a ballerina even when standing perfectly still. She was green-eyed, her beauty dark and broody. Depending on the light, her shoulder-length hair could appear almost any shade between raven and deep red. In the bright sun it shone auburn, the wind whipping it into her face.

Days when Shana came to the park with Becky were hardest of all. Nick had been with many women since returning from Afghanistan, but none of them made his breath catch in his throat the way Shana did. It was true the first time he saw her outside the memorial service for his uncle Kenny and the other employees of Three Ravens Equity at the World Trade Center. It was true for the years they dated. It was true now. No matter who shared his bed, Shana would always be the one.

It wasn't that Shana was married to another man raising Becky as his own that made these days most difficult. It was that Nick had chosen to let the charade go on. Nick, Shana, and Becky would never be a family. He could not allow Shana or Becky to become collateral to be used as leverage against him. He had too often seen collateral evolve into collateral damage. He wouldn't allow them to be hurt because of him.

Out of the corner of his eye he spotted a big-bellied cop and a woman coming toward him. The cop stopped directly in front of Nick. The woman stood behind the cop, off to his left.

The cop pointed at Nick. "This the man?"

"That's him," the woman said. "I've seen him here before. He's always watching the kids."

Marjorie Tucker was a handsome woman, a few years older than

Shana. Nick knew her name, knew her address on York Avenue. He knew who her husband, Bill, worked for and who he was sleeping with. Her son, Max, was the kid Becky was chasing. As with Odile, Nick made it his business to know.

"All right, you, stand up! C'mon. Now!"

Nick stood, hands raised, palms out. He wanted this over before they drew too much attention. *Too late.* He saw over the cop's shoulder that parents and nannies were gathering together, pointing. Shana too. He saw the emotions washing over her lovely face: confusion, fear, and anger.

"You like watching little kids, huh, buddy?"

"It's not 'buddy,' Officer . . . Frazitta," Nick read the cop's name-plate aloud. "It's Detective Ryan. ID's in my right rear pocket. I was in the academy with a Mike Frazitta. Any relation?"

Frazitta didn't answer. Instead he stepped back. He put his hand close to his pistol grip. "Show me. Do it slow, very slow."

Frazitta made a sour face at Nick's shield and ID. "Sorry, Detective Ryan. What's the deal?"

Nick put away his ID. "No deal. I'm working. Now, please get out of here before you fuck up my case even more than you already have."

"Yeah, Mikey Frazitta's my cousin." The cop turned to Marjorie Tucker. "Okay, ma'am, you satisfied?"

She nodded. After Frazitta left, she said, "I am sorry. These days, you know, you can't be too careful."

"I understand."

She seemed to want to keep the conversation going. Nick wasn't in the mood. There was only a tiny piece of Becky he could ever share. This woman's good intentions had just robbed him of it. He walked away.

Ten minutes later, in his GTO heading to the Bronx, Shana called. He knew she would.

"Nick, I just spoke to—"

"Marjorie Tucker."

There was a moment of stunned silence. Then, "How do you know her name?"

"You became friends after Max and Becky met in the park. I know a lot of things about the people in your world—about Odile, about Felix your doorman, about Marjorie's husband, Bill . . ."

"How long have you been watching Becky?" Shana's voice was brittle.

"Since I found out she was mine."

"We have to talk."

"We're talking now."

"That's not what I mean, Nick Ryan. Tonight!"

"Tonight."

He stared at his phone for several seconds before putting it down. He always looked forward to Shana's late-night visits. Always—until now.

FIVE

Nick pulled the Starlight Black GTO into a spot in front of the used-tire shop shoehorned between a vacant warehouse and an auto body shop. He had been here once last autumn. Unlike today, he wasn't contemplating the crisp autumn air or the color palette of fall foliage. He doubted that most people realized the beauty of turning leaves was an expression of death and rebirth. That night last fall was also about death and rebirth: the death of a man named Ricky Corliss and the rebirth of Nick Ryan.

Nick had set out to execute Corliss, a harmless-looking man who had murdered several young boys. Corliss had been a fastidious killer, leaving little evidence in his wake beyond charred bones and ash. After his first trial ended in a hung jury, Nick's old partner planted blood evidence. That resulted in the second trial being declared a mistrial. There would be no third trial. Corliss went free. Disgraced, Nick's old partner ate his gun. Nick couldn't let that stand, not any of it. Afghanistan had drawn razor-sharp lines between Nick's conceptions of right and wrong, between justice and injustice. Nick was never a man to point to someone else and say, "You do it." Corliss died that night. Nothing else went to plan.

A year later, the changes to the tire store's appearance were subtle.

The changes in Nick's life were anything but. Not that you could tell from outside appearances. He possessed a chameleon's gift, showing the world only what he wanted it to see. It was the reason people on the job, even those who despised him, considered Nick the best UC detective they'd ever seen. Whether it was a high school championship basketball game in Madison Square Garden, close-quarters combat in the Sulaiman Mountains, or doing buy-and-bust drug ops in East New York, the moment was never too big, the situation never overwhelming. There was the hurricane swirling around him and there was the eye of the hurricane. Nick was in the eye. It had always been so.

A man rapped his knuckles against the passenger window. Nick rolled the window down. The bracing chemical tang of solvents and paints from the body shop rushed in. The man was covered in Bondo dust, his respirator hanging around his neck. He leaned over the sill of Nick's car door. He smiled not at Nick, but at the perfectly restored '69 GTO.

"*Que bonito coche.*"

"Thanks."

"Leave the keys, *jefe*. The car stays here." He pointed at the used-tire store. "The man, he waits for you inside."

After the incident in the park, Nick didn't have a lot of diplomacy in him. He got out, locking the door and pocketing the keys. "Touch the car, I'll cripple you."

At the front counter of the tire store, a sad-faced fat man was reading *El Especialito*. He put the paper aside, tilted his head at the shop door.

The repair shop was grimy, smelling of glue and vulcanized rubber. Stacks of used tires were everywhere. The man Nick knew only as Joe sat on a green plastic garden chair, an empty chair beside him. "Please, Nick, come sit."

Joe was a fit man in his fifties. Wisps of neatly trimmed white hair were pressed tight against his tanned, balding head. Everything about him, from his tailor-made pinstripes to his gold accessories and glossy manicured fingernails to his demeanor, screamed *lawyer*.

Nick laughed. "Last time I sat in that chair my life took a weird turn."

"We've come a long way since then."

The statement was undeniable. A few hours before meeting Joe, Nick had abducted Ricky Corliss off a Brooklyn street. Once he'd gotten a detailed confession from Corliss, Nick prepared to execute him. A man he had never seen before or since stepped into the basement where he was holding Corliss and put three bullets into the child killer. When Nick got outside, two men in an unmarked police vehicle were waiting for him. One of them was Ace. They'd driven Nick here, to a lifeless commercial street in the shadow of the new Yankee Stadium.

Now as then Nick asked, "Why am I here?"

Joe shook his head. "The dumb-cop routine didn't play last year. Doesn't play now."

Nick handed Joe an envelope containing the ten sheets of paper Flannery had written out the night before. "There you go. What you wanted."

Joe barely glanced at the envelope before slipping it into his jacket pocket.

Nick was confused. "I went through a lot to get you those sheets of paper. The info on them has a lot of powerful people in this city compromised six ways to Sunday. What are you going to use him for?"

"Me? Not a thing. As I've said from the start, I am a conduit between our employers and you. And like you, I don't know and don't care to know what our employers have planned for Mr. Flannery. We both have our assignments."

That was the deal between them. Simple. If Nick would fix the problems, he would have the keys to the kingdom. Access to any intel, weapons, databases, cameras, traffic lights—anything. The problems were New York City's; the solutions were Nick's alone. What mattered to him was the chance to be more than a cog in the machine. It was why he was a cop, why he did two tours in Afghanistan. Truth was, he hadn't made a real difference until he took the job. Sometimes his hands got dirty making things right, but the city was always better off for it.

Nick wasn't in the mood to chat. "Why drag me back here to make the exchange?"

"Your car."

"What about my car?"

"It's underequipped and draws too much attention to itself." Joe walked over to the back wall. He pressed a green button and one of the two corrugated steel doors rolled up. "Come with me."

Nick followed Joe into a lighted passageway. Joe turned left toward the vacant warehouse, not toward the body shop as Nick might have expected. Joe unlocked a black steel door at the back of the warehouse and flipped on a light switch. Overhead fluorescent tubes popped on. A silver 2017 Chevrolet Malibu sat in the trenched delivery bay below the loading dock.

Nick frowned. "What am I supposed to do with that POS?"

"You of all people shouldn't need to be told that things are not always as they seem."

Joe walked down the steps to the bay floor and popped the Malibu's hood.

"An LS Seven." Nick was impressed.

"I'm told this engine produces over five hundred horsepower and nearly five hundred pound-feet of torque."

"Very nasty, but the Malibu's a front-wheel-drive car. An LS Seven in that car . . . the thing will tear itself apart if you floor it."

"Not so. It has been completely redesigned beneath the skin. The body and chassis are fully reinforced. It has six-piston disc brakes all around and is four-wheel drive. It has NASCAR-like power but handles like a Formula One machine. Enhanced power and handling are only some of its redesign benefits." Joe opened the driver's-side door and turned the ignition key. The engine rumbled to life. "Nick, please, come here."

Nick looked over Joe's shoulder. "Okay."

When Joe pressed his thumb twice against the cruise-control reset button, the mesh covering the door speaker popped open. Joe reached in where the speaker would have been, and came up with a large black handgun. Nick had never seen anything like it. Featuring a sleek grip, an angular trigger, a ridged, ventilated slide, and a horizontal magazine, it looked like something out of *Star Wars*. The futuristic pistol seemed completely out of place in an old family sedan.

"Here." Joe placed it in Nick's hand. "It's a Kel-Tec P50."

Nick hefted it. "Three pounds."

"Almost to the ounce. Why am I not surprised? Fifty-cartridge maga-zine with five point seven, twenty-eight-millimeter rounds. There are two supplemental magazines in the speaker well. The ammunition will penetrate most common body armor, or so I am told."

"Like a P90."

"Exactly. There's more." Joe reached into the car and opened the glove box. Then he pushed down on the glove box. On metal prongs at the back of the glove compartment was a weapon Nick knew inti-mately: a Glock 26. "I believe you favor this model. Hidden between the rear seat and the trunk wall you'll find a Remington 870 shotgun, two flash-bangs, and a spike strip. There's Kevlar lining the fabric of the driver's seat and at its core is a ceramic plate similar to the inserts in your military vest."

Nick shook his head. "I haven't needed any of this nonsense. If I do my job right, this is all moot."

Joe pointed to a dial just below the display screen. "See this? Turn it, push it, and it performs the functions it was designed for, but pull it out, a canister below the passenger seat will release tear gas. I suggest you not use it unless you are at a full stop and can exit the vehicle."

Nick's phone buzzed. It was Martellus Sharp calling. Sharp was Nick's brother Sean's partner at the Six-O precinct in Coney Island. "Sorry, Joe, I've got to take this."

He ran up the stairs to the loading dock, through the back door, and into the corridor. "How did my little brother fuck up this time?"

"Not calling about Sean."

"My dad?"

"Tony Angelo."

"What about Tony?"

"Dead."

"Ah, shit. Coronary?"

"Murdered."

"Murdered! Tony?"

"Wife too."

"Where?"

"His house."

"I'll meet you over there."

"Nobody's gonna want us there, Nick."

"Fuck what anybody wants. I'll be there in about an hour." Nick hung up, heading back to the tire shop.

Joe caught up to him. "We're not done yet. There's more to show you."

Nick turned. "We're done for now, Joe."

Joe saw the look on Nick's face. "What's the matter?"

"I need you to make a call for me."

"And to whom shall I make this call?"

"To the people who pull the strings."

"Whose strings?"

"Our strings."

Joe said, "What favor am I asking for on your behalf?"

"Twenty-Nine-Thirty-Nine Shore Parkway in Brooklyn."

"Is that supposed to mean something to me?"

"If it did, I'd be shocked. I want access to the scene for two. I want the whole case file."

"I can't promise anything."

"Just ask. I'll know the answer when I get there."

Nick watched Joe tap a number on his phone screen, then headed to his GTO.

S I X

Tony Angelo was the kind of guy who pronounced *jugular* like *juggler*. Half the time, context was the only way you ever knew what he was talking about. Tony mistook Venusians for Venetians, but he also spoke in naively beautiful phrases. There was the time Nick asked him when he got to sleep on New Year's Eve. Tony said, "I was blind to midnight, kid." Blind to midnight—that was how Nick heard Tony's voice in his head. That was the only place he would ever hear Tony's voice again.

The house at 2939 Shore Parkway was one of a block-long row of attached red-brick two-family units. Facing the Belt Parkway, around the corner from Coney Island Hospital, and a few hundred yards away from Ocean Parkway, it could be a very noisy street. Certainly noisy enough to mask gunfire. Nick's penthouse condo overlooking the Verrazzano Bridge and New York Harbor was a couple of miles away, also on Shore Parkway. At the moment, it felt a million miles away.

The flurry of activity and the array of strobing lights were a rubber-necker's delight. Traffic in both directions on the Belt was choked to a crawl. Only one of the official vehicles got Nick's attention—the medical examiner's van. Thinking of it as the meat wagon had rarely bothered him. It bothered him now. Martellus Sharp's long, lean body paced along the sidewalk outside the crime scene tape.

"Martellus."

"Nick."

An African American who consistently refused the bump to detective and wouldn't take the tests for promotion, Sharp was a legend. He felt he could accomplish more by shepherding young Black cops and educating white cops who came from the suburbs than by being somebody's boss. No one straddled the line between being Black and wearing blue like Martellus Sharp. He'd been on the job long enough to have worked with both Nick and Nick's dad and was now Sean's partner.

"How'd you hear?" Nick asked.

"Call came across as I was coming off shift. I recognized the address."

"Not Sean."

Sharp shook his head. "He was already gone to his meeting. I know Tony was like family. I figured you'd let him know."

"You call my dad?"

"Nope." Sharp rubbed a hand over thinning gray hair. "Not my place."

"Come on," Nick said. "Time to go inside."

The young Asian American woman controlling the perimeter, a uniform from the Six-O, smiled at the sight of Sharp.

"Hey, Sharp. What are you—" She stopped midsentence at the sight of Nick Ryan holding up his shield.

Nick said, "He's with me."

She lifted the tape for them without saying another word.

Martellus Sharp didn't like it. "Chen, you know better than to let us onto a crime scene."

"Orders," she said, pointing at Nick. "Free pass for him or anyone with him."

Nick knew that Martellus Sharp had his suspicions. While Sharp didn't know exactly what was going on, word had filtered back to him about Nick being at crime scenes where he didn't belong. Over the past year, Nick had gone from an isolated undercover detective doing drug busts to a detective first assigned to the Intelligence Bureau—a detective with juice way beyond his standing.

At the door to the downstairs apartment, a crime scene tech handed Nick and Sharp gloves and booties. Like Chen, the tech didn't ask them to identify themselves.

Nick asked, "Where?"

"You'll see."

As they stepped inside, the telltale odors of death were in the air. Once Tony retired, he'd stopped renting out the downstairs apartment. With Nick and Sean's help, Tony had turned the apartment into a man cave and woodworking shop. Nick had built the wet bar and mounted the big flat-screen. The green carpeting had white lines drawn on it, like a football field. A red, white, and blue New York Giants logo in the center of the carpet. As they walked deeper into the apartment, the scents of death grew stronger.

Outside the open bathroom door, the ME's rep knelt in front of a woman's body. The stink of urine and feces was intense. The dead were free of shame or bother. Rosa, Tony's second wife, lay with her right cheek resting on the tile, blood and a black spot where her right eye used to be. Her right arm was flung above her head. She was dressed in a floral-print sweatshirt and jeans. Her feet were in men's slippers, the left one half-off. There were two tiny red splotches on the back of her sweatshirt. The back wounds were only an inch or two apart.

Standing silent across from the bathroom, Detective Annalise Puleo nodded to Nick and Martellus. There was history between Nick and Puleo. She didn't wait to be asked to walk them through the scene.

"The shooter's behind the bathroom door. When the vic passes, she hears something, turns . . . *Bang!* The eye shot. She falls here. He stands over her, puts two through the left shoulder blade." Puleo made a gun of her thumb and index finger. "*Tap. Tap.* Any one of the shots could've killed her. The ME will tell us which."

"Tony, the husband, was first," Nick said. "She was second, right?" It was a question in form only.

"I figure she either heard something or came looking for the husband when he didn't come back upstairs. Shoulda stayed up there. The husband was already toast."

"Careful, Detective," Sharp said, pointing at Nick. "Family friend."

"Sorry, Ryan."

"Forget it. Was the husband killed in the same way?"

"Similar. Not the same. You'll see."

"Weapon?"

"Small caliber. A twenty-two or a twenty-five." She made a dime-size circle with her index finger. "Entrance wounds are tiny. No exit wounds visible. No shell casings. No nothing."

Nick said, "Quiet weapon. Shots all well placed. No missteps. He was confident, calm. Looks professional."

Puleo nodded. "Agreed. Might as well ask since you're here. How you know the vics?"

"Tony Angelo did thirty years on the job before putting in his papers. He goes—went—way back with my dad. Best friend and like an uncle to me and my brother. Rosa was his second wife."

"Where's the first wife?"

"Arizona, I think. They split up around twenty years ago. Amicable, as far as I knew."

"Enemies? Anyone you think might do this?"

"Him or her?"

Puleo gave a slight shrug. "Both."

"Rosa? I don't see how. Tony? No enemies I knew of. Sounds stupid, but everybody loved Tony."

Sharp said, "Apparently not everybody. All of us make enemies. The Ryans are really good at it."

"Thanks, Sharp."

"I don't know," Puleo said. "I hear Angelo was in uniform his whole career. Tough for me to believe he made the kind of enemy who was a pro hitter, or an enemy who had the resources to hire one. What's the worst he ever did, put cuffs on too tight? Could the wife have been the target? She's younger, pretty. A jealous lover?"

Nick was done listening. "That prick Rosen still your partner?"

"Watch your mouth about my partner." Puleo got red-faced. "He's in the woodshop."

Staring back at Rosa's body, Nick thought of Shana and Becky and collateral damage.

SEVEN

Jeff Rosen was a no-nonsense detective. Well respected. Not well liked. Nick knew all about that. Rosen stood still, watching two men unfold the fluid-proof bag in which Tony Angelo would ride to his autopsy. The stink of death in the shop was partially masked by the petroleum odor of machine oil. Rosen made an unhappy face at the sight of Nick and Sharp.

"Can I have a second with him?" Nick asked, pointing at Angelo's body.

Rosen said, "Give him a minute, boys."

The men from the coroner's office stepped back. Nick knelt down by the body. Tony's open eyes seemed to look back. Tony Angelo was family in spirit if not in blood. Smiling, affectionate, he was always the happy counterpoint to Nick's dad's dour temperament. Tony wasn't smiling now. Nick reached out to put his hand on the dead man's shoulder, stopped. "Forever blind to midnight, Uncle Tony. Blind to midnight."

"What was that?" Rosen asked.

"Nothing important." Nick stood.

The two tiny red dots on his yellowed T-shirt were an inch apart, both through the heart. Nick shook his head, thinking that Tony's heart was so big that the wounds could have been a foot apart and they still would have hit their target.

Nick stepped back. "Thanks, Rosen."

Rosen said, "The lathe was still turning when the uniforms got here. Noise must've masked the hitter's approach. I figure he walked right up behind him." Rosen held his gloved thumb and forefinger an inch apart and touched the back of his own neck with his other hand. "There's a clean horizontal slit about this wide between two vertebrae at the back of the vic's neck. Paralyzed him. Eventually popped him in the skull before finishing him with the two in the heart." They all looked at the rectangular blank of wood in the lathe. "The gouge was found next to his right hand. His eye protection fell off when he hit the floor. CSU has already bagged them, but they'll be useless. The killer was meticulous."

Martellus Sharp pointed at the wood blank in the lathe jaws. "Wonder what he was gonna make."

Nick said, "Guy's got to be pretty skilled and confident with a blade to do that when he could just shoot his victim."

"He does. My guess, he's done this before. Enjoys his work." Rosen shook his head.

"Maybe the shots were secondary." Nick shrugged.

"You're an observer, so keep your opinions to yourself. The neck wound stays off the radar. That's holdback. I see it mentioned anywhere in the media—"

"We know what holdback is, Rosen. It won't leak from us."

Rosen wasn't satisfied. "You two, upstairs with me."

As Nick walked past her, Puleo made a quizzical face at Nick. There was sadness in it, some yearning too. Their time together had been brief and intense. They both understood they would be seeing one another again for the worst of reasons.

The contrast was stark on the upper floor. The three men went into the brightly lit kitchen; the aroma of bacon-wrapped meatloaf hung in the air. Nick felt the ambient heat from the oven, the dinner never to be eaten still inside. A Pandora station was still playing over their stereo. "That's Life" was the unfortunate tune Sinatra was singing as they sat down.

Rosen didn't appreciate the irony. Sinatra was silenced. Rosen turned to Martellus Sharp as they sat down at the kitchen table. "I'm told you went way back. That right, Sharp?"

"Tony and me, we did."

"You, Ryan, what's your story?"

"He was close to my dad. He didn't have any kids or much family, so he was like an uncle to my brother and me."

Rosen ran through the questions Puleo had asked about enemies or potential suspects. He got the same answers they gave Puleo. He asked a few more detailed questions. When was the last time Nick had seen Angelo? Did he know the state of their marriage? Had Rosa been married before? What was Tony's relationship with his ex? Like that.

He closed his notepad, shut off the record function on his phone. "Look, Ryan, I don't know what kind of marker you called in to get access to my case. I figure someone owed you big-time. What I want you to know is that it stops here."

"What does?"

"What I said downstairs holds. You'll get to look over my shoulder. I'll give you access to whatever I have, but this isn't your case. Understood? Puleo and me, we work the case. You're in the stands, not on the field with the players."

"Relax."

"Nah, nah, it's not like that, Ryan. I know about your rep. Don't placate me by telling me what I want to hear."

"Is that what I'm doing?"

Rosen ignored the question. "Ryan, you know what a maven is?"

Sharp answered. "It's Yiddish for an expert."

"Very good." Rosen applauded, turning back to Nick. "My brother Arty is a sales manager at a Honda dealership on the island."

"He has my condolences," Nick said.

"Hear me out. What Arty says is that the worst buyers are the ones that bring a maven along. You know, someone who has car sales experience. What he says is that the mavens always feel pressure to prove how wise they are. They feel they have to outsmart the salesperson with their acumen. He says mavens screw up more deals than anyone or anything else. You catching my meaning here?"

"I promise not to bring an expert with me if I ever buy a Honda."

"You trying to be funny, Ryan?"

"I might be if you had a sense of humor."

"Fuck you, Ryan."

"I don't need parables. I got it."

"Make sure you do. I don't need a maven fucking up my case."

"Do your job and it won't be a problem." Nick stood. "Are we done here?"

"Wait a second. Did I hear an 'or else' in there?"

Nick laughed. "You need a parable?"

"Get out. I've got work to do."

Nick placed his card on the table in front of Rosen. "Email what you've got to that address."

Martellus Sharp was already heading out the door when Rosen grabbed Nick by the wrist. Nick shook loose but stopped.

"I know about you and Annalise. Don't confuse her and don't ruin her career by asking for things you shouldn't be asking for. You do that and we'll have real trouble. You're not the only one on the job holding markers on people."

Nick knew that Rosen's loyalty to Annalise was coming from the right place. He admired it. Partners could be closer than spouses. He left without another word. He had somewhere to go and something to do.

EIGHT

Nick rang the bell to the basement apartment. Visits with his dad were always unpleasant. This one would be worse. Worse because it would be about something more than his father's roiling resentment and self-pity. Nick Ryan Sr. was dressed in dirty sweatpants and a faded blue NYPD T-shirt. He was surprised to see his eldest son standing in the doorway. The surprise quickly surrendered to its default expression of resignation.

"It's you!" he said, disappointed. "I'm waiting for the pizza guy. What did your brother do this time that you're here?"

His father turned his back and walked inside. He plopped down in his recliner, the only piece of furniture that had made it from their old house in Brooklyn to the basement apartment in Bayside. A red plastic cup and a half-empty bottle of Jameson sat on a white plastic end table. The TV was tuned to the St. John's–Villanova basketball game on ESPN.

The place was as it was the last time and the time before that. The fold-out couch was a mess of creased sheets. The coffee table was covered in old newspapers, used paper plates. It smelled of home-heating oil fumes. Unlike Tony Angelo's workshop, it stank not of death but of dying. Nick Sr. was committing slow-motion suicide, the weapons of choice Irish whiskey and regret. The furnace rumbled the linoleum tiles under their feet.

"You were good," his father said, pointing at the flat-screen. "You and Chris Mullin, the two best ballplayers Xaverian ever produced. Your mom and me were so proud of you when you played at the Garden. You had, what, six scholarship offers from D-one schools?"

"Yeah, Da, I coulda been a contender. Didn't matter. I was always going to be a cop anyway."

"Ryans and cops, synonyms. You can look it up," he said, pouring a few fingers of Jameson into his plastic cup. "My brother Kenny, God love him, would be alive today if he'd only come on the job like he was supposed to, like a Ryan. *Sláinte!*" He drank. "Want some?"

"Sure."

That put a smile on his father's face. He found another red plastic cup and poured his son a double.

"Let me ask again, what did your brother do this time?" Nick Sr.'s smile had since disappeared. "Marie kick him to the curb again? Did he fall off the wagon or is it the gambling?"

"I'm not here about Sean."

"Then what? Oh, it's to be one of those visits, is it? You had a shit shift. Some asshole said something about me, so you're here to berate me again."

Nick knew this subject was bound to rear its head because it always did.

"Da, it's not—"

"What would you have had me do? Half the guys I worked with were protecting the three drug gangs in my precinct. They were tipping off those shitbirds to raids, sending Narcotics in the wrong direction . . . For fuck's sake, boy, they were providing security for their shipments, collecting for them. Word was, Eddie Crane whacked some street dealer for the Asesinos."

"I've heard this all before."

"What, you wanted me to wait until the Argent Commission subpoenaed me?" Nick Sr. slammed down his emptied cup. "You wanted me to hide, to have an excuse."

Nick had long ago ceased trying to stop his father's rants. Once he began, it was going to play out like an old eight-track tape. Their interaction had become as ritualized as the dance of bees.

"Did I say that, Da?"

"I know. I know, I killed your mom because she lost all of her friends after I testified. I ruined your and your brother's careers. No one on the job trusts you guys. The sons of a rat are no better than a rat. A rat is a rat is a rat." Nick Sr. poured himself another, drank it, and threw the remote at the TV. He missed.

"You done?"

"Yeah."

"Tony's dead." Nick got it out before his father could get going again. "That's why I'm here, to tell you."

His dad stared at him as if he had spoken in Zulu. "Tony?"

"Tony Angelo, Da. Uncle Tony." Nick retrieved the remote and shut off the TV. "Murdered. Rosa too."

Nick Sr. paled, made a gut-punched face. "Tony and Rosa. Jesus." He crossed himself. "How? Why?"

Nick bit his lip about the knife wound. "Pro hitter. Small caliber. Three pills for each."

Nick Sr. dispensed with the glass and drank straight from the bottle. "I don't get it. Tony . . . you know Tony your whole life. He had a heart the size of an elephant. Guy was a sweetheart. He loved you kids. He was on the job for years when he took me under his wing. In all the time we worked together, he never had a bad word for anyone."

"Cops make enemies, Da."

"Not Tony. Only rough period in his life come right after Nine-Eleven. That was a bad, bad year for him. Drinkin' and fuckin' around. It's what caused the break between Candy and him. He got suspended twice. They assigned him to the rubber-gun squad for a few months. Good thing he met Rosa. She helped straighten him out."

"I don't remember that."

"Why would ya? You were what, sixteen and mourning Kenny? You were pretty distracted that year, dating Shana and all. God, what a beauty, that girl. That year was rough for the whole city, whether you were in the bag or a civilian." Nick Sr. got a sad, wistful look in his eyes. "That day fucked us all up. After that, a lot of good cops took a turn. It was after Nine-Eleven that the guys in my precinct went south. It was like people forgot who they were inside."

"Not you."

"I was never a saint, but yeah, even me. I was a little erratic after the towers fell. I was angry and sad about my brother getting killed. I got a little too rough sometimes. I guess I was like people who get mugged and don't fight back. It eats at them afterwards. They question themselves and they don't know what to do with their anger and disappointment. Worst feeling in the world is believing you are a coward."

Nick said, "You acted out."

"If you say so."

"Detectives Rosen and Puleo are probably going to speak with you. Rosen's a prick, but he's good. Puleo is quiet and smart. Don't hold back with them unless there's something you want to tell me that you think will hurt Tony's rep."

Nick Sr. scratched his scalp, screwed up his lips as he thought. "Only weird thing is that after Nine-Eleven he tried to enlist."

"Tony?" Nick laughed. "Fat Uncle Tony?"

His dad laughed too. "Can you believe that shit? He was in his late thirties and already carrying an extra forty pounds. I'm surprised the recruiters didn't wet themselves at the sight of him."

"I guess a lot of people had a patriotic impulse after the attacks," Nick said. "If I'd been a year older, I would've tried to join up. It was one of the reasons I enlisted eventually."

"Don't go there, boy. You threw away too much by joining up. Shana most of all."

Nick bit the inside of his cheek. This lecture about Shana was another part of the dance between him and his father. Today of all days, he wasn't in the mood. "Enough, Da."

Nick Sr. frowned. He seemed to have more to say but kept it to himself. "You going to tell your brother?"

"You do that." Nick looked at his watch. "I have to be someplace."

His dad came over to him, patted his son's cheek. "Thanks for coming to tell me. That was a good thing of you to do."

"I wish I didn't need to come."

"Where did wishing ever get us?"

"About as far as hoping."

"Exactly right, boy. You sound like your mother when you say things like that. You hear anything more, you let your da know."

"See you at the wake."

Nick ran into the pizza delivery guy coming his way. He gave the kid thirty bucks and took the box. This time when his father answered the door, there were tears in his eyes. He'd only ever seen his father cry once before, at the cemetery when they were burying Nick's mom. *Appropriate then. Appropriate now.* Nick handed him the pizza and left without a word. The loudest words between them were those unspoken.

NINE

Vampires. Apt because they could love only under cover of night. Death brought them together the first time. It rescued them a second. He remembered Shana at sixteen, her long, graceful strides cutting through the late-September wind, how the wind blew back her hair, how for the only time in his life he'd felt overwhelmed. He didn't know who she was. Didn't know that her father owned Three Ravens Equity, the firm his uncle Kenny had worked for. Didn't know their destinies would be intertwined.

He heard her slide the key into his lock, listened to it turn. Watched her step into the condo, lean against the door, pushing it closed behind her. Her eyes on Nick the whole time. The lines of her exquisite face registered as sadness, not rage. It was a night for sadness. There was a disquieting stillness between them.

Shana broke it. "What's wrong?"

"Tony Angelo and his wife were murdered."

"Tony?" She was confused. "Your dad's friend? *Uncle* Tony?"

"Yeah."

"God, Nick, I'm so sorry." She seemed to realize how hollow a word *sorry* was. "He loved you guys. He was always so sweet and he was a major-league flirt. I loved it. When he hugged you, he really hugged you. He could make the whole world seem safe and warm. And the way he mangled the English language . . . He was like Yogi Berra."

"He liked you from the get-go. 'Hold on to that girl,' he used to say. 'You let her go and you're a bigger dope than I think you are.'"

"Who would want to murder Rosa? What did she ever do to deserve—"

"To quote Clint Eastwood, '*Deserve's* got nothing to do with it.'"

"Huh?"

"I'm pretty sure it wasn't about Rosa. She was in the wrong place at the wrong time."

"Then who would want to hurt Tony?"

"Same question I've been asking myself for hours. Whoever it was, was a pro or could afford to hire a pro."

"To murder a retired street cop?" She walked over, knelt by him, and placed her head in his lap. He stroked her hair, taking in the citrus and raw-honey hints of her perfume.

Nick said, "You have something to tell me."

"No. I have a question." She stood, took off her brown leather jacket, tossed it onto the sofa.

"Ask."

"Why have you been watching Becky?"

"Because she's perfect."

"That's not an answer."

"Watching her in the park with you and Odile was the only piece of her life I could share."

"But it isn't. You know I would be with you and Becky. Brad wouldn't stand in the way. He isn't a stupid man. He knows he's a compromise. All you have to do is ask."

Nick turned to the window facing out on the Verrazzano Bridge and the Narrows beneath it. "I can't ask for that."

"There's a difference between *can't* and *won't*."

"You're right, there is."

The second death that brought them together was Ricky Corliss's.

The day he set out to kill Corliss, Nick visited Shana for the first time since returning from Afghanistan. Thinking he might be heading to prison if he was caught, he came to have the goodbye they never really had. That was when Becky came running into the living room. He knew she was his.

"Why won't you ask, Nick?"

"Can't. Can't!"

"All right, why can't you?"

"Because there's always someone."

"What?" She was lost.

"You asked who would want to hurt Rosa."

"I did, but—"

"She was collateral damage. The killer wasn't there for her, but she stumbled into it. If she had stayed upstairs in the kitchen. If she hadn't married Tony. If she had stayed in Puerto Rico. You and Becky or even Brad can't be Rosa. I won't let you be collateral damage."

Shana smiled. "I was right."

"About what?"

"It's *won't*, not *can't*."

"You always did love winning."

"Says Nick Ryan, Catholic high school championship game MVP, war hero, decorated detective."

"Says he."

"It doesn't make any sense, Nick. We were together when you were on the streets in uniform in Canarsie. When you were in plainclothes riding the subways as a target. After your father testified and you had as many enemies on the job as on the streets. If I had promised to wait, you would have been at war and that would have been okay with you? But not now. Why not now?"

"Things have changed. It would be more dangerous for you and Becky."

"How can it be more dangerous than all the other times?"

"I can't explain."

She laughed joylessly. "There's that word again—*can't*."

"It's can't *and* won't. Just explaining it would put you in danger and that's not going to happen."

"I can't do this anymore, Nick. I thought I could be a vampire for as long as you needed to come around, until you gave in and asked us to be with you. I've slinked around behind Brad's back for a year because when we're together the rest of it goes away. But it comes rushing back with the sun, my other life. This morning . . . when Marjorie called the cops, it hit me so hard I knew I couldn't avoid it any longer. I want one life. I want that one life with you and our daughter."

"I know you were raised wealthy and that you're used to getting what you want—"

"Stop it, Nick. Now you sound like everyone else, the people who doubted us for all those years. I don't always get what I want. I don't always win. You know that better than anyone. Remember, it was you who left me behind."

"You gave me an ultimatum."

"I'm giving you another one."

"You're going to get the same answer," he said, threading his arms around her waist. He cupped her chin in his hand, forcing her to face him. "Don't do this, Shana. Don't force my hand. We're happy together."

"I can't reserve my happiness for once every few weeks or wait until Brad is out of town. I love you, Nick Ryan. From the minute you held the door for me outside the memorial, I have loved you. We were meant to be together. So let's be together."

He loosened his grip. "Maybe someday."

She pushed her hands against his chest. "I'm tired of maybes and somedays. Today is someday."

"No."

"Never, then." She stomped over to the sofa, grabbed her jacket. "Don't let me see you in the park again."

"Okay."

"Okay?"

"What do you want me to say?"

"You know what I want you to say."

"I can't."

Shana threw her set of keys at him. She left, slamming the door behind her. Nick listened to the echo of her footsteps on the terrazzo floor leading to the elevator. When he heard the elevator door close, his "other" phone rang. He wanted to throw it out the window. He wanted to leave Joe and the city's messes behind him. There was no turning back. Even if he walked away, he had already made the kinds of enemies who neither forgave nor forgot. Although he didn't know who the people were who passed his assignments to him through Joe, knowing that those people existed put him at risk. He answered the phone.

TEN

The sun was flirting with the eastern tip of Long Island when Ace pulled his blue Ford to the curb in front of Tony Angelo's place on Shore Parkway. There had been a passing snow shower overnight that was already beginning to melt away. The light dusting hadn't hidden the ugliness beneath it. Nothing hid blood for long. Besides, snow in the city hit the ground dirty.

"Condolences. I heard the news about your friend and his wife," Ace said as Nick climbed into the front seat. "How long you been out there like that?"

"About an hour. I spent a lot of happy days in that house." Nick pointed to the Angelos' place. "I just wanted to see it again like this, with nobody around. Look at it. Yesterday, there were people crawling all over the place. Everyone's moved on to the next crime scene, the next body, the next whatever. Not me. Tony and Rosa aren't going to become numbers on the Six-O's weekly stat sheet and then forgotten."

The truth was deeper than he cared to share. Nick had come to mourn not only Tony and Rosa but also the loss of Shana and Becky. Tony and Rosa were gone and there was no getting them back. Shana and

Becky were different. They were there for the asking. Only he couldn't ask. That made it all worse somehow.

"Happy days." Ace pulled away from the curb, getting onto the westbound Belt Parkway. "Be nice if we could appreciate them while they was happening instead of just looking back at them."

Nick ignored him. "We're going to the Bronx, right?"

"We are."

The relationship between Ace and Nick had started off badly. Now they were allies. Although they had come to a workable arrangement, they knew very little about each other. Arm's length was a layer of protection. Uneasy allies or not, they had done things that bound them together in a way that couldn't be undone.

Ace kept quiet until the Verrazzano came into distant view. Nick saw that Ace was pressing his mouth shut hard, forcing himself not to speak. They had spent a lot of silent time in each other's company over the past twelve months, enough time to decipher each other's distinct silences.

"Say what you've got to say, Ace."

"I haven't been sleeping lately."

"Skip the preamble."

Ace shook his head. "No easing into shit with you."

"There are days I'm in an easing-in mood. Today isn't one of them."

"I've been thinking a lot about . . . you know, what we did last year."

"We did a lot of things last year."

"That thing at the Scarborough Houses, Ryan. That other shit we done—that stuff was on the side of the angels. Them who got fucked earned it. Most were lucky they didn't get worse, but that other thing . . . I just can't get past it."

Nick glimpsed something in the passenger-side mirror. "You see those three vehicles behind us, the ones changing lanes?"

"Uh-huh." Ace nodded. "The Subaru, the red Vette, and the old Voyager? Yeah, I been watching them since we got on at Ocean Parkway."

"That's the third time they've changed lanes in unison."

"Drug caravan?"

"Doesn't feel like it. Experienced transporters wouldn't call this much attention to themselves. Let them get ahead of us. There's a speed trap coming up after the bridge."

Ace eased off the gas and moved right. "You know the man ain't gonna be happy if we're late. Why don't we let this shit go and let the regulars handle it?"

"Let him be unhappy. If I wanted to punch a clock, I'd work in a factory."

"Whatever you say, Ryan. But since we're doing this, you wanna call in the tags?"

Nick dug his phone out of his pocket. Ace's car had no standard computer, camera, or radio installed. Because they operated in the shadows, Nick and Ace had to avoid electronics that could track them.

A few hundred yards past the Verrazzano and before Nick could use his phone, the Vette swung out from behind the Subaru. It was doing over a hundred by the time it zoomed past Ace's Fusion. The driver weaved in and out of traffic, blasting his horn as he went.

Ace said, "Shit, he couldn't call more attention to himself if he was on fire."

Just as Ace finished speaking, a highway patrol unit proved his point. Siren blaring, grille and dashboard lights flashing, an unmarked NYPD Charger tore off the shoulder. Its rear tires spat out wet turf as it fishtailed onto the roadway. The Vette veered left onto the Gowanus heading toward the East River crossings. The Charger was close behind. The Vette wasn't stopping.

"He's scrubbing attention away from the other two vehicles." Nick tilted his head at the other two cars. "Let's stick with the Subaru and Voyager."

Ace smiled, something he rarely did. "Been a long time since I done real police work. Wonder if I even remember how. You sure about this? Like I said, the man don't like to be kept waiting."

"Too bad."

"Easy to say when you're the king."

"King, not me. You and me, Ace, we're the guys who scoop up the horse shit after the parade passes by. Only difference between us is that I've got a fancier shovel."

The Subaru and the Voyager kept to the speed limit, peeling off right from the Belt Parkway onto 278 in the opposite direction. Ace kept his distance, the rising sun's reflected orange glow off lower Manhattan's skyline in his rearview.

Nick said, "They're taking the back door onto the Verrazzano. They didn't want to get onto the bridge to Staten Island before they knew if they were hot. Once they were on the bridge, there'd be no retreat." Nick called in the tag numbers, waited, clicked off.

"What's the word?"

"Tags are clean. The Voyager is registered to a Carmine Gabrelli of Levittown. The Subaru is registered to a Robert Terrio of North Babylon. No stolen-car reports. No pending violations. No warrants pending for either man. Nothing."

"Just some nice Long Island boys out for a ride, huh?"

"They're dirty."

"Agreed. You know Staten Island's only a short hop to Jersey. They cross into Jersey and—"

"Don't start talking to me about jurisdictions."

On the other side of the Verrazzano, they were all caught in a red sea of brake lights. Ace was good with that. "Easy to keep track of them in this. We can't go nowhere and neither can they."

When traffic opened up, the Subaru and Voyager kept together in the right lane. They got off the Staten Island Expressway, exiting onto the West Shore Expressway. Ace followed a quarter mile back, making sure to keep seven or eight cars between them.

"Ryan, you know this road goes to the Outerbridge Crossing, right? New Jersey is on the other side."

"There's a lot of Staten Island between here and Jersey. We'll have an answer soon enough. Look at the blue-and-white on the shoulder."

"Another speed trap. Maybe these guys just want everybody to make their ticket quotas."

The Subaru pulled into the left lane and rocketed ahead. Like the Vette before it, the Subaru weaved in and out of traffic. And just as before, the cop gave chase. The Subaru was no match for the highway patrol. It didn't take long for the white-and-blue unit to overtake the Subaru and force it off the roadway.

"Whatever this is about is in that Voyager," Nick said as they passed by the NYPD cruiser and the Subaru.

Ahead of them, the Voyager pulled off onto the West Service Road. Ace slowed so that the minivan was barely in sight.

"Jesus, Ryan, what's that smell?"

"It's Fresh Kills, once the biggest landfill in the world. Now just a moldering pile of old garbage they're turning into parkland. They're already building regular road access."

"What is it with Staten fucking Island, man? Todt Hill, where all those Mafia guys live, means 'death hill' in German. And all these kills— why couldn't they just call them creeks or inlets like everywhere else? They trying to be ironic or some shit? Look, the Voyager is turning onto the old landfill access road."

About a minute later, Ace turned down the same road toward the security booth at the landfill entrance. There they found the body of a security guard face down in the mud. The lower half of his body was still in the booth. The back side of his head was missing. His blood-soaked baseball cap was pinned to the fence by the wind. Nick called it in.

Vast tarps had been laid over the mountains of garbage and a system had been set up in the pile to burn off the methane gas, but the odor of decay was still strong. Whirling flocks of hopeful birds flew circles above them. When Nick and Ace caught up to the Voyager, the old minivan's tailgate was raised, and the driver-side door was open.

"You stay here." Nick pulled the Glock off his hip.

Ace had his Colt Python at his thigh. "I'm coming with you."

"No, you're not. Wait here for the backup or they won't know where to look."

"Why should I listen to you?"

"I got the fancier shovel, remember? Don't worry about me. Watch your back."

"My back is just fine. It's your ass I'm gonna be protecting."

With that, Nick Ryan headed down a muddy path toward the creeks and estuaries separating Staten Island from New Jersey.

ELEVEN

Nick focused on the two sets of prints in the soil dampened by last night's snow. One set—men's size 10 or 11 work boots—left deep impressions in the mud. Their pattern was consistent, the gait regular and unhurried. The other prints told a different story. Those prints—a smaller man's bare feet—zigzagged. At points, Bare Feet had turned to face Work Boots. There were places where the prints came together and there were impressions in the mud that indicated the smaller man had fallen to his knees. A bit farther on, there were long shallow ruts and claw marks from where Work Boots must have dragged Bare Feet. The ruts lasted all the way to where there was an opening in the weed-lined path.

Nick slowed his pace. The overgrown weeds turned to sedge and reeds. He was getting close to the waters of Fresh Kills. He heard human voices just above the ambient traffic noise and the squawks, caws, and shrill bleats of the circling birds. When Nick stepped into a marshy clearing at the water's edge, he saw where the voices were coming from. The two men were about twenty-five yards to his right.

Work Boots, the man Nick figured was Carmine Gabrelli, was short, heavyset, and dressed in dirty, too-tight tan coveralls. He held a big revolver in his pudgy right hand. The muzzle of the six-inch satin-finished steel barrel was pressed into the thick black hair of a much younger man—Bare Feet. The younger man, a kid really, was dressed in wet, filthy boxers. His legs, face, and torso were partially covered in mud. Nick knew that Work Boots wasn't a pro. A pro would already have done the kid and thrown the body into Fresh Kills. Instead, he hesitated. His gun hand was shaking hard enough for Nick to see from seventy-five feet away.

The kid was pleading for his life. "Please, mister, don't do this. Please, I'm sorry. Whatever I did, I'm sorry. I don't know what I did. Just tell me what I did and I'll make it right. My father, he'll make it right. He's a powerful—"

The kid had said just the wrong thing. Gabrelli stiffened, slamming the revolver hard into the side of the kid's head. Bare Feet went limp, nearly toppling over into the water.

"Don't you fucking mention your motherfucking father to me," Gabrelli screamed. He was red-faced, spit flying out of his mouth. "He's why you're here. And there's no making up for what he did to my family."

The tantrum had let Nick get to within forty feet, close enough for an accurate shot. Gabrelli raised the pistol, a .357 Ruger. *No wonder the security guard was missing the back of his head,* Nick thought. A .357 with hollow-point ammo did ugly things to flesh and bone.

"NYPD!" Nick held his shield up in his left hand, then pocketed it. "Drop the weapon now, Gabrelli, or I'll fucking kill you where you stand. Get on your knees."

Seemingly confused that the cop knew his name, Gabrelli turned slightly toward Nick. "No third chances, Carmine." Nick lowered his voice, waving his left hand toward the ground. "Drop it."

Gabrelli dropped to his knees, lowered the Ruger, but held on to it. "His father killed my brother, Jimmy. His body's back there in the dump. My brother's in there with all that garbage! For years we didn't know what happened to him. My folks died not knowing. Now this kid's gonna pay that debt."

Nick inched closer. He was no more than thirty feet away. "Look, I don't know about any of that, but the security guard, he didn't kill your brother."

Gabrelli bowed his head. "I'm sorry about that, really, but . . ."

Twenty feet. "What do you think the guard's kid should do? Should he kill your kid?"

"I'm sorry."

Fifteen feet. "Come on with me, Carmine. My name's Nick. I'm not going to lie to you. This is a bad situation, but it doesn't have to get worse. You have a family, right?"

"Yeah, course I do."

Ten feet. Nick stopped, gave another downward wave. "Carmine, drop the weapon and come with me. Come on. Don't make me have to make it any worse for your people than it already is."

"Okay." Tears rolled down Gabrelli's cheeks. He loosened his fingers on the Ruger's grip.

It all went to shit. The kid stirred at Gabrelli's back. He scrambled to his feet and ran. He didn't get ten feet before slipping on the mud. Two shotgun blasts and pistol fire echoed in the distance through the morning air. Ducks and geese took off from the kill. Above them gulls, crows, magpies, and pigeons panicked, somehow missing each other as their orderly circles broke into thousands of winged fragments. Gabrelli ignored the chaos. He turned, raised the revolver. Nick fired until Carmine's coveralls were soaking through with blood. Gabrelli fell backward, his knees still under him. Nick raced to him, kicking the big Ruger away.

Carmine's eyes were wide open, blood and bubbly white foam pouring out of his mouth. He moved his lips. Only wheezing sounds came out. With a shudder and heave, his chest collapsed. The light went out of his eyes. The tension in his body vanished, taking the hatred and vengeance with it. Nick felt for a pulse he knew wasn't there.

"Listen, kid, you okay?" Nick asked, retrieving the Ruger.

"I guess. He was gonna—"

"Listen. Hide in the reeds and stay there until me or another cop comes for you. I gotta see what that shooting was about."

Nick took off back the way he came. Sirens filled the air as he came out the other end of the path where the Voyager was parked. A bullet whistled past his ear. He hit the ground, scanned the area. Ace was down on his side in a puddle of blood, pounding the dirt in pain. The Subaru, driver's-side door open, was parked behind the blue Ford. Nick saw the top of Robert Terrio's head above the door sill.

"Hear those sirens, Terrio?" Nick shouted. "First, throw out your weapon where I can see it, walk out from behind that door, hands raised. Carmine's dead. The kid's alive. The man you just shot is an NYPD detective. If he dies, you will too. No trial. I'll just fucking kill you. You want to live, do what I say. Throw out the weapon."

Nick began to combat-crawl toward Ace. He was about halfway to him when Terrio stepped out from behind the car door, a handgun in his waistband and a pump-action shotgun in his hands. *Boom!* The buckshot hit a few feet in front of Nick, kicking up wet soil into his eyes. He was partially blinded. Nick raised his Glock, pictured where the shooter was, and squeezed the trigger again and again until the weapon locked out.

Terrio gasped. There was a muted thud as he went down.

Nick tossed the Glock, pulled the big Ruger from his waistband, and crawled the rest of the way to Ace. With the sirens almost on them, Nick wiped his jacket sleeve across his eyes. His vision still blurred, he turned Ace onto his back and checked for where he had been shot. Blood was leaking out of several small wounds in the right side of Ace's chest and shoulder. There were too many for Nick to stanch even with both hands, so he pressed his palms down hard on as many of the chest wounds as he could cover.

"I told you to watch your back," Nick said, smiling at Ace.

"Fuck you, Ryan. He didn't hit me in the back."

"You're a funny man."

"I'm a dying man." Ace's chest heaved. "Don't let me die like this."

"Shut up."

"This is the NYPD," a voice called out over a speaker. "Drop your weapons. Now! Get on your knees facing away from us and lock your fingers behind your head."

Ace's eyes got wide. "Please, Ryan, don't let me . . ." His voice barely a whisper before he drifted into unconsciousness.

Nick screamed. "NYPD. Ten-thirteen. Ten-thirteen. Officer down. Officer down. Get a bus here now!"

He tossed the Ruger, held his shield behind his head, and waited.

TWELVE

Nick was bone weary. He'd spent ten hours at Richmond University Medical Center, then helicoptered over to Bellevue with Ace. He had recounted the specifics of what went down so many times he'd lost count. There was also that he'd killed Carmine Gabrelli and put Robert Terrio—Carmine's brother-in-law—in a coma. If Afghanistan had taught him anything, it was that killing gets easier, but never easy, and that with each kill you died a little too. All this piled on the loss of Shana and Becky and before he'd had a chance to come to terms with what had happened to the Angelos.

His GTO was still parked around the corner from Tony Angelo's house, but he decided he needed sleep more than his car. When the white-and-blue unit dropped him in front of his building, Nick thanked the uniforms and headed for the entrance. He never made it. Two men—both Nick's height, in their forties, white and stony-faced—stepped out from between the hedges that lined the walkway to the building. One blocked his way. The other blocked his retreat. Nick could tell by the silent, athletic way they moved that they were dangerous. He half-turned to keep both in sight. Both men held SIG Sauer P229s in their right hands. They made sure to stand out of range of Nick's arms and legs and far enough apart so that if Nick went for one, the other would have time to react.

"Detective Ryan?" asked the man to Nick's right.

"Who's asking?"

He raised his gun hand. "My name is Carver. I assure you this is a friendly invitation, weapons notwithstanding. There's someone who wants to chat with you. This . . ." He waved the gun. "Well, let's just say it's more persuasive than a heartfelt request. Our employer can be somewhat impatient."

"Notwithstanding, huh? Very fancy."

"Let's do this without incident so you can get some rest. Oh, and I'm glad to hear Detective Meadows will recover from his wounds."

Meadows! Nick thought. *Ace's real name.*

That comment about Ace's recovery impressed Nick. Because of the nature of Nick's unique status, a tight lid had been put on the details of what had happened earlier on Staten Island. But Nick didn't waste too much time being impressed. He was busy calculating the odds of escaping unscathed. He would have liked his chances better had his own weapons not been confiscated by the unit assigned to investigate officer-involved shootings. All he had available to him was his hawkbill knife. He was confident he could handle one of these guys, but not both.

"Okay," Nick said, "where're we going?"

Carver laughed. "First things first. Willoughby is going to pat you down. Don't do anything foolish."

Willoughby found the folded hawkbill tucked inside Nick's waistband. He handed it to Carver and stepped back.

Carver eyed the hawkbill before slipping it into his jacket pocket. "You could do some real damage with that knife. One cut to the femoral artery . . ."

"You do realize pointing a weapon at an NYPD detective and abducting him are pretty serious felonies."

"No one's pointing a weapon at you and no one's abducting you. You're coming along voluntarily."

"You've got a liberal interpretation of *voluntary*."

"Let's say voluntarily, like when you were in the army." Carver smiled. He spoke into the cuff of his jacket. "Location one." A black Chevy Suburban pulled to the curb where the white-and-blue unit had parked only a few minutes earlier. "Please, Detective Ryan. Your carriage awaits."

Nick said, "P229s. Chambered for .357, right? You're ex–Secret Service."

"I prefer *retired* to *ex*. Now, Detective, please . . ."

His odds of escape took a turn for the worse, for there was a fourth man, in the Suburban's front passenger seat, in addition to the driver, Willoughby, and Carver.

He hesitated before getting in. "I don't suppose saying I hate the middle seat will do me much good."

"I'm afraid not, though I agree that the middle seat is the least comfortable." Carver checked his watch. "I know you won't be reassured, but sit back and relax. This time of night, it should be about an hour, give or take."

———

With one eye on the route they were taking, Nick kept a drowsy eye out as the Suburban headed east on the Belt Parkway toward Long Island. If they had wanted him dead, there were easier ways to achieve that goal than a polite abduction off the street in front of hundreds of potential witnesses looking out their front windows. These guys were too detail oriented for that.

The Suburban slowed as it turned off the Long Island Expressway onto Route 107 north. Nick knew Long Island. Shana's dad had a summerhouse in East Hampton and his brother, Sean, lived in North Massapequa. This part of Long Island marked the southern boundary of what New Yorkers referred to as the Gold Coast. Nothing about the huge walled and gated estates or the country-club golf courses they passed along the two-lane road did anything to give the lie to the name *Gold Coast*.

The Suburban slowed. Looking out the window, Nick saw a long row of perfectly trimmed hedges. Behind the hedges was a six-foot-high stone wall. Now almost at a crawl, they turned left. Two imposing wrought-iron gates swung open.

"This is it, Detective Ryan," said the driver.

"Old Brookville," Nick said. "Almost as fancy as Carver's vocabulary."

Carver laughed. "The vocabulary used around us at the White House must've rubbed off."

They drove another quarter mile up a long, curved, sloping driveway, past a cottage to a manor house the size of a jet hangar. The mansion was all red bricks, white columns, and peaked roofs. Above the huge double front doors, suspended from a thick black chain, was a light fixture that looked like a glass coffin. As Nick walked beneath it, he thought of the sword of Damocles. The front doors opened.

"Go on in, Detective Ryan." Carver gently urged Nick forward. "We'll be here to take you back to Brooklyn."

"Not coming?"

"Try to be polite. It's been a rough day for her too."

Her?

The moment he stepped through the vestibule into the great entrance hall, he understood. On the wall in front of the sweeping curved staircase to his left was a family portrait. A tall, elegant-looking man of forty stood beside a younger blond-haired woman who would have been equally at home on the cover of *Vogue* or *House Beautiful*. Seated in front of them were two teenage children, a boy and a girl. The girl, older than her brother, had her dad's looks. The boy, his mother's. Nick recognized the boy. The photo array on the Steinway grand piano confirmed it. The kid was older now. He wasn't covered in mud, nor was he begging for his life.

THIRTEEN

She was in her midforties now, more petite than she appeared in the family portrait. Dressed in a gray blouse, black slacks, and heels, she possessed a beauty undiminished by age. If anything, it had added a depth to her looks that surgery and Botox never could. Her shoulder-length hair had turned a silvery gray and her eyes were a startling violet blue. She seemed to read Nick's mind.

"The portraitist made us pose for hours," she said. "Yet somehow, the moment it captured seems so much more fleeting than a photograph. I detest it, but Jonathan demands we keep it up."

"It doesn't do you or your son justice."

"Lovely of you to say, Detective Ryan." She came and stood by him. "No, I don't suppose it does. Excuse my rudeness." She looped her arm through his and maneuvered him out of the great room.

This close to her, he caught a whiff of her. Wealthy women smelled different. A lesson he had learned from Shana and her friends. Their makeup and scents were custom blended. No doubt this woman had been to one of the exclusive perfumeries in Grasse, France. Whoever created her scent must have had a man with Nick's tastes in mind. Her unique blend had hints of patchouli, notes of crushed sage, and undertones of a late-spring garden after a rain shower.

She had walked him to a paneled pocket door and slid it back. The room they stepped into would have been called a study: part library, part home office, part bar. There were white marble busts of Shakespeare and Julius Caesar in one corner and a black marble bust of Homer on a bookshelf. A large verdigris armillary, its arrow pointing to the heavens, stood next to an even larger antique globe. The books on the built-in shelves were gilt-lettered and leather-bound. East of the huge side-facing stained-glass window was a mahogany desk. On the opposite side, a dry bar.

She let go of his arm and moved toward the bar. "I'm Victoria Lansdale. As you deduced, it was my son, Jon Jr., you rescued today. I'm told your partner will recover fully from his wounds. I'm glad of that. I wanted to thank you in person."

"A card would have been easier."

She laughed. "Brave and funny."

"Thanks are unnecessary. Ace—Detective Meadows—and I were doing our jobs."

"You know, Nick. May I call you Nick?"

"That I'm standing here proves your asking for permission is academic. I know a man who says that it's easier to ask forgiveness than permission."

"A wise man, your friend."

"A rich man. My experience has been that wealth gives the rich a false sense of sagacity."

She laughed. Her nose crinkled when she did. "Wealth comes with its privileges."

"Hazards too, apparently. If it didn't, we would never have met."

Panic flashed across her face. She pretended to ignore it, pouring herself a glass of red wine. "Drink?"

"Bourbon, neat."

"Weller Wooden Cork?"

"Please. I've never tried the Wooden Cork."

"I wouldn't know the difference. I don't much care for amber alcohol, but Jonathan has a taste for showing off the best of things."

"Like you?"

She laughed again, sadly. "I suppose. And like me, he tires of them."

"How is your son?"

She handed him the heavy crystal tumbler. "Cheers." She took a large swallow of wine.

"*Sláinte.*" He sipped the bourbon. "Very good."

Victoria Lansdale finished her wine before his second sip of the bourbon.

"To answer your question, Nick, Jon Jr. seems all right. He has a nasty bruise, scrapes and cuts, but was released from the hospital. He's recovering at his sister's town house in the city."

That raised an elephant-in-the-room question. Why wasn't the kid here?

"He won't be fine tomorrow," Nick said. "When the shock wears off, the depth of the trauma he suffered will set in. He came pretty close to getting killed. You don't get over that by wishing it away or hanging out with your big sister. Mrs. Lansdale, you should be prepared for the fallout. Find someone who specializes in treating ASD and you might be able to lessen the blow."

"ASD?"

"Acute stress disorder. It's PTSD's nasty first cousin."

"Thank you, Nick." She looked directly into his eyes. Hers were suddenly red and moist. "How is it you know so much about it?"

"Two tours in Afghanistan." He finished the bourbon.

"Another?"

"Yes, please." He handed her the glass. "Tell me what today was all about."

"You're asking *me*?"

"Seems a natural question."

She poured his second drink halfway to the top of the tumbler. She poured herself more wine from its handblown, wildly shaped glass decanter.

Nick pointed at the decanter. "Chihuly?"

"No, one of his former studio assistants. I'm impressed you know Chihuly."

"A misspent youth."

She laughed, nose crinkling. "I doubt that. So, as I was saying, the details are a bit sketchy. Apparently, Jon Jr. was coming home late from a party when he was grabbed off the street by three men outside the house he shares off-campus at Hofstra. I didn't even know *that* much until the police called me afterwards. I was hoping you could fill me in on what happened. The police weren't very helpful in that respect and Jon didn't seem inclined to discuss it. All he would say is that he is furious at his father."

"Where is Mr. Lansdale?"

"Australia." She didn't explain further. "Details, please."

"I don't think so. I know the rich very well," he said, placing his glass down on the bar. "I don't mean what most people think of as rich. I mean go-fuck-yourself rich—rich like you. I'm unimpressed by money. That means I won't play by your rules because you think the rules are what you make them."

"You are an exasperating man."

"You won't be shocked to hear that I've been called that before. You wanted to thank me. You've thanked me. With two glasses of this fine bourbon, I consider your mission thoroughly accomplished. Now, if you could ask Carver to take me back to Brooklyn, I'd appreciate it."

"I'm sorry, Nick . . . Detective Ryan . . ." She put down her glass and latched her hand around Nick's wrist. "Please, I know I went about this in completely the wrong manner. You're right, of course, I am used to getting my way. I will have Carver do as you ask, but understand, my son means everything to me and I will be indebted to you always."

"We can try this again if you go about it like a mere mortal. I'm sure you can find your way to Brooklyn. If you do, then I'd be glad to answer your questions."

She smiled an electric white smile. "Brooklyn?"

"Do you know it?"

"I might have heard of it once or twice. Does travel there require a visa?"

Nick returned the smile. "Remember, get your son some help. Don't wait."

She stood on her toes and kissed Nick on the cheek. "Thank you."

Victoria Lansdale let go of his wrist and left the room. His wrist felt as if her hand were still on it. Two minutes later, Carver entered.

"Back to Brooklyn?"

"Yeah," Nick said. "Hubbard Street and Shore Parkway."

"Come on, I'll drive you."

"No Willoughby and the gang?"

Carver handed Nick his knife. "Do I need them?"

"On most days, probably. The way I feel tonight, I think you're safe."

FOURTEEN

He'd fallen into a dreamless, alcohol-infused sleep, a half bottle of Weller 12 on the kidney-shaped glass coffee table next to the sofa. The ride back to Brooklyn with Carver had given him a chance to let killing Carmine sink in.

"What's it like, killing a man?" Carver asked. "I was in the marines, but I was never deployed."

"It's not *like* anything. That's the problem."

"Secret Service, our job was to prevent killing. I'm a hunter, though."

"It's not like hunting because with humans, both sides know the stakes. The guy I killed today, he knew I was going to have to do it if he made a move. He made the move anyway. A deer or boar is acting out of survival instinct. This man did the opposite."

"Doesn't that mean something, that he forced your hand?"

"Net result's the same. I shot the shit out of him and he's dead." Nick turned to Carver. "Do I get a question?"

"Sure."

"How did the Lansdales make their fortune?"

Nick could see that Carver was uncomfortable with the question. "Venture capital. Invests in huge projects and businesses all over the world."

"Like in Australia."

"Like that, yes."

"What does a man like that have to do with a guy like Carmine Gabrelli's brother?"

"You had your one question."

Nick pressed him. "Okay, then why would Lansdale need retired Secret Service agents working for him?"

"It's a secret." Carver snorted at his own joke.

"The wife?"

Carver shook his head. "Again, you got your question."

They rode the rest of the way in silence. Nick's thoughts were anything but silent.

When he got back home, he'd had a drink for Tony and Rosa. For Shana. For Becky. He'd stared at the photo of Shana and him taken at her high school graduation party at the Waldorf Astoria a thousand years ago. It was his favorite picture of them. There was still innocence in their eyes, the belief that they could prove the doubters wrong. It was them against the world. The world had finally won.

The photo was still on his chest when he was roused by Joe's phone. He let it ring. Joe would call again. He always did. Nick put the photo on the coffee table. He looked out at the Verrazzano Bridge and saw by the slim shadows it cast that the morning was nearly over. The clock on the cable box confirmed it. Yesterday's incident meant he was off the job until the investigators cleared him of the shootings. But he was never off from his unofficial duties. Joe's phone rang again. Nick picked up.

"What?"

"Unfinished business."

"The Inspector Gadget car?"

"Among other things. The other things are currently more pressing."

"How's Ace?"

"Ornery."

"Good. When can I see him?"

"I'll let you know when I know. How are you? You sound . . . off."

"Not your business. Where?"

"Valentino Pier."

"Not Citi Field or Totonno's Pizzeria?"

"It's no longer worth my while to try to impress a man unwilling to be impressed."

"I liked Totonno's that morning. Pizza for breakfast is hard to beat. If we could do that again . . ."

"I don't have time for this now."

"When?"

"An hour."

"Two hours."

"Two hours, then." Joe clicked off.

———

He got to the pier early, Mack, as always, in tow to watch his back. Like everyone else in his life, Nick trusted Joe on a situational basis. Trust was the thing he missed about the army. The survival of each individual in a unit depended on every other person in the unit. Enemies were clearly defined. Not in Nick's new world. It was too easy for players to switch sides without changing jerseys. Lesser men might have been eaten alive by paranoia. Not Nick. He kept vigil at the edge of his blind spots.

Valentino Pier in Red Hook was a concrete finger sticking out into New York Harbor. A secret to most New Yorkers, an afterthought to others. Nick leaned over the rail; the Statue of Liberty seemed close enough to touch. Ahead of him, along with the greened copper statue, Ellis Island and the cranes from Port Newark. To his left, Staten Island and the Verrazzano. To his right, the competing glass towers of Lower Manhattan and Jersey City. There was no serenity to be found here. The water stank of things unknown, of things unseen beneath the oil slicks floating on its surface. Tugboat and ferry horns blared. Helicopters *thwap-thwap-thwapped*, their blades beating the air above him.

He turned away from the rail. Joe was coming up the pier toward him, a thick accordion file pinned under his right arm. Nick thought of Joe as little more than a well-appointed messenger boy delivering word from on high. The wind blew out the side wings of his white hair. A vain man, Joe tried to slick them down. Finally, he let the wind have its way.

They didn't shake hands. *You don't shake hands with the UPS driver, do you?*

"What's wrong?" Nick asked.

The surprise played across Joe's permanently tanned face. "Wrong? Haven't you learned that the easier question to ask in this city is 'What's right?'" Joe walked past Nick, hitched his foot on the rail. He gazed out at the Statue of Liberty. "Ryan, I told you early on, no freelancing. Was I not clear about that?"

Nick leaned his back against the rail, looking in the opposite direction down the pier toward the old brick warehouses of Red Hook. "Perfectly clear."

"What is it about the words *keeping a low profile* that you fail to comprehend? What were you two thinking about yesterday?"

"We were being good cops."

"You were being cowboys."

"*Yee-haw!*"

"That's not funny, Nick. I know you must have instigated it, because your partner wouldn't've."

"He's not my partner and I know his name is Meadows."

Nick was suddenly curious about Joe's true identity. Maybe it was knowing Ace's real name or Joe's slightly off manner. Whatever the reason, he trusted his instincts.

Joe snapped his fingers at Nick. "Pay attention. Yesterday's ugliness in Staten Island had your fingerprints all over it. Meadows knows better. He understands how to follow orders."

"Look where that got him. If he was a little more of a cowboy, he'd still have my job."

"He was never up to the task," Joe said. "Water finds its own level."

"We saved a kid's life."

"At significant cost. You killed a man, put another in a coma he'll never come out of, and you got Meadows shot. Every time you draw outside the lines, you garner too much attention, and we're forced to work overtime to put a lid on things. It makes it more difficult for you to do the jobs for which you are uniquely suited, the ones this city needs you to do. There are thirty-four thousand, nine hundred ninety-nine other cops to do the rest."

Nick held out his right hand. "You were told to deliver a wrist-slapping. Delivery accepted."

"Next time you feel like being a *real* cop, call it in."

"If we just called it in, there'd be a dead kid floating in Fresh Kills."

"Be that as it may—"

"Did you get me here just to scold me?"

"Vlado Markovic?"

The name rang a faint bell in the recesses of Nick's memory. As he tried to retrieve it, he turned and stood shoulder to shoulder with Joe. "Sounds familiar."

"I never get over seeing the Statue of Liberty," Joe said. "My grandparents, like your great-grandparents, saw it as they came over from the old country. They were different old countries, to be certain, but I think about how it must've made them feel."

"She's more welcoming to some than to others."

"No argument there."

"Vlado Markovic." Nick smacked the pier rail. "He was the one homicide vic in the city on Nine-Eleven outside of Manhattan."

"Correct. He was stabbed to death on a subway platform on his way to work."

"Hate crime, right? Revenge for the terrorist attacks. Markovic was full-bearded and spoke with an accent, so it's assumed the killer or killers mistook him for an Arab."

"If I were your teacher, I'd give you a gold star." Joe nodded to the east. "The Smith and Ninth Street station. He bled out alone on the Manhattan/Queens–bound platform."

"What about him?"

"You need to get to the truth of what happened that night."

"Why?"

"Wrong question. You don't get to ask why, remember? Even if I were inclined to answer you, I couldn't. I don't know why and I don't wish to know. End of story."

"What makes them think I can do what homicide detectives have failed to do?"

"Because you're batting a thousand. If you were a baseball player, they'd build you a separate wing in Cooperstown."

"Fuck flattery." Nick reddened. "Accolades and medals are as meaningful as wet cotton candy. I chucked the last medal I got from the department down a sewer in Chinatown."

Joe shook his head. "You'll do it because it's your job."

"I've got something more important to look into than a cold case nobody gives a shit about."

Joe laughed. "Oh, I assure you, someone very much gives a shit."

"Tony and Rosa Angelo matter more to me."

"The bosses are aware, but you need to focus on Vlado Markovic."

Nick tugged the accordion file out from under Joe's arm. "Heavy."

Joe said, "Your Glock 19 and 26 are in there. They've already been tested. You may need them. As always, any other resources you may require to find Markovic's killer will be at your disposal."

"When will I be cleared to go back to work?"

Joe shrugged, smiled like the devil. "Yet to be determined."

"Punishment?"

"Incentive."

"I've never needed extra incentive to do my job."

"No one asked for my input." Joe took a step, stopped. "Oh, I almost forgot these." He reached into the pocket of his camel-colored vicuña coat. He handed Nick a car key fob, an electric door opener, and a slip of paper. "The Malibu is parked in a garage at that address. It's an unused safe house, so you don't have to worry about arousing suspicions. There are instructions in the glove box. Please, avail yourself of its use. Your car is becoming too conspicuous. Use the Chevy for your own good."

Nick let Joe get halfway down the pier before dialing Mack's cell.

"Christ, Ryan, will you let me do me job."

"Never mind that, Mack. See Joe coming down the pier?"

"I could scarcely miss the fooker in that coat. Must've cost the bastard some serious wedge."

"Follow him?"

"Far as I can tell, that Joe fella came alone. You know, Ryan, sometimes I find myself wishing I'd taken me arse to Chicago and left you and your machinations behind."

"Funny, Mack, sometimes I find myself wishing the same thing."

"I've got to shift it, boyo. Vicuña Coat is headed this way."

Nick turned back to the Statue of Liberty and wondered if she was the reason Joe had chosen to meet him here.

FIFTEEN

Nick realized he seldom visited Lenny except under the cloak of darkness. There was more human activity on Ocean Parkway now than during those late-night visits. Cyclists puffed out streams of cold steam as they pedaled along the bike path. Long-skirted women in obvious wigs pushed strollers before them. Black-hatted men in long black coats, side curls, and unruly beards walking in groups. Coming in the opposite direction, Bangladeshi men, eyes downcast, wearing full-length tan frocks, matching pants, and skullcaps, their arms wrapped around themselves as a hedge against the chill.

At the basement door, Lenny looked at the accordion file under Nick's arm. "I don't know who or what that file is about, but how could I possibly add to anything so obviously comprehensive?"

Lenny Feld was not averse to an occasional display of false modesty. He was acutely aware that Nick needed him to find the things that no one else could. It wasn't about what was in the files Nick brought to him. It was about what *wasn't* in them. Lenny's physical disfigurement was easily reconciled with his abiding vanity. Lenny's vanity was about the gifts of mind. Nick was careful never to hit the subject too hard. They both knew that Lenny blamed his brilliance for the death of his family as much as he blamed the arsonist.

"I have something for you." Lenny smiled with the functional pieces of his face. "Come."

At the door to Lenny's room, Nick noticed another file on the metal folding chair. As Lenny put a pot of water on the hot plate, Nick placed the file on the floor and sat.

Lenny spooned instant coffee into the bottom of two cups. "Just when I think I understand you, Nick, you confound me."

"How so?"

"You killed a man yesterday—Carmine Gabrelli."

"How do you know—"

Lenny laughed, coughing afterward as he always did. "You're not seriously asking me how I know things I shouldn't. That's why you're here, is it not?"

"Point taken. Yeah, I killed a man yesterday and put another in a permanent coma."

"Yet here you are."

"Here I am."

Lenny faced him. "I think about the man who murdered my wife and daughter. Sometimes it's all I think about. I wonder if the next day he just went on with his life the way you seem to. Did he go home, shower, and sleep well? Does he think about the murders as much as I do? Does he think about it at all?"

"I don't know the answers. I can only answer for me. Yesterday I did it to save someone's life. That matters, but only a little. There's a price to pay. That price would be the same whether I kept doing my job today or sat at home pondering it."

"Pick up the file from the floor. Take a look."

When Nick did, he saw a photo of a smiling Carmine Gabrelli in a volunteer firefighter's uniform.

He said, "I didn't ask you for this."

"I'm not a golden retriever, Nick. I didn't earn two PhDs and seven patents by being told to fetch. I was curious about the man you killed. Read the file."

Nick flipped the photo. Beneath it was a grainier photo of a man who resembled Carmine. Younger, squat like Carmine, better looking. He wore blue US Air Force coveralls with sergeant's stripes on his sleeves. "His brother, Jimmy?"

"Correct. You should be a detective."

"Practicing again for open-mic night at the Improv?"

"There's the Nassau County Police missing-persons report and the case file. Interesting reading."

"For you, maybe."

"Doesn't it matter to you why the man kidnapped a college kid and was going to kill him?"

"He thought Jonathan Lansdale had Jimmy Gabrelli murdered and he was going to pay him back by killing his son. He told me that."

"But you should read the file. It might still interest you."

"Whatever you say, Lenny. I've got more things to get to than jets stacked up over Kennedy."

Feld poured the hot water into the cup, stirred, added milk. They sat quietly for a few minutes, sipping. Then Lenny looked at the LED time readout on one of his devices. He tilted his head at Nick. "Did you come for the stuff from Flannery's phone? It's early in the day for one of your visits."

"For Flannery, yeah, but for some other stuff too."

"Other stuff?"

"Does the name Vlado Markovic mean anything to you?"

"Should it?" Lenny's voice couldn't mask his excitement. Despite his off-the-charts IQ, Lenny was like most people. He longed to be needed. After the fire, he needed to be needed more than most.

"On Nine-Eleven there was only one homicide in the city that wasn't part of the terrorist attacks."

"Vlado Markovic."

"You should be a detective."

"I wouldn't want to put you out of a job. Give me a few days." Lenny read Nick's face. "There's more?"

Nick told him about Tony and Rosa Angelo.

"I'm so sorry, Nick. I heard on the scanner but had no idea you knew them."

"How could you know?"

"What do you need?"

"Besides the usual background stuff you find, I need you to monitor this cell number."

"Who does the number belong to?"

"Annalise Puleo."

Lenny's eyes got wide. "That name I know. Weren't you two—"

"We were, but that was a few years ago. She's working the Angelos' homicide."

"Speaking of phone numbers . . ." Lenny went to his workbench, got another file, and handed it to Nick.

"Flannery?"

Lenny nodded. "Something curious turned up."

"What?"

"I hacked the numbers on Flannery's phone, then hacked the numbers on those phones. One number turned up that might interest you."

"Whose?"

"Yours."

That pushed Nick up off the folding chair. "Mine?"

"Yes, your cell number. It's all there, Nick. You've got a lot of reading to do."

Nick thought about questioning Lenny further but realized the answers were in the files. "Thanks, Lenny."

"Nick," Lenny called after him.

"What?"

"Take the Markovic file with you. I don't need it."

"You sure?"

"Truthfully, Nick, when you bring me files, I never read them. I let you leave them to give you comfort."

"Why am I not surprised?"

"There's something else," Lenny said, his face deadly serious. "You keep putting your promise to me at the back of the line. My end of our bargain has a shelf life."

"Understood."

"I hope so, Nick. I hope so."

It was night outside when Nick emerged. It seemed darker than it should be.

SIXTEEN

Nick parked his GTO in his building's underground garage, uncovered the Norton, and fired it up to make sure the damned thing still ran. He understood his uncle's love for the GTO. He had grown to love it too. Nick was less sure about the Norton.

"There's something about English motorcycles," Uncle Kenny once said to him. "It's like Jaguar E-Types. They're so fucking beautiful it doesn't matter that they're mechanical nightmares. In a world of shit, beauty counts for a lot. Remember that, kid."

He remembered. Didn't make him love the Norton any better. In another of those twists life kicks your ass with, it was only after seeing Shana for the first time that he got what Uncle Kenny meant about beauty. That he never got to tell his uncle he finally understood was a singular regret. Well, now with Becky, there were more regrets. Nick scolded himself. *Where have regrets gotten you? As far as wishes, hopes, and dreams. Nowhere.*

He collected Lenny's files and rode the elevator up to the penthouse condo. Of the four things he'd inherited from his uncle—the GTO, the Norton, the money, the condo—Nick loved the condo best. It was what his uncle had liked least. Kenny always saw it as a stepping stone to a loft in SoHo or a brownstone in Chelsea. Not Nick. His root ball was firmly planted in Brooklyn, buried down deep beneath the soot, soil, and concrete.

When he stepped out of the elevator, something was off. Someone was waiting for him, hiding at the other end of the short hallway between his penthouse and the door to the roof. He knew who it was by the scent in the air. There was a gold-labeled bottle of champagne in an ice bucket on the mat in front of his door.

"Come out of there, Mrs. Lansdale."

Victoria Lansdale stepped into the light, her heels clicking on the terrazzo floor. Her wardrobe motif was black on black with a splash of red: a waist-length kid-leather jacket over a silk blouse, over slacks, over Louboutin pumps that added several inches to her height. Her silver-gray hair was dazzling against the field of black. Her makeup was as perfect as if it were anatomical.

"How did you know?"

"Shadows can't hide a woman's scent. Patchouli, sage, spring flowers. Mixes nicely with the smell of expensive leather."

"Bravo. I thought Carver and his men were perceptive, but you . . ." She applauded quietly as if he had sunk a birdie putt.

"How'd you get up here?"

"Same as you—the elevator." She laughed, nose crinkling. "The front door was easy. Press enough buttons . . ."

"Where's your Secret Service detail?"

"I know where they aren't."

"Don't you feel exposed all on your own?"

"I feel perfectly safe with you and I'm pretty good all on my own."

"Strange. I've found that wealth makes people pretty paranoid." Nick walked up to the ice bucket, took out the champagne. "Louis Roederer Cristal 2004." He replaced the bottle in the bucket among the small plastic cold packs. "Expensive?"

"*Expensive* is relative when you have money."

"Even more so when you don't."

"The bucket cost more than the bottle. So you tell me."

"If you couldn't tell last night, Mrs. Lansdale—"

"Vicky."

"If you couldn't tell last night, Vicky, expensive gifts don't pull much weight with me."

"I know. I've lived in a bubble so long I've forgotten how to be a person. I handled last night atrociously. I simply wanted to say I was sorry for that and to thank you."

"Like I said, a card would've been less complicated."

"But I'm here, so do me the courtesy of letting me take you to dinner. After that, we can forget the sorrys and thank-yous."

"Good. I'm hungry. First, let me throw these files inside."

"Can I come in and see?"

"Wait there." His life was already too complicated. He stepped around the bucket, opened the lock, and placed the files to the left of the door. He reached back for the champagne bucket.

She said, "Don't do that."

"Why? What've you got in mind?"

"Let me come in and I'll show you."

"I meant for dinner."

"Grab the bucket. The champagne's for sharing. You'll see."

He cradled the bucket in his arm.

———

Outside, Nick followed Victoria Lansdale to a white SUV, a Maserati Levante.

"Put the champagne on the floor in the back, will you?"

Nick did as she asked. "Aren't you going to ask me what kind of food I'd like?"

"You're a Brooklyn boy, right?"

"I am."

"Then I don't have to ask."

As they pulled away from the curb, Nick asked, "How's your son?"

"He's seeing a Dr. Kassinove. He's supposed to be the best in New York at treating acute stress disorder."

"Good. Last night you asked me about what went on yesterday."

"Carver got me the details."

"Why would a man like Carmine Gabrelli or his brother have anything to do with a man like your husband?"

She snorted. "My husband wasn't always a man like my husband, if you get my meaning."

"You mean he didn't always have money to invest in other people's dreams?"

"When we met, he already had money, but not the kind of money he's come into."

"You have an interesting way with words, Vicky. Very lyrical."

"My father fancied himself a kind of poet," she said, as if that explained the forces of nature.

They headed east on the Belt Parkway and got off at Cropsey Avenue a few minutes later. She turned left onto Surf, turned right on Ruby Jacobs Walk, and parked at a meter.

Nick laughed. "Nathan's? You're taking me for Nathan's Famous hot dogs?"

"And french fries, of course. Where else would a St. Brendan's Brooklyn gal take a guy who went to Xaverian?"

"So that stuff last night about needing a visa was bullshit?"

"I grew up on Sheepshead Bay Road, Nick. Lived in an apartment over a kosher deli."

"Leo's." Nick smiled. "Ate there plenty of times. Closed years ago. What happened to your accent?"

"Gone like Leo's. It cost my modeling agency a shit ton a money to make me lose this freakin' accent," she said, slipping easily into Brooklynese. "You know what I mean?"

"You are a surprising woman, Vicky."

"I hope so. C'mon, let's eat."

They had two hot dogs apiece, shared a large fries. They made mimosas out of orangeade and champagne.

"Memory's a funny thing," she said, her eyes staring into the past. "I remember this stuff tasting better when I was a kid."

"Back then it was a treat. Now it's a curiosity. You're not who you were. None of us is."

"A philosopher."

"Not nearly. I spent a lot of years living between two worlds: one world like you live in and one down here at street level."

"Shana Carlyle's world."

Nick didn't react. "No secret about Shana and me. You don't need a man like Carver to find out about us."

"No wonder money doesn't mean anything to you. Talk about money! You walked away from what could have been an easy life."

"No life is easy. Money softens the blows. It doesn't stop them from coming."

"You're wrong, Nick Ryan."

"How's that?"

"You *are* a philosopher."

"You wanna get some real drinks?"

"Sure," she said. "You drive."

SEVENTEEN

From the jar of pickled eggs atop the bar to the cheese-and-onion sand-wiches to the Guinness on tap, the Black Harp was the real deal Irish pub. Like McSorley's in Greenwich Village, it had dust on its fixtures dating back to the turn of the twentieth century.

Nick enjoyed the bemused expression on Victoria Lansdale's face at the sight of the patrons.

"I've never seen this many tattooed women, man buns, ugly clothes, and unkempt beards in one place."

Nick said, "Williamsburg's a bit different from when you lived in Brooklyn above Leo's Deli."

"I know about Williamsburg, you schmuck!" She slapped Nick's arm. "Jon Jr. wanted to live here when he graduated. It's just so strange to see a place like this in the midst of Hipsterville."

"It was here even before Brooklyn was part of New York City and it'll be here when Williamsburg turns poor again."

They sat on rickety cane stools at the end curve of the long bar. A barrel-chested, big-bellied barman came over to them. He wore a wary expression on his bearded face.

"Nick Ryan! I didn't expect to see you here, boyo."

"Mack, I'd like you to meet Vicky."

Mack winked at her, his smile warm enough to heat the building. "What's a beauty like you doin' with a reprobate like Ryan here?"

She winked back. "Turn off the blarney, Mack, and get us a drink, will ya?"

"Feisty, are ya? What's your pleasure, darlin'?"

"Irish coffee, heavy on the Irish and light on the coffee, a dab of cream. None of that crème de menthe or sugarcoated-rim crap."

"And for you, boyo?"

"Same."

"Give us a minute. I'll brew you up a fresh pot." Mack headed down the bar.

When he'd gone, Nick said, "Your son *wanted* to move here. Past tense?"

"His father invested in some big real estate projects in the neighborhood. That ruined it for Jon Jr."

"I know all about fathers and sons."

"Carver told me about your father's testifying in front of the Argent Commission. Must make things at work hard for you."

"Afghanistan was hard." He changed subjects back to where he started. "Your son's troubles with his father—is that why he's at his sister's and not recuperating in Old Brookville?"

She ignored the question. "Where's the ladies'?"

"Other end of the bar, make a left."

"When I get back, can we please talk about anything else besides my husband?"

"Sure."

Mack appeared in front of Nick as soon as Victoria Lansdale had gone out of view. He handed Nick a sheet of paper. "Joe's info is all there. His address, tag number. His coat's not the only fancy thing about that fooker. Drives a gray fifty-five 300 SL Mercedes."

"A Gullwing?" Nick laughed. "That motherfucker!"

"Am I missing something, Ryan?"

"He's always on me about *my* car being too conspicuous."

"As conspicuous motors go, you two are a matched pair. Your Vicky, she's cracker. Christ, she's got quite the pile from the hardware she's sportin'. The stone on her ring is the size of a baby fist and I could retire on the wee stones in her wedding band. You gonna give her a ride?"

"Like the lady said, Mack, get us a drink."

The barman winked. "As you wish, ya chilly-hearted bastard."

Nick was sipping his coffee when Victoria Lansdale emerged from the ladies'. She was slipping her cell into her back pocket. Nick could see by her walk that the phone call had changed things. She was carrying weight on her shoulders that hadn't been there when she left for the bathroom.

"What is it?" Nick asked. "Is it your son?"

"No."

"Maybe the coffee will help. Well, it's more like coffee-colored whiskey."

She didn't sit. "Nick, do you think you can get yourself back home?"

"Sure, but—"

She held her palm up to stop him. "It's not your concern."

Nick threw two twenties on the bar. Waved to Mack that he was leaving. Turned to Vicky. "Let's go."

"No, that's fine. You stay and have your drink. Have both. I'm perfectly okay on my own."

"That may be, Vicky, but there's the matter of my champagne bucket."

It was an excuse. They both knew it. She seemed relieved to have his company.

"Please, will you do me the courtesy of making my apologies to Mack when you see him next?"

Her old Brooklyn accent had gone the way of her smile. The stiff-spined facade and proper manners were back in place.

———

With the buzz from Williamsburg Bridge at their backs, they turned the corner off Wythe Avenue onto South Fourth. The street was empty. The Maserati was parked at the end of the block near Kent.

"Amazing view." Vicky pointed across the East River at the light show of Manhattan. "It looks close enough to touch. I remember as a kid thinking I could never get there. That I could take the D train or the F and I could visit, but it could never be mine. Now we own two apartments there. I sometimes wish I could undo it all."

Before he could respond, Nick's radar popped on. He heard something—footsteps, many footsteps—beyond the noise from the bridge. He grabbed Victoria Lansdale's right biceps. She got the message, stopping in her tracks.

"What is it?"

He swung her around to face him. "Look at me unless I tell you otherwise. Play along." He stroked her cheek, stared into her eyes. "There are at least two men behind us, one in front of us between the back of your Levante and the van parked behind it. Now he's coming our way. When I kiss you, look across the street and tell me how many men you see." Nick cupped her chin in his hand, tilted her head, leaned down, and kissed her softly on the mouth.

"One," she said, pulling back. "He's wearing a black balaclava." She kissed him again.

"They all are." He whispered, "Take this." He slipped his Glock 19 out of his hip holster into her palm. "Do you know how to use it?"

"Yes, but—"

He kissed her ear, whispered, "Depress the trigger a little and you'll feel when you can fire." He kissed her again as the footsteps drew closer. "There's a doorway behind you. That's where you'll be. If they get past me, don't hesitate. Don't negotiate. Shoot for their torsos. Keep shooting until you empty the magazine. There won't be more than two of them to deal with. One if I'm lucky."

"How can you know that?"

He didn't answer, kissing her, urging her backward into the unlit doorway. When he was sure Victoria was hidden by the shadows, he stepped forward. The hawkbill knife was in his right hand, his shield in his left.

"Listen, assholes, get the fuck out of here," Nick yelled, flashing his shield. "Walk away now! I'm not in the mood."

Before Nick got the last word out of his mouth, the man who'd been approaching from the left kicked the shield out of Nick's left hand. Nick dropped, rolled behind the man, and sliced through his left Achilles tendon. The man toppled backward, grabbing at his useless leg, screaming in pain. Blood soaked through his sock. Nick leaped back to his feet just as the two men who'd been behind them charged. He surprised them by running straight at them. Instinctively they separated. *Big mistake.* The one on his left got ahead of the other. Using the pinky side of his left hand, Nick threw a short-chopping blow into his attacker's throat. The man went down, choking, gasping for air. Before the other one got close to him, Nick side-kicked his right knee. It collapsed inward with a sickening snap of connective tissue. There was more screaming. *Three down, one to go.*

Nick stepped backward toward Vicky. He whispered over his shoulder, "Put the gun in my hand."

She did as he asked. When his hand emerged from the shadow, the Glock was in it, pointed at the fourth man, who had positioned himself in the middle of the asphalt on South Fourth. He too held a pistol in his hand.

"Mrs. Lansdale," he talked past Nick. "Tell your husband that his bill is long overdue and that his little army of Secret Service men will do him no good. That yesterday and today are his final notices." He spoke with a cultured Eastern European accent Nick couldn't identify. It wasn't Russian or Polish. That much he knew. "It will be much worse from today forward. No more polite prodding. So I beseech you, for your own good and the health of your children, do deliver this message. Now, Detective, if you let me collect my incompetent men . . ."

"Too late, motherfucker. You attacked me and you're threatening this woman. You had your chance to walk away and you didn't take it."

The balaclava muffled the man's laugh. "In the universe there are endless chances. Only a foolish general expends all of his resources during his first assault. Please, look to your left and right, Detective Ryan. These are my most competent men. It is now your chance and Mrs. Lansdale's to walk away. My message has been delivered. You are unharmed. The lady is shaken, yes, but intact. The same cannot be said of my people. Be as smart as you are good at hand-to-hand combat. Holster your weapon and go."

Nick saw masked men on either side of him, both holding MP7s with sound suppressors.

"We're leaving," Nick said, holstering the 19. He reached behind him. Victoria Lansdale grabbed his hand. Her palm was sweating and her hand was shaking.

"Do as I ask," said the man in the street. "No one will bother you, but I urge you, Mrs. Lansdale, pass the message along and save your family much heartache."

Walking toward the Maserati, Nick bent over to retrieve his shield. As he did, the man with the severed tendon spat at him. Missed. He cursed in a foreign language. Nick didn't have to speak the language to understand. Cursing is the universal tongue.

As Nick raced the Maserati away, he said, "Call Carver and have him meet us at my place."

She seemed not to hear. She stayed stone-still and silent the entire ride back to Bay Ridge.

EIGHTEEN

The moment they stepped through Nick's door, Victoria Lansdale broke into pieces. She fell to her knees, her whole body shaking. He let her be, knowing she needed to shed some of the panic she had forced herself to swallow. He poured her a glass of red wine from a bottle Shana had brought over for last week's late-night visit. A lot had changed in a week. Vicky got off her knees and sat on the leather sofa. Nick handed her the glass. He sat beside her.

"You were good out there," he said.

Vicky Lansdale cradled the glass in two hands and drank the wine in a single gulp. "This is very good wine."

He laughed. "That's what you're thinking about, the wine?"

"I don't know what I'm saying. It's true about the wine, though."

"Opus One."

She turned, a quizzical look on her face. "On a cop's salary?"

"I live in a penthouse."

"Right, Carver told me . . . your uncle. I'm sorry."

"The wine was a gift."

She repeated, "I'm sorry."

He took the glass out of her hand, lifted her chin, stared into her eyes. "Look, Vicky, tough isn't having a gun. Tough is how you handle having one stuck in your face. There are some things you can't prepare for. You think you'll be ready for them because you play the scenarios out in your head, but when the time comes—"

"Like what?"

"Like the first time I was in combat. I'd been shot at on the streets. I'd worked undercover in the Seven-Five and the Seven-Seven, so I thought I would be ready."

"Did you panic?"

"I'm not built to panic."

She stared back at him. "I liked you kissing me."

"I liked kissing you, but—"

She put her hand on his mouth. "I came here tonight to sleep with you. I could sleep with anyone I wanted since I was fifteen, man or woman or both. It's been a long time since I met someone real."

He pushed her hand away. "You wanna sleep with the pool boy, sleep with the pool boy. I'm not here to scratch your itches or reintroduce you to the real world."

"The people in my circles—they all think of themselves as masters of the universe. Not one of them could have handled what happened tonight without begging or bargaining. Not one of them could've or would've saved my son. They would have tossed his life away if it bought them another five minutes."

"I know the people in your world. Money is like power. There's no shame in having it, only in what you do with it."

"You're awfully smart."

"For a cop, you mean."

Her lip twitched. "Don't tell me what I mean. I already have a husband for that."

Nick didn't like where this was going. He sensed that her coming here tonight was about many things, her attraction to what he represented being only a tiny bit of it. He admitted to himself that sleeping with her would also have been more about losing Shana again. He took the glass from her hand and poured her the rest of the bottle.

Handing it to her, he said, "Give me your phone, Vicky."

She hesitated but gave in, reaching into her pocket. "He's listed under Station Taxi. It's silly. Carver says it's for my protection."

Nick went into the guest bedroom he used as an office. "Carver, this is Nick Ryan."

"Why are you calling on her phone?"

"Come get her. She's in my apartment. Bring the troops."

"Something wrong?"

"Very wrong, yeah."

"Ryan, I'll call when we arrive. If there's trouble, work the phrase *that's funny* into the conversation. Then I'll know what approach we have to take."

"Okay. It's not tonight you have to worry about."

"What is it?"

"We'll discuss it when you get here." Nick clicked off.

When he returned to the living room, Vicky Lansdale was gone. Her empty wineglass was on the coffee table. He found her in his bedroom, naked, leaning back on her elbows on the edge of the bed. Her clothes were in a neat pile at her feet. It was no surprise to him that naked she was even more unearthly beautiful.

"Put your clothes on, Vicky." He handed them to her. "This isn't going to happen. Carver and his team are on the way."

"It'll take him an hour to—"

"If it took him a week, it wouldn't change my mind."

She tossed her clothes aside, stood up, and pressed herself against him. "If time won't change your mind, I will."

He gently grabbed her shoulders and pushed her away. "Listen, Vicky, you're freaked out and want some comfort."

"I'm lonely and suffocating. It's not comfort I want."

"No, you want to be rescued."

"Maybe."

He stroked her cheek. "One rescue per person *per night*. Get dressed."

She smiled at him, collected her clothes, and found her way to the bathroom.

NINETEEN

Carver came into Nick's apartment with his SIG at his thigh. Nick peeked over Carver's shoulder. Willoughby and two other men Nick didn't recognize were in the hallway—Willoughby by the elevator, the two others at the roof access door. All the men in the hallway were armed with the immediately recognizable P90 submachine gun.

"Where is she?" Carver stared into Nick's eyes. He shifted his gaze to read Nick's body language, searching for any sign of danger or an indication where it might come from.

Nick understood. He would have done the same. "She's in the bedroom, sleeping." He threw his thumb over his shoulder. "She's fine. For now. See for yourself."

Carver swung his leg back. He used his heel to open the door wider. His nod was almost imperceptible. Willoughby and one of the other men stepped quietly forward into the apartment, P90s raised. Using only hand signals, Carver directed the remaining man to stay with Nick and told Willoughby to follow him. Carver raised his SIG. Willoughby stood close to Carver's left shoulder. They each covered the other's blind spots as they swept the entire apartment.

"Clear," Carver called out once he was satisfied there was no one in the apartment other than his men, Victoria Lansdale, and Nick.

Willoughby stayed with Victoria Lansdale. The unnamed man went back out to the hallway.

"I hope you understand," Carver said.

"Doing your job. I would have done the same thing."

"So . . ."

Nick explained about the incident on South Fourth. He repeated verbatim the message the man in the balaclava had asked Victoria Lansdale to deliver to her husband. Nick went over it a few times.

"He said the bill was long overdue." Carver repeated it back to Nick. "Was it your sense he was talking about money or was he being metaphorical?"

"Unclear. My instinct is that money is involved, but this is about more than money."

"Were the threats viable, do you think?"

"Very. They were well organized, well armed, and pretty bold. They understood tactics. If they had wanted her dead, she'd be dead. Me too. And they know about you and your men. I believe they had something to do with Jonathan Lansdale Jr.'s abduction."

Carver was skeptical about that. "Doesn't sound like a match to me. Carmine Gabrelli owned a plumbing business. His brother-in-law worked as a laborer in a bonded customs warehouse at JFK. His son, the man who drove the Corvette, is a wedding DJ. Until yesterday, none of them had any issues with law enforcement. Gabrelli had a carry permit. Both the handguns were his and registered with the Nassau County Police. Doesn't sound like a criminal enterprise."

"Think about it. Why now? Why after wondering what had happened to his brother for years did Gabrelli choose to act yesterday? He acted because someone convinced him that Jimmy Gabrelli was killed by your employer. I could tell that this was news to Gabrelli. Someone had stuck a pin in his balloon and the pent-up rage exploded out. Why the son and not the father? Maybe he had been warned the father was too well protected. Tonight, I think the guy with the accent was making a point that he could get to the Lansdales in more ways than one."

"Possibly. We'll consider it. Is it your intuition Mrs. Lansdale knows what this evening's attack was about?"

"She seemed genuinely surprised."

"Seemed?"

"I'm not one of those detectives who thinks he's got a built-in lie detector. Carver, this isn't my business. I would have been fine if I had never seen you or her again. My life's already too complicated for my own good. There is one thing. She got a phone call a few minutes before the incident. It changed her mood and demeanor completely."

Carver checked his watch. "We have to get going."

"Mr. Lansdale?"

Carver ignored the question, whispered into his sleeve.

Nick smirked. "So, that's a yes. The husband is coming back from Australia. That must've been the call at the bar . . . from you. No wonder you didn't ask who the call was from."

Again Carver didn't respond.

"How many vehicles do you have here?" Nick asked.

"Two."

"I thought so." Nick handed Carver a key. "That gives you elevator access to the garage. Have your chase vehicle meet you down there. That key's a spare. Mail it back."

"Mrs. Lansdale," Carver spoke past Nick, "please step out into the hallway with Willoughby. I'll be along momentarily."

Nick turned. He saw a woman whose face showed none of the telltale stress fractures one might have expected on someone whose life and whose family's lives had been threatened. The fear was reserved for her eyes. Nick wasn't a believer in the whole eyes-as-windows-to-the-soul thing. He had seen fear in all its permutations. He knew where to look for it, where even the bravest people hid it.

"No, Carver," she said, her voice strong and steady. "You wait in the hall. I'll be out shortly."

"Ma'am, your husband—"

"Get out! I won't be a minute."

Carver and Willoughby stepped out. She pushed the door closed behind them.

"I'm sorry, Nick, about . . . before."

"No need. I'm sorry about the pool-boy crack."

"I enjoyed the evening until . . . Thank you for everything."

"Thanks for the champagne, orangeade, and hot dogs. You ever want to come back home for a visit, let me know. Next time it's on me."

She smiled, her nose crinkling. "Pizza?"

"Di Fara's on Avenue J."

"Maybe we'll have more luck with that."

"Maybe."

She kissed his cheek. "Thank you."

"Remember," he said, opening the door for her, "it's easier to send a card."

He watched them get onto the elevator before locking the door.

TWENTY

Nick sat down with a glass of bourbon. Swishing a mouthful from cheek to cheek, he placed three files on the floor before him: the two from Lenny on Flannery and the Gabrellis, and the one on Vlado Markovic from Joe. He had questions about all of them. His heart wanted him to ignore all three, to laser-focus on the murder of the Angelos. He smiled just thinking about Tony. His murder could not rob Nick of the man's joy. How at Christmas he would play "Dominick the Donkey" over and over again just to get under Nick Sr.'s skin.

"Christ Almighty, Tony, will you shut that fucking record off."

That was when Tony would grab Nick's and Sean's little hands and circle-dance, singing along about the Italian Christmas donkey in his raspy, out-of-tune voice. No number of bullets could silence that voice.

"God knows I love your dad like a brother," he would tell them, "but he's as sunny as a cow's balls."

A cow's balls! One of Tony's favorite expressions, something he didn't stop saying even after Sean pointed out that cows were girls.

Tony put Sean in a playful headlock. "Listen, kid, don't let them brains go to your head. You'll fall over."

Nick's gut pointed him at the Gabrellis' file. He needn't have killed

Carmine to be curious about what was actually going on between Gabrelli and Jonathan Lansdale Sr. Once before, in Afghanistan, Nick had killed up close. Much closer than the distance between him and Carmine—close enough to feel the heat of the man's dying breath on his cheek. It was what got him decorated and discharged. He rarely thought about it. Never talked about it. Neither did the US Army. He finished the bourbon, poured another, shifted his attention away from the distant past to the events of earlier that evening. He knew that what had happened outside the Black Harp had nothing to do with him. He took getting attacked personally just the same. Nor could he get the vision of a naked Vicky Lansdale out of his head.

He was also curious about why his phone number had turned up in Lenny's extended search of Flannery's phone records. He was curious about a lot of things, not the least of which was Joe's real identity. With the intel Mack had given him, that would now be easy enough to discover. Nick wasn't sure he wanted to know. The system, such as it was, had worked for a year. Joe funneled the jobs to be done from on high. Nick fixed the problems. An unaware city kept safe. Knowledge was power, but some knowledge was more dangerous than it was worth.

He had his assignment—Vlado Markovic. Nick never let himself be distracted when there was a job at hand. As with the killing in Afghanistan, he did things his way. Always. It was what made him so good at UC work, what made him the perfect man for the shadows. His calm, his unpredictability, his ability to solve complex problems on the spot made him an outlier. Outliers were as despised as they were valued.

"Watch your back, Nicky," his coach used to tell him. "The way you are . . . it makes people uneasy. I'm not talkin' hoops here. You'll make weak men feel small and small men feel worthless. The Japanese have an expression. The nail that sticks out from the board will be hammered down. Watch out for the hammers, Nicky. For you, they'll be everywhere."

He picked up the Markovic file. Markovic had been a month shy of his thirty-second birthday when he was murdered on 9/11. In his passport photo, he was clean-shaven, hollow-cheeked, and pale. His light-blue eyes, like Vicky Lansdale's earlier, were repositories of fear. For a Serb national who had lived in Sarajevo when war broke out, the traces of fear made sense. By the time he was killed, Markovic had put on some weight, a small percentage of it from a thick black beard. A baker at a commercial bread factory in Queens, he had immigrated to the United States in 1999. He'd lived, by all accounts, a quiet, unobtrusive life. No trouble with the cops. No trouble with his employers. No trouble with Immigration. From the file, it seemed his first trouble in the United States was his last.

Nick studied the crime scene photos. Markovic had died with his eyes open, the fear and everything else he felt as a living man gone. A good portion of his blood was gone too. According to the autopsy notes, there were eleven distinct premortem stab wounds in and around Markovic's abdomen. There were a few postmortem wounds as well. The autopsy photos showed that the naked man's torso, especially his belly, was a mess of slits and slashes. Having been stabbed with a piece of glass less than a year ago, Nick winced. He was glad he could only remember how much it hurt without actually reliving the pain.

"Someone was seriously pissed off with you, Vlado," Nick said aloud. "Seriously pissed."

Multiple stab wounds or gunshots were usually giveaways that rage was involved. It was unlike the cool, efficient murders of the Angelos.

Nick immediately noticed two things: a burn scar on the dead man's right biceps, and a swollen and bruised right ankle. The ME had simply commented on the scar's presence and moved on. The ankle got his attention as well. In the transcription of his autopsy notes, he said, "The X-rays confirm a fracture of the right fibula at the lateral malleolus." Nowhere in the ME's or the detectives' reports was there mention of any cast, boot, or bandaging of the break. The break was fresh. The detectives figured he'd broken the ankle running from his attacker. Simple enough. Nick didn't like it. There was more not to like.

There were no defensive wounds on Markovic's hands or arms. Nick didn't like that the victim was found face up. Didn't like the fact that despite how much blood he had lost, the crime scene seemed clean, too neat. There was no blood anywhere except immediately beneath and around Markovic. And then there was the body itself. It was as if it had been placed there, not like it had fallen. If not for his open eyes, Markovic could have been mistaken for a sleeping drunk.

As Nick continued reading through the file, his mind drifted back to the Angelos. He had an idea how he might be able to make progress on their case while working his assignment. Nick put the Markovic file on the floor, took another sip of bourbon, and went into the guest bedroom that he sometimes used as an office. He punched the keypad to his safe, swung the door back, and removed a white business card. On it was a phone number. Nothing else. He twirled the card around in his fingers. He had two calls to make, but to call the number on the white card would cost him. Possibly money, but definitely a piece of himself.

TWENTY-ONE

When Nick was certain the link between his phone and computer was working, he punched in the number.

"Hello, how may I help you?"

The voice on the other end of the phone was electronically distorted to sound male. Nick knew better. They'd met only once, on opposite sides of Pete Moretti's grave. That meeting had ended abruptly as Nick reached for his off-duty piece. She darted him with a tranquilizer gun. He didn't know her name. Had never seen her face uncovered. Didn't know where she was from or where she lived. What he knew about her was that she was blond or dyed her hair that color. She was athletic and spoke perfect unaccented English. Most importantly, he knew this: she was a mercenary, an assassin, a murderer.

Nick had seen her handiwork close-up. According to her, Nick was a member of her tribe. It wasn't a moral judgment. You take the step into that abyss, there can be no moral judgments, only professional assessments. Last year, with her help, Nick had taken the step. It hadn't been about money or survival, but about vengeance. According to this woman, vengeance as a motive didn't make the act blameless or clean. He understood as much.

He asked, "Do you know who this is?"

The chill in her laugh cut through the distortion. Then, switching off the distorter, she said, "Nick Ryan, I am pleased to hear your voice. As I predicted when last we spoke, we would speak again."

"Good on ya. You were right."

For two people with such limited contact, they had a very complicated relationship. By her own admission, she was responsible for planting an explosive device in McCann's, Nick's local bar. The bomb was there for Nick's benefit, to teach him a lesson drawn in blood and battered bodies. One of the dead, Angeline Compton, was a woman with whom Nick had had a brief relationship. In turn, Nick had killed the man who paid for the bombing.

Nick ignored that. He had more in mind than soliciting her assistance. "I need your help. Doesn't that count for something?"

"This is beneath you, Nick. You disappoint me with your pleas. Previously, I owed you a debt from the death of the woman, Angeline. I consider that obligation satisfied. Business is business. Pay the retainer. This is not up for negotiation. Go to your computer. The routing information in the email will vanish in thirty seconds after opening. I hope we will speak again."

The line went dead. Nick looked at his phone. It dinged with an email notification. He scrambled for a piece of paper and a pen. Just as he finished writing the information down, the email vanished as if it were never there. He didn't bother trying to find it in his trash file. Lenny had taught Nick how to send ghost emails like the one she had sent him. He had used the technique himself.

———

The next call was in some ways a more difficult one to make.

"Nick?" There was surprise in her whisper, other things too.

He was pleased his number was still in her contacts. He hadn't been sure it would be. "Annalise."

"Um . . . what is it? It's . . . two fourteen in the mornin'. Kinda' late to be calling about—"

"This isn't about the Angelos. Well, mostly not."

There was a long uncomfortable pause. "Then what are you calling about?"

"Is someone there?"

"You don't fucking get to ask me those kinds of questions no more, Nick."

"You're right. I'm sorry."

"Okay."

"I need your help on a case."

"You need help? You don't never need nobody's help. What, the pod people come and steal the real Nick Ryan?"

"It's a homicide, a cold case. You're an expert, I'm not."

"Whatchu need?"

"Can you come over?"

There was a longer, more uncomfortable pause than before. "You're not . . . you know."

"You walked away from me, AP, not the other way around. That mess was your mess, not mine."

"AP," she repeated. "Nobody but you calls me that."

"I won't if you don't want me to."

"It's okay. It's just that, you know, I haven't heard it since . . . Is this important, Nick?"

"I wouldn't ask otherwise."

"Gimme a half hour."

"No problem."

She didn't click off immediately. She had stuff to say that hung unsaid in the air between them. Nick ended the call. If they had things to say, they'd have their chance in about twenty-nine minutes.

TWENTY-TWO

When Nick got home from Afghanistan, his North Star pointed him at wherever Shana wasn't. It pointed him at Annalise Puleo. She was raised by the streets and had the ghosts of gang tats to prove it. She had worked hard at masking her background. All you had to do was scratch the facade a touch to see the South Bronx come through. Rugged and smart, unconventionally pretty, she was short, and a little heavy when they met. She kept her impossibly thick black hair trimmed and wore minimal makeup. Nick understood. There were lots of women in the NYPD, but it was tougher for them. For Black women, for first-generation women—Dominican, Chinese, Haitian, Korean, Indian—it was tougher still.

"You sure them pod people ain't switched you, Ryan?"

Annalise stood in the doorway, black Schott motorcycle jacket slung over her right shoulder, a matte-black Bell helmet tucked under her left arm. She wasn't the same person she had been four years ago, the last time she'd been to Nick's. She wasn't the same detective either. He'd noticed as much when she walked him and Martellus Sharp through the killing of Rosa Angelo. Annalise was confident, no longer keeping her head down to try to ward off unwanted attention for her brains or gender. You didn't earn a spot on a homicide squad by being silent or being a mouse. She had let her hair grow out to shoulder length. At the Angelos', she had it tied back in a ponytail. She'd spent time in the gym but still kept the makeup to a minimum.

"Place looks the same," she said, stepping inside.

"Nothing gets by you, AP."

"Fuck you, Nicky!" She smiled a broad white smile. It was that smile that had first gotten Nick's attention. She threw her jacket on the sofa and placed her helmet on the coffee table. "You got some Coke or soda or something?"

"Sure. The file's on the table next to your helmet."

Nick came back into the room with her Coke. Annalise sat on her knees, the file photos spread out on the floor in front of her. There was more than curiosity on her face when she looked up at Nick to take the can.

"Should I even ask how you got this file? Or why a UC detective from East New York is interested in this?"

"I'm in IOAS these days."

"You, in the Intelligence Bureau? What the fuck, Nicky? How's that shit work? Nobody got any love for you. With what your daddy did . . . you know."

"No love, not even from you?"

Annalise turned her head and touched her neck. It was a tic she had when she was excited or uncomfortable. She shot to her feet. "If we're goin' there, I'm goin' home."

"Sorry, AP. Let's reset. My bump and reassignment was payback for that thing at McCann's last year," he lied. He didn't like lying to her. It was lies that had come between them. The lies had been hers, but still . . . He couldn't tell her the truth.

"The bombing, yeah. That's right. I was real proud of you. The way you took charge of that whole mess. Another medal for your collection."

"I lost that medal down a sewer."

"I never did understand you. Like why you was with me to begin with."

"I thought we weren't going there."

She put her hand on her chest and bowed her head slightly. "*¡Lo siento! ¡Perdón!*"

"Forget it. You still riding that Raider?"

"No way. I ditched the Yamaha. I picked up a Ducati XDiavel at a police auction. You still riding that Norton piece a shit?"

"Hardly. I keep it because it was my uncle's and he loved it." Nick pointed at the photo spread.

"The photos, yeah, so." She drank the Coke in two gulps. "What about them?"

"Anything bother you?"

"Some of it looks like it don't seem right."

"Like what?"

"It's too neat. There's a shit ton a blood, but the vic is layin' there like there wasn't no struggle. Blood's all in one spot. No defensive wounds nowhere on him. What he do, stand still on a broken ankle and let the motherfucka stab him eleven times without movin'? And when the perp was done, what, the vic lay down and happily bled out." She looked up at Nick, worry on her face. "But, Nicky, this ain't jus' any homicide you got here. This is Vlado Markovic."

"I know. But I had some of the same thoughts about the crime scene. It didn't feel right."

"What's this got to do with Intel?"

Nick shook his head. "Please look through the whole file and write down the questions you would ask. What bugs you about it and why. Like that."

"You gotta gimme more than *please*, Nicky."

"You trust me?"

She bowed her head and did that neck-touching thing. "It wasn't you who lied to me. You stood up for me and took my ex's shit when it came down. So, yeah, I trust you."

"Then don't ask me that question again. This time, let *please* be enough. I'll also owe you."

"So you'll owe me." She laughed. "You got to Intel and a bump, but you ain't got no juice, not so long as you're your daddy's boy."

"Don't be so sure."

"Whateva you say. Look, I gotta tell you, shit don't always fit. Murder scenes don't always make sense from pictures or even in person. It ain't always like at the Angelos'. Sometimes your sense tells you something's wrong, but then the guy confesses and it makes sense."

"Since you brought it up, what's going on with the Angelos' investigation?"

She wrinkled her lips, thinking about how to answer. "Not much. Preliminary bullshit, you know. The neighbors didn't see nothin', didn't hear nothin'. Everybody loved them. Tony because he said funny shit and would snowplow his neighbors' driveways. Rosa because she would bake or cook stuff when somebody on the block got sick. It was like they was a couple outta the Bible."

"Enemies?"

"None that we can find so far, but we're diggin' into his record now."

"You might want to take a look at his record around Nine-Eleven."

"Why?"

"My dad says that was the only time he can remember Tony acting strange."

"I'll tell Rosen. He's looking at the records. I'm gonna interview your dad tomorrow."

"I'm glad it's you doing it."

"There's something else, Nicky. Rosen says I'm not supposed to tell you."

"What."

"You, your brother, and your dad are Tony's beneficiaries after the wife. With her dead too, you get the house, the insurance policy, the investments."

"Rosen probably thinks we did it."

"Sean was working his shift. We have your GTO's E-ZPass scanned going north on the Triborough Bridge around the estimated TOD."

"You've checked?"

"SOP. Who benefits from the death is always at or near the top of the list."

"Da never leaves that shitty apartment."

Annalise laughed again. "Rosen got no love for your daddy, but we know he was the vic's best friend. We don't figure it was your father."

"You want another Coke or something else?"

"I'm sorry, Nicky." Her face was grave.

"For what?"

"You took a lot of crap at the end there you didn't deserve. It was me who didn't tell you I was married and that my ex was a controlling jealous *mamagüevo*."

He smiled sadly. Put his hand on her cheek. "Don't apologize, AP. You didn't tell me, but I figured it out pretty early on. We were both going through stuff. It was good we had each other."

"No regrets?"

"None."

"How about that Coke?"

"When you in tomorrow?" he asked, delivering the soda.

"Don't worry about it."

"Okay, I'm half-dead. Leave the questions on the coffee table. Let yourself out. Thanks again, AP."

She opened her mouth to say something, but just turned away.

TWENTY-THREE

Groggy, staring up at the ceiling, he thought about how much was on his plate, how he would manage it. He had to get to the truth of Markovic's murder. The preposterous nature of his job was that he rarely knew exactly why he was doing what he was assigned to do. Sometimes it was obvious, like the thing now causing Ace's insomnia. What they had talked about before he was shot. Nick had been thrown into a nightmare scenario. He'd somehow have to prevent the racial tension in the city from exploding after yet another police shooting of an unarmed Black man.

Did he like what he'd done to keep the lit fuse from reaching the powder? He supposed the answer would be no, if he gave it much thought. Unlike Ace, Nick put it behind him. Afghanistan had taught him that every big decision is a calculation and that you can't run from your choices. There was no profit in questioning what had already been done if you took the lessons with you moving forward. People's fascination with time travel was almost always about the past. Nick's concern was the now and what was to come.

Sometimes, like with Flannery, the endgame was less clear. Leverage was involved, but Nick would never know who would wield it, when, or why. That wasn't the point. As long as Nick could see the angle where the little guy was helped, he would be on board. He was on board anyway. Once you had done the things he had done, there was no turning back.

Annalise was gone when Nick strolled out of his bedroom. Several sheets of lined paper were stacked on the coffee table next to the Markovic file. He recognized AP's neat cursive writing on the top sheet. The living room smelled vaguely of leather and cigarette smoke. They were familiar traces of her. When they were together, Annalise gave up smoking on even-numbered dates and started again on the odd ones. Nick looked at the date on his phone and laughed. Not everything about her had changed.

He turned away, noticing the ice bucket Victoria Lansdale had given him. He considered calling her to see if she was safe. He didn't call. She was Carver's concern. Victoria Lansdale was trouble. If there was anything in the world in abundant supply, it was trouble. Nick didn't need to borrow any, though he couldn't get the image of the naked Vicky Lansdale completely out of his head. Beauty left scars too. Nick turned his thoughts from Vicky's beauty to the men who had attacked them last night. He thought about the Gabrellis and how it was all connected.

He thought about it until he got to his computer. Nick had faith in Annalise and knew that Rosen was a dogged son of a bitch, but the Angelos meant more to him than Vlado Markovic, the Lansdales, and the Gabrellis stacked one atop the other. Meant too much for him just to sit on his hands and wait. He looked at the routing information he'd written down from the ghost email, fanned the paper in front of his eyes.

Between the offshore accounts he had set up for the fictitious Marty Berg and the now-screwed Shea Flannery, Nick had the hundred-grand retainer with money to spare. Because his bosses avoided all risk of being discovered, those moneys were untraceable except to a man who did not exist. *Perfect!* He would transfer twenty-five out of Berg's numbered account and seventy-five out of Flannery's. As Shana's father used to say and as Vicky Lansdale agreed, it was easier to ask forgiveness than ask permission. He'd always hated that phrase. It was a rich man's concept of the world. The rich always assumed there would be no consequences or, if there were, they could be dealt with as Warren Zevon suggested, with "lawyers, guns and money."

First, he recovered the file containing the recording of his phone call with the assassin. He ran it through several voice recognition programs including the NYPD's and Interpol's. They all turned up with the same result: "No Match." It was what he had expected. That done, Nick got busy completing the transfer of funds.

Within ten seconds of his tapping the key to complete the transfer, his cell buzzed. A number with a foreign country code showed on his screen. He knew who it was. He knew that the country code was a computer trick, another one Lenny had taught to him.

"That was very expeditious," said the distorted voice. "You must be impatient for my help."

"Back to using the distorter?"

She laughed. When she spoke again, it was in her oddly accentless voice. "An old habit, but a useless one with you. You certainly recorded our most recent conversation and ran it through voice recognition programs. No matches. Sorry to disappoint you."

"No, you're not. You were showing off."

"I have my pride, yes."

"Pride or vanity?"

"Never vanity. Vanity is weakness. You will learn."

"If you say so."

"What is it you require of me?"

"A meeting."

There were a few beats of silence. Nick smiled. The hesitation was what he had hoped for. She was considering it. She thought the debt she owed him for the death of Angeline was paid. Nick didn't see it that way. She had killed or maimed several people with the bombing at McCann's. Men and women who had nothing to do with Nick. For her, collateral damage was part of the cost of doing business. For Nick it was anything but. Yes, he wanted her help in tracking down the Angelos' killer. He wanted her too. Wanted to see her off to prison.

"Never."

"That's not true, is it? You stood across Pete Moretti's grave from me. I can still feel the dart in my neck sometimes."

More hesitation. He knew she was fascinated by him, not attracted necessarily. More like invested in his career. She had said as much during their only meeting. She had also said they'd crossed paths in their pasts. He still couldn't think where.

"I will call again."

She clicked off.

TWENTY-FOUR

He called Joe.

"Progress on Markovic?"

"You'll be the first to know." Nick asked, "Where's Ace?"

"Have you acquainted yourself with your new vehicle?"

"No."

"Then I suggest you do so. My patience has limits. When you've done that, call again and I will give you Meadows's location."

Nick knew they wouldn't have left Ace at Bellevue. He would be somewhere the press and the public couldn't access him in case word of the incident in Staten Island leaked out.

"Have I been cleared in the shooting yet?"

"You're too intelligent to ask that, Nick. Finish the task you've been assigned. Who was responsible for the homicide of Vlado Markovic? That's the question you should concern yourself with."

Something was up. Joe didn't usually push him like this. Nick was tempted to push back, to use some of the leverage in his possession. He now knew Joe's real identity, where he lived, what he drove, and more. That, and he had held back some of the information Flannery had spewed out in the hotel the other night. But such valuable cards were best held in reserve for bigger payoffs.

"I'll call you from the Malibu."

———

Renowned for its Christmas light displays, Dyker Heights was an atypical part of Brooklyn. Bordered by Bay Ridge, Bath Beach, and Bensonhurst, it was a suburb within the city, an area of single- and two-family homes with driveways and private yards. There was even a well-known public golf course, Dyker Beach, in the neighborhood. Golf! Very un-Brooklyn indeed. Nick knew the area intimately. He'd grown up here. He could almost smell his mom's lamb and herbed potatoes roasting in the oven. What he smelled instead was snow in the air and the water from the Narrows.

The safe-house garage in which the Malibu was parked was only a block away from the red-brick house once owned by the Ryans. When he was growing up, his paternal grandparents lived upstairs. Nick's family lived on the main floor. Uncle Kenny lived in the basement. He wondered if Joe knew about the proximity beforehand or if the location of the safe house was coincidental. Nick mistrusted coincidence. After his mom died, his dad had sold the house. He'd been living off his pension and the proceeds since. Nick hadn't been back.

There was a dummy For Sale sign up in front of the two-story Tudor-style safe house with the small leaf-covered lawn. The driveway was littered with plastic-wrapped pennysavers and the mailbox was cluttered with letters addressed to "Current Resident." Nick shook his head, knowing that if the house were actually for sale, it wouldn't have stayed on the market for ten minutes. Dyker Heights homes were hot properties even in bad economic times.

Nick backed his GTO up the driveway to the detached garage at the rear of the house. Out of his car and settled in the driver's seat of the Malibu, he depressed the ignition button. The engine roared to life. He had to confess to loving that incongruous full-throated rumble coming out of the seemingly innocuous Chevy.

Before grabbing the instruction manual out of the glove box, Nick reviewed the things Joe had shown him in the Bronx. He hit the cruise-control reset twice. The door speaker screen dropped down to reveal the Kel-Tec P50. For the next fifteen minutes, he practiced pulling the futuristic-looking weapon out of the door. He used his left hand. Used his right hand over his lap. He practiced dropping the side-loading magazine out and putting in a fresh one. He repeated this process with the Glock 26 that was clipped to the back side of the glovebox. He checked under the seat for the tear-gas canister. There was a Taser under the driver's seat, a tactical knife hidden in the sidewall of the center console. There were things in the car that weren't mentioned in the handbook—unseen things that Nick knew were there and wanted no part of. To help rid the car of them, he called his friend Louie Randazzo. They'd grown up together, played basketball together at Xaverian. After graduation, Louie had taken the opposite path at the fork in the road.

"Nick fuckin' Ryan, what's shakin'?"

"Louie Two Shots, how's the family business these days?"

"You assholes are makin' it tough for people to earn."

"I'm crying for you, Louie."

"Yeah, I hear you drownin' in your own freakin' tears. What can I do for you?"

"I need the Sweeper."

"House or car?"

"Car."

"It'll cost you."

"Did I ask how much?"

Louie laughed. "You comin' to him or—"

"He's comin' to me." Nick gave Louie the address.

"The old neighborhood, huh? How's your dad and your shithead brother doin'?"

"Same."

"That bad?"

"Fuck you, Louie."

"Yeah, I love you too, Nick."

"Should I pay him or send it directly to you?"

"Use PayPal."

"Too late in life for you to develop a sense of humor."

"You're a pain in my ass. You know that?"

"One more thing."

"Christ, Nick, what?"

"We need to talk. Face-to-face. I'll come your way."

"Tonight. Rossini's at seven. You foot the tab and I'll handle today's bill. Okay?"

"Works for me."

"Hey, Nick, I almost forgot. I heard about Tony Angelo and his wife. Rough, man. Any idea who it—"

Nick cut him off. "None."

"Don't bite my head off. The guy'll be there in an hour. See you tonight."

Nick didn't know the Sweeper's name. Didn't have to. Didn't want to. What he knew was that the man was an ex-intelligence officer with a particular expertise in electronic surveillance. The mob were so paranoid about their decimation over the past few decades that they spared no expense in making sure their homes, cars, social clubs, and offices weren't bugged. Lenny Feld was good with electronics. He'd even made some equipment for Nick that allowed him to find the more obvious transponders, but Lenny's genius was for computers and data manipulation. Besides, Lenny rarely ventured out of the synagogue basement. Nick sensed that finding tracking devices in a car rebuilt by his bosses would be a job for a professional.

Two hours after Louie hung up, the Sweeper showed Nick three transponders. "Whoever planted these is good. Not as good as me, but good. They made one very obvious and one much less so. Old trick. You work so hard to find the second one, you think, 'Gotcha!' You're so sure you've found the hidden one, you stop looking. And this one here," he said, holding up the third transponder. "This one has its own power source. This is a lithium thionyl chloride battery. No need to hook it up to your vehicle's power source."

"That's it, these three?"

The Sweeper, an anonymous-looking man with a receding gray hairline, gave Nick the stink-eye.

Nick raised his palms and apologized.

"Apology accepted. By the way, there's some interesting wiring in that car. In fact, that whole car is pretty interesting."

"Your interest in it is over right now," Nick said, his tone of voice conveying the threat.

"What interest?"

"I thought you'd understand."

———

Nick's next call was to Joe.

"Have you finally acquainted yourself with—"

"I'm sitting in it now."

"Good. And you have—"

"Stop asking me questions and tell me where Ace is."

"I don't understand you, Nick. You don't even like Meadows."

"No, Joe, it's not me you don't understand. It's *cops* you don't get. It's not about like or not like. It's about having someone's back."

"How's that work?"

"It's about whether you can step into a dangerous situation and know someone will be there behind you. What Ace and I feel about each other is beside the point. The other day in Staten Island, he stood up for me when it counted. He had my back. Even the UC people I worked with who hate my father and think my dad's stink is on me had my back when I was in a bad spot. It's the only way this works."

"Mea culpa. I didn't know you felt so intensely about this issue."

"You're apologizing to me? Must be the end of days."

Joe laughed.

"It wasn't that funny," Nick said.

"It's not that, though you are sometimes amusing."

"Then what?"

"Ace is very close."

"You getting cryptic with me?"

"Not at all. Meadows is on the top floor of the VA hospital."

"The VA hospital right here on Poly Place?"

"You can probably see it from the front of the safe house. I'll leave your name at the nurses' station so you can see him."

"Thank you."

Instead of "you're welcome," Joe reminded him, "Markovic. The clock is ticking."

"Joe, one more thing. Don't ever mistake my faith in Ace as blind trust."

"I don't catch your meaning."

"Sure you do. Don't use him against me."

"That sounds awfully like a threat."

Nick didn't deny it. "When I have something on Markovic, I'll be in touch."

TWENTY-FIVE

Nick came back from Afghanistan pretty much intact, physically and psychologically. The same couldn't be said for many of the people he'd served with. Some came home as cracked and scrambled as Humpty Dumpty. Others had left actual pieces of themselves over there. It didn't take long once he was inside the white brick hospital to be reminded of the nightmare of war. A man about fifteen years Nick's senior and legless just above his knees impatiently rocked his wheelchair back and forth as the two of them waited for the elevator.

"Getting fitted for some new improved legs," the man said, slapping his thighs. "Wore the old ones out. You?"

"Visiting a friend."

"Army?"

Nick nodded. "You?"

"Marines. Where'd you serve?"

"Afghanistan. Two tours."

"Iraq. Two tours plus." The legless man's smile was gut-wrenching. "IED made sure I didn't make it through my third."

The elevator came. They rode up a few floors in silence.

"This is me," said the guy in the wheelchair.

Nick patted his shoulder. "Put the new pair to good use and stop wearing out the prosthetics. You're costing the taxpayers too much money."

They both laughed.

War changed everyone. For Nick it had drawn sharper lines between right and wrong, justice and injustice. It was what allowed him to do the job he did. In war things were writ large. Morality got tested in ways not even a big-city cop could comprehend. Doing the right thing meant something very different to Nick when he stepped off the plane that brought him home than it had when he got on the plane to leave.

The top floor was quiet—nothing like the noisy, busy floors below he'd glimpsed when the elevator doors opened. It was quiet up there, but the hospital odors were inescapable. The pine-scented cleaners, the tang of alcohol clashing against the all-too-human scents of bodily waste and decay.

The nurses' station was short on nurses. One of "Joe's men" was there. Except for Ace, Nick didn't know any of them by name. He occasionally recognized one of them, but these men—he'd yet to see a woman among them—were there to protect Joe and do his bidding. Even when Nick didn't see them, he knew they were there. Mack, who always watched Nick's back during meetings, had confirmed as much. The only time they weren't present was at Joe and Nick's get-together on Valentino Pier. Maybe Joe had finally realized that anyone who was there as backup could also report on your own movements. Maybe not.

This guy was new to him. Big, well-dressed, and ex-military in carriage. He was Black, kept his hair short, and kept his face coldly expressionless. There was always something threatening and inhuman about that look. Nick ignored the cold stare. He could see that Joe's man recognized him. None of them dared fuck with Nick. The guy simply pointed down the hall to his left.

Seated at the window, Ace was dressed in a hospital gown. He was staring out at a view not very different from Nick's view out his living room window.

"Nice view, isn't it?" Nick said.

"Fuck that bridge." Ace didn't turn. "If we'd stayed on the Brooklyn side a few days ago, I wouldn't be in here."

"Can't argue that, but the word *if* has a thousand faces. If we had stayed on this side of the bridge, there'd be a dead college student floating in the water at Fresh Kills. Carmine Gabrelli would be alive and his brother-in-law wouldn't be in a coma. If, if, if . . ."

Ace turned. "No candy or flowers?"

"Next time, Meadows. Meadows! You had to get shot for me to find out."

"That's Baxter G. Meadows to you, Ryan."

"What's the *G* for?"

"*G* is for go fuck yourself."

They laughed.

"You're still Ace to me."

"Good. I like that better."

"When they letting you out of here? I need you."

"Why's that?"

Nick caught Ace up on most of what had happened between the shooting and the present moment.

Ace took it in. As was his way, he said little in response. If Nick wanted feedback, he'd have to ask for it.

"I'm here for a while, then to rehab," Ace said. "You and the Irishman will have to do it on your own. That buckshot wrecked my shoulder. Can't lift my damn arm."

"There goes your chance at the championship belt." Referring to Ace's past as a boxer generally got a smile out of the usually stoical cop. Not this time.

"Nah, I was only ever good enough to lose. You know what I mean?"

"You were the guy at the next step, the one who would give the promising boxer a tough fight on the way up."

"That was me, all right. The stalking horse who never got the mare. Like with you and me. I was only a placeholder until someone like you showed up. Why you here anyway?"

"To tell you I won't forget what happened. If Gabrelli's brother-in-law had gotten around you, both the kid and I would be dead."

Ace shook his head slowly. "Watch it with that *if* word. Someone once told me it had a thousand faces. Besides, your remembering don't mean shit. All you got is a fancier shovel than me."

"You're right, Ace. That's all I got."

"Next time you show up here, bring something to eat."

"Name it."

"There's a barbecue place in Red Hook."

"I know it. What you want?"

"Surprise me."

Nick walked across the room and shook Ace's hand. "You're nobody's stalking horse or placeholder. I owe you. I won't forget."

As he walked out of the hospital, his phone rang. He didn't recognize the number but sensed he should answer. "Ryan."

"I have some information for you, Nick." It was a now-familiar woman's voice in his ear.

"How much?"

"For this, it will cost you only the price of a coffee. Tomorrow. Cadman Plaza by the war memorial at ten a.m."

"You want to meet?"

"I speak several languages, Nick. I thought I spoke in English."

"How do you like your coffee?"

"I will let you figure that out for yourself."

Before he could say another world, he heard an annoying beeping in his ear.

TWENTY-SIX

A red-sauce Italian restaurant with wall paintings of Sicily, candles in old straw-covered Chianti bottles, and checkered tablecloths, Rossini's was a dying breed. It smelled like garlic bread and vinegar and bubbling tomatoes and fresh-cut basil. There used to be a place like Rossini's in most New York City neighborhoods. These days, Italian restaurants had either been subsumed by pizzerias or gotten bigheaded.

Louie Randazzo was already seated at a four-top table in the rear of the restaurant, his back to the wall, two strides from the swinging kitchen doors. He could see anyone coming toward him and could get out through the kitchen if he needed to. Louie stood and they embraced. It was a genuinely affectionate hug, not perfunctory or pro forma. Then Louie, who was six five, held Nick by the shoulders at arm's length.

"Look at you. Still in great shape. You could step on the court right now. Me . . ." Louie let go of Nick and patted his own belly. "I couldn't be a ball boy."

"I don't know, Louie. You look like you *swallowed* a ball."

"Fuck you, wiseass."

"I see you're still sitting with your back to the wall near the kitchen. No offense, but you're not exactly Crazy Joe Gallo. Nobody gets whacked

in public these days. On the street in front of your house in the dark—
that's the thing."

"Old habits, Chilly. Old habits."

"No one's called me Chilly since high school."

They sat. There was a carafe of red wine on the table, a bowl of ice,
and a plate of lemon wedges. Randazzo poured the wine into water
glasses.

"Old man Rossini is dead, but they still make their own wine. How
many places you think still make their own?"

Nick dropped two ice cubes in his glass and squeezed in some lemon.
"Probably a few on Arthur Avenue."

"Screw the Bronx. I'll take Rossini's any day. *Salute!*"

They drank. Nick said, "Smooth as gravel."

"I love this place. They still call meat sauce 'meat sauce.' They don't
call it ragù or Bolognese and charge you thirty bucks for a buck's worth
of dry pasta. This is old-school Brooklyn. I don't even recognize Brooklyn anymore. Anyways, I ordered already. Calamari, antipasto, garlic
bread, the lasagna, sausage, and veal parm combos. You want anything
else, just ask."

"I'm paying anyway. Besides, you look like you ate already."

"One more fat joke and I'm leaving. We gonna do business now or
after we eat?"

"Never on an empty stomach."

Ninety minutes later, after two espressos, Nick slid some photos
across the table to Louie. "The top ones are of Tony and Rosa Angelo."

"Neat work."

"Precisely. See how the two body shots are so close together, but the
real identifier is a small incised wound in the back of the neck. See?"
Nick pointed to the photos of Tony's body. "I think he sometimes likes
to paralyze his victims first."

"Why not the wife?"

"I don't think she was a target. She stumbled into it after he'd already
killed Tony. She was collateral damage. Anyway, could you ask around
and see if this is the work of anyone . . . you know."

"I know." Louie squirmed in his seat. "Not really the kinda thing we do, Nick. If your uncle Tony was connected and he fucked up, I can't get in the middle of that. Besides, I thought Tony was a clean cop. He was in the bag his whole time on the job, right? What use could he have been to . . . my friends?"

"Tony used to say that nobody never knows nobody. Do I think he was clean?" Nick shrugged. "Sure, but he didn't get killed by a pro for giving someone a ticket for an expired meter."

"You lookin' for revenge, here, Nick?"

"I got my reasons. Revenge isn't one of them."

"I'll ask around, but—"

"That's all I'm asking."

"Who are these guys?" Randazzo asked, holding up the next two photos.

"The one in the air force uniform is Jimmy Gabrelli. The other one is Carmine, his younger brother. I had to kill Carmine in Fresh Kills the other day."

"Holy shit! That was *you* killed that guy? I heard there was some trouble over there, but no one could find anything out. Why's that?"

"Above my pay grade," Nick lied. "It's one of the reasons I'm asking you. The brass put a lid on it. But I know that Carmine claimed some-one had his brother, Jimmy, killed years ago and buried him in—"

"I get it. You know, Nick, not everyone with a vowel at the end of his name's connected and not every corpse that wound up in Fresh Kills or Fountain Avenue was a mob hit."

"I'm just being thorough is all. No accusations from me."

Louie waved the waiter over. "I'll have a sambuca with three coffee beans and my friend will have . . ."

"Bourbon?"

The old waiter eyed Nick with disdain.

"I didn't think so. Grappa."

The waiter smiled approvingly.

When the old man walked away, Louie said, "Forget the bill and forget about the Sweeper. I like it better that you owe me a favor."

"You watching *The Godfather* again?"

"Look, you owe me one or not?"

"Sure, Louie. Just watch what you ask for. We all have lines we don't cross."

The waiter brought their drinks. As Nick drank, he thought about what he had said about crossing lines, and which ones he had yet to cross.

TWENTY-SEVEN

The homeless man on the bottom step of the World War II memorial stirred. Dressed in a frayed desert-camo jacket, he pushed against the cardboard-box mattress that had shielded him from the cold granite. He peeked over the edge of the shelter he'd fashioned from black plastic garbage bags, stones, and a rusted bicycle frame he'd found on the Court Street sidewalk. There was a dusting of snow all around him. He looked up at the huge grayish-tan wall behind him, the larger-than-life figures of a soldier at one end and a mother cradling her child at the other. There were some words carved into the limestone about bravery, death, suffering, and peace. He'd seen a movie once where a character said that the quickest way to forget a war was to build memorials to it.

He blew hot breath into his cupped red, chapped hands and pulled his grimy green-and-white woolen New York Jets hat down as low on his head as it would go. His unkempt hair stuck out several inches, falling halfway down his neck. He ran his fingers through his mountain-man beard, scratched at the skin beneath it. He dug a half-smoked, lipstick-stained cigarette out of the backpack on which he had rested his head. He put it between his yellowed teeth and lit it with a disposable lighter he'd found in a garbage can at the edge of the park. He sucked the smoke in so deeply that half the cigarette burned away with a single draw. He blew the smoke and steam out into the gray morning. The cold had kept most of the people out of the park and off the great snow-covered lawn spreading out before the memorial.

In the homeless man's ear, there was a whisper. "Lone figure approaching from your three o'clock." The whisperer had an Irish accent.

The homeless man spoke into the tiny microphone taped to his wrist. "Is it her?"

"You tell me, boyo. Definitely a woman, but is it her . . ."

"I have to hear what she has to tell me, then we move."

The homeless man tossed his cigarette. It hissed in the snow. He crawled back under the black plastic roof of his shelter, listened to the gentle shushing of her footfalls as she approached. He watched her walk past him, pace, then stand still. She stood to his left, facing the wall, apparently reading the words carved into it. She was the right size, moved as he had seen her move the night of the bombing at McCann's. But he couldn't be sure it was her. Her face was obscured below the nose by a silky black scarf, dark glasses hid her eyes, and her fur-trimmed hood was pulled down tight over her watch cap–covered hair. She kept one hand in her pocket. The other was gloved in tight black leather.

"Noble words," she said, still looking at the wall. "But there is nothing noble in war. Wouldn't you agree?"

"Only nobility in war is between soldiers, and then, not always," said the homeless man, sliding out from his shelter.

"You forgot my coffee, Nick."

"I'll owe you one."

"You are incredibly skilled at disguise and might have fooled anyone but me. You use the things you find on the street rather than props you bring with you. The yellow teeth and the body odor—very nice touches. You make sure to arrive early and scout out the area. You bring backup. These are things many in our profession get wrong."

He still couldn't figure out where she had learned English. It wasn't quite robotic, but it was free of any local accent he had heard and the intonation pattern was subtle.

"Our profession," Nick repeated. "We aren't in the same profession."

"You are very insistent on this point, but repeating it does not make it so. In any case, here we are."

"Here we are." Nick kept his hands in his pockets. He knew not to step too close to her. "I'm curious."

"Your curiosity is something you must learn to control or it will make you vulnerable. And you are already too vulnerable."

"Yes, Yoda."

She snickered.

The fake yellow teeth smiled. "So, you are human. That's something."

"What are you curious about, Nick?"

"Why the face-to-face? It doesn't fit your profile. It would be one thing for you to show up at my door unexpectedly, but letting me know in advance . . ."

"For two reasons. One, to see you again. As you know, I have taken a particular interest in you."

"Care to explain?"

"Someday possibly."

"The other reason."

"To warn you against trying to set another trap for me. I will excuse it this one time because I realize you feel you must try. I wanted you to get it out of your system. You haven't yet completely shed your policeman's mindset."

"You said something about me coming with backup."

"The Irishman, Mack." She turned, faced a stand of trees to her left, and waved. "I could easily have taken care of him and left you more vulnerable than you already are."

Mack shouted into Nick's wig-covered earpiece, "For fook's sake, Ryan! She's *waving* at me!"

Nick ignored Mack. "Why *didn't* you take care of him?"

"Again, to make a point about traps. Please, so that we may continue as service provider and client, remove your empty hands from your pockets and tell Mack to lower his weapon."

"Why would I do that?"

"Nick, you have forced me to do something I would have wished to avoid. As I mentioned, you are already too vulnerable. I am going to remove my bare hand from my parka pocket. In it will be only an iPad. I will stand close to you so that you may view it. I urge you not to act rashly. I am aware of your skills at martial arts and hand-to-hand combat. Be assured, mine are more than equal to yours. Do you agree?"

Nick got a very uneasy feeling. He removed his hands from his pockets, leaving the Taser in his left pocket and the Glock 26 in his right. He spoke into his wrist. "Stand down, Mack." He stepped close to the woman holding the iPad in her ungloved hand, the screen turned to him.

"Tap the screen, Nick."

He did as she asked. A drone view of a park appeared, but it wasn't Cadman Plaza Park.

"A park, not this park. So?"

"Tap the screen once more."

He did so. This time the camera on the drone zoomed down at a children's play area. On the slide was a little girl in a puffy coat. Her dirty-blond hair stuck out from under her fake-fur hat. A few feet from the slides stood a tall, stunning woman. Her hair was dark and shiny even under a gray sky. She wore a sheepskin coat, unbuttoned, and a long beige scarf over a black sweater.

Before Nick could speak, the woman said, "I have killed women, as you know. I have never killed a child and I will harm neither of them. But if you ever again try to do foolishness as you have attempted today, I may be moved to hurt the husband. That might even please you, though I doubt it. Do we have an understanding, Nick Ryan?"

"We do."

"Very well." She held the tablet so that only she could see the screen, tapped, and typed into the virtual keyboard. She turned the screen. Staring back at Nick was the image of a man in his mid- to late forties. He had an oval face with small ears. A graying beard and black mustache surrounded prominent lips. He had a prominent forehead accented by a hairline receding on either side of a patch of salt-and-pepper hair. His eyes were cold and dark and misaligned, the left one turned outward.

The eyes framed an unremarkable nose. "He's Croatian, Franjo Petro-vic. Although he does not categorically use a small-caliber weapon, the cervical cut is his signature. He is known as the Swede."

"Why the Swede?"

"Perhaps he has a passion for IKEA furniture. I do not know."

"What about him?"

"When you can access your computer, there will be as full a dossier on him as is available. I am uncertain if he is the man you are seeking, but as I stated, he is known to do his work in the manner you described. He is like a cat, I am told. He enjoys toying with his prey. Now, Nick, our transaction is complete."

"What should I call you?"

She tilted her head, confused. "What?"

"If we speak again, I need to be able to call you something, a name."

"A trick?"

"I would never endanger Becky or Shana that way. I just need to call you something. It will help me think of you as other than an assassin."

"Tuva. You may call me Tuva."

"Turkish?"

If Nick thought that would throw her off somehow, he was wrong. "I could as easily have said Tina, Teresa, or Tatiana. It is just a name in a million."

As the last word came out of her scarf-covered mouth, they both stood stone-still. The world was hushed. She tensed, eyes wide, alert—a cat ready to pounce. She seemed to sense that something was about to take a bad turn. Nick recognized the body language. Maybe Tuva had a point about them being alike. Without a word uttered between them, they both took off up the steps to find cover behind the memorial. As they ran, Nick gently pushed her so that his body was between Tuva and the memorial wall.

They didn't hear the shot fired, but they heard it whistle past them. The second shot hit the granite step at Tuva's heel, ricocheted. A shard of the stone tore through the front of Nick's dirty jeans, slicing into his shin. There were two more shots. Both missed, not by much. They huddled behind the statue of the soldier.

"Those shots did not come from Mack's position," Tuva said, scanning the tall buildings that surrounded the triangular-shaped park. "Did anyone but Mack know about this meeting?"

"No."

Mack was again shouting in Nick's ear. "What the hell is going on?"

Nick asked, "Mack, can you tell where those shots came from?"

"Opposite side of the park is the best I can figure."

"Okay, Mack, clear out."

"You sure, boyo?"

"They blew their chance. They're probably long gone by now. I'll be in touch."

Tuva said, "Do you trust Mack?"

"To a point, but there's no upside in this for him. If he wanted to split, he could just leave. No need to eliminate me. And if he wanted to do me harm, there are less awkward, less flashy ways than this."

"Agreed."

"What about you?"

If someone could look insulted beneath a scarf and dark glasses, she did. "No one knows anything about me or my movements. I have no close attachments, no vulnerabilities in my life to be threatened."

"Then we're where we started."

"No, Nick. We are not. I will not forget." She leaped up and took off.

Nick didn't follow. There was little point. She was right. Her skills were more than equal to his and he had other things to focus on. Walking out of the park, scanning the surrounding buildings, he wondered what Tuva's last words meant. With her flat intonation, it was impossible to know whether she was grateful or angry.

———

Nick took a circuitous route back to the Malibu, parked in a garage on Montague Street. He'd taken it because . . . well, because he had to try it out. More importantly, Tuva had no way to connect him to the Malibu. If she had eyes on him, she would be looking for his GTO or the Norton. As he made his way to the car, he ducked into a Starbucks on Court Street. In the bathroom, he cleaned his bloody shin, using toilet paper as a makeshift bandage. He replaced the homeless-vet outfit with grimy coveralls and a watch cap he pulled from his backpack. He already had the work boots he'd worn as the homeless man. He kept the mustache part of the mountain-man beard.

What made him great at disguise was what made him great at UC work. It wasn't the clothing, the facial prosthetics, the beards, the colored contact lenses, or the wigs. Those things worked with people who were distracted or didn't care. To convince people who were looking at you hard, your inside had to mirror your outside. It wasn't enough to change your posture or your gait. You had to look the part, smell the part, *be* the part. Most cops who did UC work sucked at it because they were still cops underneath it all.

When Nick emerged from the bathroom, he gave the three baristas twenty bucks each to let him use the basement and exit onto the side street. Fifteen minutes later, he was seated in the Malibu. He reached into the glove box and took out one of the burner phones he'd put there early that morning.

"Well done, Santo," Nick said.

"Cool. You got me covered, right?"

"Nobody's called nine-one-one."

"I'm good doin' this shit as long as you don't want me to hit nobody. But *jefe* if the money is right . . ."

"I got your number."

Santo Contreras had been a sniper attached to Nick's unit. Nick had no love for snipers, but war took on a life of its own regardless of what was fair or right or what any one person thought. Nick had managed an uneasy friendship with Contreras because they were both New Yorkers. Sniper school had taught the man a lot of skills useful in war, but useless in Jackson Heights. So Nick had a good idea Santo would say yes when he offered him the gig and supplied the old-style Remington 700.

"Look, Ryan, what was that about?"

"Answers or the rest of your money, not both."

"Can't pay the rent with answers."

"Good choice."

"Later."

"Later."

Nick knew that Tuva wouldn't be trapped with peanut butter like a common gray squirrel. He had to play the long game. It would be a gradual process of gaining her trust. That was what today had been about—trust.

TWENTY-EIGHT

Coveralls off, mustache removed, Nick showered and properly patched his shin. He put on a suit and tie. Nothing fancy. Just a dark-blue polyester-blend jacket and pants, a rumpled white shirt, and a too-wide black tie that made him look like a typical overworked NYPD detective. It was as much a disguise as what he'd worn earlier. He was no more a typical detective than he was a homeless man.

Before leaving, he sat at the desk in his spare bedroom that doubled as an office. He opened the email Tuva had sent him, and read about Franjo Petrovic. A nasty piece of work, he was a former member of the BSD, the Croatian version of the Navy SEALs. Since then, he'd left a trail of bodies throughout Central and Eastern Europe. Most recently he'd expanded to the whole continent. He was known for paralyzing his victims with a single well-placed cut. The attached psychological evaluation painted a grim picture of a man who enjoyed the ugliest aspects of his work. There was also an English translation of a transcription of eyewitness testimony to one of Petrovic's murders in Bosnia:

After Hamza collapsed, the man with the knife straddled him. He had a huge smile on his face. He grabbed Hamza's face and made him stare up at him. "Look at me. Look at me," he repeated. "Your pain is over, my friend. I want you to watch me. Watch me or I will take my time with you. It won't hurt. There's that. But I assure you, watching me dissect you is not how you want to go into paradise." Hamza could not hold his head up and was struggling to breathe. The man slit through Hamza's trousers and underwear. [*witness sobbing*] I am sorry. The man then . . . [*witness sobbing*] he cut off his . . .

Nick got the point and stopped reading. He forwarded the file to Lenny Feld and to Annalise Puleo.

He didn't need to add anything to his email to Lenny. Lenny would know what to do. To Annalise he wrote:

Don't ask questions I won't answer. If you need a source, say you came to me and I got it through the Intel Bureau. This might be who you and Rosen are looking for. The reasons will be obvious when you read the attached file. Run his photo. Check with TSA, ICE. It's worth a shot.

The series of odd coincidences wasn't lost on Nick. Strange that Petrovic and Markovic came from the same corner of the world. As he sat there, he replayed in his head the scene of the attack on Vicky Lansdale on South Fourth Street. The man who led that attack didn't fit Franjo Petrovic's physical description. The man from South Fourth obviously had the capacity for violence, but he seemed more interested in the ends than the means. Petrovic seemed to Nick a man who relished violence.

Nick moved his lips, trying to recreate the cultured Eastern European accent of the man who had issued the threat to Vicky in Williamsburg. That was another of Nick's skills—his ability to mimic regional accents. Didn't do you any good to look the part and still sound like someone from Brooklyn. He remembered snatches of what the man had said, and repeated the words aloud.

"Tell your husband that his bill is long overdue and that his Secret

Service men will do him no good. That yesterday and today are his final notices."

Nick recited it again. Again. Again and again until he felt he was getting closer. His first attempts sounded too harsh, too Russian. He softened it some and it strayed toward Hungarian. Then, finally, he added a bit of Italian intonation. When he thought he had it, Nick Googled *Serbian accent*. He watched and listened to three brief videos and repeated the words of the speaker on-screen. He repeated the process for Croatian speakers. Despite the two nations' proximity, their accents were different. The man on South Fourth Street was definitely a Serb. The Gabrellis, the Lansdales, the Angelos, Vlado Markovic, a Serbian gang, a Croat killer for hire—none of the puzzle pieces fit together in anything more than an unfortunate grouping of coincidences. Whether Nick trusted coincidences or not, he didn't see how they could be anything else.

The rest of the day and the days to come would be solely devoted to the Markovic homicide. With that out of the way, he could turn his attention back to the murders of Tony and Rosa Angelo. Because Markovic's homicide was a unicorn—the only one in the city on 9/11 not directly connected to the terrorist attacks—his case had garnered a lot of press in the decade that followed. Stories would appear in the papers and on TV in the days on either side of the 9/11 anniversary. There were the breathless on-scene reports, some of which went so far as to include reenactments of what was alleged to have happened. All of which cemented in the public's mind the accepted version of the event.

The segments were all of a type. The reporter, most often an attractive female, would stand alone on the night-darkened platform at the Smith and Ninth Street subway station. She would turn, point down at the concrete, and say, "This was the spot on which Vlado Markovic, a hardworking Serbian immigrant, was viciously and brutally stabbed to death in the hour before midnight on the most traumatic day in modern American history. Police have concluded that Markovic, who wore a full beard and spoke in thickly accented English, had been mistaken for an Arab by someone looking to find a convenient target for their anger." Then the segment would cut to prerecorded excerpts from an interview with an NYPD spokesperson—occasionally one of the detectives working the case.

People weren't thinkin' straight that day. There was a lot of displaced anger and people didn't know what to do with it. I was always amazed more innocent people didn't get hurt. Says a lot about New Yorkers, I think. The viciousness of the attack, the number of stab wounds indicate to us that there was blind rage involved here. Think of how many relatives and friends of the victims of the attacks on the Trade Center must have wanted to get revenge and might've been out for blood that night. The way we figure it, Mr. Markovic was the innocent victim of someone who was looking for a target. Wrong place, wrong time. But if anyone knows anything, we've set up an eight-hundred number . . .

The newspaper items were less sensational and more detailed, but they too repeated what Nick thought of as the "wrong place, wrong time" narrative. After actually reviewing the file, seeing the photos, and reading Annalise's notes, he no longer accepted it as gospel. In recent years, there were fewer stories about Markovic. They still read the names of the victims and rang the bell at Ground Zero on September 11, but Vlado Markovic was now an afterthought, an increasingly obscure historical footnote. Although people didn't exactly want to forget 9/11, there was a hunger to move on.

———

Carla Markovic had remarried and had two kids in college. She was now Carla Ruvolo. Nick caught up with her at the Park Slope offices of Richard Neer, DDS. He flashed his shield, asked to speak to Mrs. Ruvolo.

"You get bored or something? Been a while since one of you guys came around," the receptionist said, shaking her head. "Let me go see what she's doing."

A few minutes later, a slight, gaunt-faced woman in her midfifties, dressed in blue scrubs, came through the door into the waiting room. She had a winter coat slung over one shoulder, and her bag over the other. She had a lovely smile. The smile didn't last.

"C'mon," she said, "I've got a half hour and there's a deli around the corner we can sit at."

Nick bought her a turkey-bacon wrap and a Diet Coke. He had coffee. Carla inhaled half of the wrap, eyeing Nick suspiciously as she did.

"None of you guys ever bought me lunch before," she said. "And don't you usually travel in pairs? It was always Tweedle Dee and Tweedle Dumber. Same stupid damn questions, same results. Nothing. Always seemed to me they had made up their minds and were going through the motions. Every other year it would be two new detectives; then they stopped coming around . . . until you."

"I'm not here to promise you I'll do any better or that my questions will be original. What I can promise is that I haven't made up my mind."

She was understandably skeptical. "You won't be angry with me if I tell you I've heard that line before?" She picked up the other half of her wrap.

"How did your husband break his ankle?"

That got her attention. She put the sandwich back down, tilting her head up at him like a confused puppy. "What do you mean?"

"You didn't know he had a broken ankle?"

"No. I mean, he was kinda weirded out that whole day. He was panicked, trying really hard to make sure he could get to work that night. Vlado had that immigrant thing about never missing work and fear of losing his job. He even got out his bicycle from the basement, but the tires were flat. He was walking just fine. Why didn't I know he had a broken ankle?"

"The detectives . . ." Nick looked at his notes. "Breen and Harris, probably just assumed he had broken it running from his attackers because there was no cast or bandaging found at the scene. It makes sense."

"Okay." She nodded in agreement. Nick could see she was warming to him. She liked him asking the question no one had posed before.

"You said he was weird that day. Weird how?"

"You know he came from Serbia, right?"

"I do. How did you guys get together?"

After a brief hesitation, she explained they'd met at a bar. *So cliché, right?* They dated for about three months before he proposed. He was sweet and treated her well. She told the story as if it was a series of rehearsed lines repeated many, many times. Nick noticed her affect; her body language didn't seem to match the words coming out of her mouth.

He asked, "When was this?"

"'Ninety-nine. We got married that June."

"You said he was weird the day he was killed." Nick turned the conversation back around.

"It was hard for him. He got forced into a militia group during the war over there. I don't really understand it, the whole Croatia, Serbia, Bosnia-Herzegovina thing. When I asked about it, Vlado, he really didn't want to talk about it. Sometimes when he got drunk . . . he'd say stuff."

"Stuff like?"

"About how in the militia they did bad things. That's what he would say, 'bad things.' He wouldn't ever elaborate. But sometimes he would talk about someone he called Zmaj. I Googled it. It means *the dragon.* When he talked about that Zmaj, Vlado got all jumpy. I think the attacks on Nine-Eleven brought his war experiences back to him."

"So," Nick said, "he was fine until that day?"

"You know, thinking back, he'd been a little tense for a few weeks before that day. He was drinking more than normal."

"What was normal?"

"On the weekends, but since late that August he was drinking every day. You know, not to get drunk."

Nick nodded. "Like to calm his nerves."

"Yeah, like that exactly."

"I noticed he had a burn scar on his right biceps. What was that from? The bakery?"

"Oh, that." She frowned. "No, he had that when we met. It was from his time in the militia. He didn't explain it more than that and I didn't ask."

"Now I am going to ask you the questions everybody before me asked."

"That's fair."

"Enemies?"

"None I knew of. He was to himself a lot. That's why he liked the bakery. He could do his job, keep his head down, and support us. He worked really hard to do that."

"Relatives?"

"None here, or at least none I knew of."

"Friends?"

"Our friends were my friends mostly. There was one guy at the bakery who got him the job."

"What was his name?"

"Petar Stankovic."

"Do you have contact information for him?"

"I did at home somewhere." She shrugged. "We kept in touch after Vlado's . . ."

"Here's the ugly question," Nick said. "Was either of you unfaithful?"

Carla laughed. "You know, I can't say that I loved Vlado. I liked him a lot. He was kind to me, caring, you know? The sex wasn't bad. A little unimaginative, but not bad. I never cheated on him, I think because he was so earnest, so grateful. I don't think he cheated on me. I can't think of when he would've had the time."

"You said he was grateful. Grateful for what?"

Nick could see that the question made her uneasy. She squirmed in her seat, looked everywhere but at him. She was obviously thinking of some evasive way to answer him.

"Carla, I've got no interest here except solving Vlado's murder. Nothing else matters to me. Whatever you say outside of that scope stays between us."

"It was a green-card marriage," she said, her face reddening with embarrassment. "He . . . um . . . he paid me to marry him."

"I'm not here to judge you, but I need you to be honest with me. How much?"

Carla Ruvolo bowed her head. "Twenty-five thousand dollars."

"In cash?" Nick purposely kept the surprise out of his voice. "Where did he get that money?"

"I didn't ask. It was that kind of marriage. There was a lot I didn't ask and a lot he didn't tell."

Nick patted her forearm. "That's okay. Like I said, I'm not here to judge you. When Vlado died, what was his estate worth?"

There was her embarrassment again. Nick changed tactics.

"I've been patient, Carla, but if you're going to start lying to me, that will change. Unlike the guys who came before me, Vlado's murder means something to me. I may not find the person who did it, but I'm trying, and no one should stand in my way, especially not you. You do that and I'm going to start looking very hard at you."

"Okay, okay."

"The truth. All of it."

"He left me a small insurance policy that came with his benefits from the bakery. Ten grand. A coupla hundred bucks in those silly savings bonds. We had a few thousand in a joint checking account and he had a separate savings account with fifteen hundred bucks."

"But . . ."

"He wasn't the love of my life, but it took me about six months before I could get the courage to go through his things. I found a safe-deposit box key from the bank we used. I hired a lawyer, I filled out a ton of forms, and with the death certificate—"

"How much?"

"Eighty thousand dollars."

"In cash?"

"Hundreds, banded together."

"And the detectives didn't ask you about this?"

She shrugged again. "Like you said, Detective Ryan. They'd already made up their minds about why Vlado was killed. I don't think they looked at me for more than five minutes."

Nick leaned forward and gave Carla Ruvolo a long, cold stare. "Should they have looked longer?"

"I swear I had nothing to do with Vlado's murder. On my kids' lives, I didn't know about the money. I wouldn't know how to go about killing someone or hiring someone to do it. I don't even watch *Law and Order*."

"Relax. I believe you. No way you could have known in advance about how perfect Nine-Eleven would be for his murder. Any idea where the money he paid you to marry him or the money in the deposit box came from?"

"None. I was shocked. I mean, he made out okay at the bakery, but we just managed our expenses and saved a few bucks between us."

"What did you do with the twenty-five he paid you and the eighty grand from the box?"

"Nothing mostly, at least for a few years. Then I bought a car, a red Mazda Miata." She smiled a big smile, remembering that car. "I traveled a little. The rest . . . I put it into a college savings account when I got remarried and we had kids."

Nick gave her a card. "Call me if anything else you think will help comes to mind. I may be back in touch."

She grabbed his wrist as he got up. "You won't say anything about—"

"Not unless I find out you lied to me. Otherwise, no worries."

She smiled up at him. It was a cracked and unconvincing smile.

TWENTY-NINE

Markovic's case had been kicked around for nearly two decades, and the evidence wound up back at the Brooklyn Property Clerk's Office on Front Street. Nick's shooting on Staten Island had yet to be declared righteous, but the folks at the Brooklyn Property Clerk were either unaware or uncaring. The woman at the desk looked none too pleased when she saw the date on the request form.

"You kidding me, Detective?"

"Sorry."

"It's gonna take a while. Prepare to wait and then get dusty." She pointed to a row of chairs across from her. "Have a seat."

Nick sat, watching the woman make a call and read off the request form. He texted his father, asking for details about the funeral arrangements. Before he could put the cell back in his pocket, it buzzed in his palm.

It was Louie Randazzo. "That you, Nick?"

"You called me, remember?"

"Don't be a dick. You got a phone we can talk on? Really talk on?"

"I'll call you back."

Nick pulled out the burner phone he'd used that morning to call Santo. "What you got?"

"On the hitter, I got nothing. No one around uses anyone with that MO, at least not that they're sayin'."

"Okay, Louie, thanks for try—"

"I said I got nothin' on the hitter. I didn't say I got nothin'."

"Sorry."

"Jimmy Gabrelli was a douchebag, a small-timer with a big mouth. He worked for the Malzones outta Nassau County as a kid. He did gofer shit. You know, running messages, dropping off envelopes . . . He was goin' nowhere. He was half a moron."

Nick pointed out, "Gabrelli made sergeant in the air force."

"God knows how that happened. Makes you wonder about the military, don't it?"

"Watch it, Louie."

"Sorry. You want me to say thank you for your service or some shit like that?"

"You were saying about Jimmy Gabrelli."

"Had a big mouth. When he come outta the air force, he talked about a big score he made over there that was gonna show all the guys who used to bust his balls that he wasn't a doormat anymore. Showed up at the old social club in a Porsche. Then . . . poof! Jimmy went bye-bye, like, a few days later."

"Any idea who disappeared him?"

"Nah. Could be the Malzones or one of the crew leaned on Jimmy to find out where the money for the Porsche came from, but it don't seem like it. I checked. Nobody in the crew bought a new house or car or a diamond for his girl or nothin'. Nobody kicked any money up and the Malzones were old-school about loyalty to their people, even schmucks like Jimmy. I heard the old man was really upset when the *strunz* went missing."

"You friendly with the Malzones?"

"Friendly enough. Why?"

"If it's not too much trouble, ask if the name Jonathan Lansdale ever came up in conversation with Jimmy."

"Who's this Lansdale?"

"That thing at Fresh Kills. The guy I put down claimed it was Lansdale had Jimmy whacked and put in the dump."

"Interesting."

"That's one word for it."

"I'll ask."

"Thanks, Louie. I owe you one."

"More than one, but who's countin'?"

"You, apparently."

Louie clicked off. As soon as he did, Nick's regular phone buzzed in his pocket. It was the text back from his dad.

> Wake at Molloy's Funeral Home on Coney
> Island Avenue tonight.

> Service tomorrow at St. Mark's in
> Sheepshead Bay.

Nick's finger hovered above the arrow to forward the text to Shana. She would want to know. Remembering the drone footage Tuva had shown him, he decided against it. He thought it safer to keep up the wall between Shana and Becky and himself. The less anyone associated Nick Ryan with Shana Carlyle and her daughter, the better.

Twenty minutes later, the woman at the desk called to him. "Detective Ryan, your evidence boxes are here. Go through that door." She pointed to her left.

Inside the room, a weary-eyed cop stood next to a table on which two boxes sat. As the woman at the desk had warned, the boxes were dusty. They had been sealed with tape and resealed several times.

The cop asked, "What's the Intel Bureau want with this case anyway?"

"We're bored over there with counterterrorism and security for dignitaries. You know how it is."

The cop cut through the sealing tape and matched what was inside the boxes with the inventory made by the detectives who previously had the evidence in their possession. Two of the bagged items got Nick's attention. He didn't say a word.

"Here's the inventory of what's contained in the box. When it comes back—"

"I know the drill."

"Sign here." He held a clipboard out to Nick.

Nick signed. "Thanks."

"Asshole," the cop mumbled under his breath.

That was exactly what Nick wanted. Let the guy focus on him instead of the evidence. No one needed to be any more curious about what was going on than they already were.

When he got the boxes to the Malibu, Nick gloved up. He waded through the evidence bag. In some sense, this was all that remained aboveground of Vlado Markovic: a cut-up, blood-crusted lined denim jacket, blood-crusted chinos, a worn pair of Nike running shoes, a wallet, a key ring, a few loose coins and subway tokens, a blue Mets cap. In that way, Markovic was luckier than some of the other 9/11 murder victims. Many of them had been pulverized, leaving only memories behind. *No*, Nick thought, *dead is dead*. The preamble had it backward. We weren't all born equal. Only in death was equality truly achieved.

There were two items he was particularly interested in: the wallet and the key ring. While he was sure every detective before him had gone over the contents of the wallet, Nick knew there might be something for him to see that the others had missed. After talking with Carla and discovering that Vlado had secrets, Nick thought the key ring might be more interesting than the wallet.

He opened the bag containing the wallet and its contents. It was a cheap green synthetic fabric trifold. Inside was a wedding photo of Markovic and Carla. Carla was a pretty bride. Markovic was beardless, a bit heavier than in his passport photo. There were a ten-dollar bill, three singles, a bank debit card, a credit card, a shred of paper with a series of numbers and letters scrawled on it in pencil. The numbers were too long to be a phone or social security number.

Nick was curious. He called Lenny and read the numbers and letters off the shred of paper. As he did, he heard Lenny tapping on a keyboard.

"It's a Nifty Car Rental reservation number—an old one. They've been out of business for years."

"Do you think you can pin it down?"

"Silly question."

"I'll be at the wake for the Angelos tonight. I won't be too far away from you."

"Wait, let me check my social calendar. Yes, I think I can squeeze you in sometime between right now and forever."

Nick didn't want to play into Lenny's self-pity. "Okay, later."

The key ring was next. It wasn't the keys themselves that first caught Nick's attention. The clear plastic fob attached to the ring displayed a shield with a black-and-gold background on which were displayed a red cross and a stylized two-headed white eagle. Above the eagle was a gold-handled, upward-pointing silver sword. The image was surrounded by white Cyrillic lettering. Nick took a photo of it and sent it to Lenny.

The keys themselves, though less attention-grabbing than the fob, were not without their interesting aspects. There were two house keys, a flat key—probably from his locker at the bakery—and two padlock keys: one a Master Lock, the other a Yale. He didn't figure the keys would get him anywhere. Nick realized he had padlock keys on his own key ring for locks he'd lost track of years ago. He put everything back in the boxes. As he drove back to the safe-house garage to collect his GTO, Nick realized he had many more questions about Vlado Markovic than when the day began. That was a good thing.

THIRTY

A thoroughfare of delis, convenience stores, funeral homes, ethnic restaurants, gas stations, used-car lots, and grimy brick apartments above empty storefronts, Coney Island Avenue defined Brooklyn ugly. Molloy's Funeral Home was a tired-looking building on the corner of Avenue M and Coney Island Avenue. Nick parked the GTO a block away. The crisp air stank of car exhaust and buzzed with traffic noise. His phone vibrated in his pocket.

"Nick Ryan."

"Detective Ryan, it's Carla Ruvolo. I found our old phone book with Petar Stankovic's number and address."

"Can you text them to me?"

"I'll do that now."

"Thank you."

"Detective Ryan."

"Yeah."

"I realized afterwards how I must've sounded to you. The way Vlado and I . . . you know."

"How's that?"

"Like a mercenary or . . . a whore."

"I don't think that, but my guess is, part of you does. No one is harder on us than ourselves."

"I haven't thought about the money for years and now that I look back, I never told anyone about it before today."

"There's nothing back there for you to undo or change, Mrs. Ruvolo. No one forced anyone to do what they did. What does the other stuff matter?"

"Thank you for saying that. I'm texting the number now."

The phone call ended and the text came through.

He got to Molloy's early. He had his reasons.

The first things he noticed were the matching rosewood coffins, lids closed, at the front of the room. There were flowers all around. The flags by Tony's coffin: the gold-fringed Stars and Stripes, the New York City flag, the green, white, and blue NYPD flag. The room smelled of the flowers, not of the dead. He wondered if that was the original purpose of flowers at a wake—to cover the stink of the dead when they were laid on ice out in the family's parlor. He spotted Puleo and Rosen at the back of the room. Their presence was SOP. No one realistically expected the killer to show, but there was always a chance. Nick nodded to the partners. Annalise nodded back. Rosen stood up, coming around to Nick.

"Got a minute?"

"Sure."

They stepped into the reception area.

Rosen said, "Thanks for the heads-up on Franjo Petrovic."

"Anything from the FBI, ICE, or TSA?"

"A guy like Petrovic isn't going to come into the country under his own name. Nasty piece of work, that guy. As for the feds, I'm not sure they'd tell us even if they had something."

"Thought I'd ask anyway."

"So what's your angle, Ryan?"

"What are you talking about?"

"I figured you'd be all over us with you being so close to the vics. Besides the intel on Petrovic, nothing from you. Puleo told me you've only called her once and that was for something else. I know you better than that."

"Trust me, Rosen, you don't know me at all. I've got my own cases to deal with. This may really surprise you, but I trust Annalise and know you're a dog with a bone. I'll keep out of your way as long as I think you're doing your job."

"Just keep it that way."

He looked over Rosen's shoulder. Nick saw his father, his brother, Sean, and his sister-in-law, Marie, coming through the front door.

"Rosen, keep your warnings for people who give a shit." Nick stepped past him.

The Ryans weren't huggers by nature, keeping their greetings to handshakes and hellos. He kissed Marie on the cheek. Nick Sr. looked truly shaken. His breath smelled of Jameson and the cinnamon-scented mouthwash that failed to mask it. For a rare change, Sean seemed happy to see his big brother. They stepped into the room. One after the other, they knelt in front of the caskets, Rosa's first, and said their goodbyes.

Nick had gotten here early because he thought he wanted to take his time bidding Tony farewell. When he got to Tony's coffin, crossing himself, putting his knees down on the padded rail, Nick realized he had only one thing to say. "Blind to midnight, Uncle Tony. Love ya."

Out of respect, the Ryans sat in the second row. No family came to sit in the front. The Ryans were his family. Rosa's family filled the other side of the room. That was where all the tears were shed. Martellus Sharp and his wife and a few of Tony's old cop friends showed. They gathered at the back of the room, drinking from not-so-well-hidden flasks and telling stories. Nick joined them. His father didn't. Even among the retired cops, Nick Ryan Sr. was a pariah. Nick Jr. got cut some slack because of the war-hero thing and because of his actions at the McCann's bombing.

For fifteen minutes, Nick listened to them telling stories about Tony's mangling of the language, his sense of humor, and his generosity. All the tales began with "There was this one time Tony . . ." Rosen stood back a little, listening too. Nick noticed none of the guys were telling stories from around the time Tony had hit that rough patch. There was nothing linking his murder to that time, but Nick was too smart to think they couldn't be related.

He asked, "Any of you guys work with Uncle Tony in the early two thousands?"

The circle of Tony's old cop buddies went stone silent. *So, Da was right about Tony going through a tough period in those days.* No one wanted to speak ill of the dead, especially not at the man's wake. Funny stories, sure, but nothing demeaning. Nick excused himself and headed for the bathroom. He figured, if any of Tony's buddies had something to say, they might say it quietly to him alone. He figured right.

"Hey, Ryan, slow down, for chrissakes!" A heavyset man in his midsixties caught up to Nick at the foot of the staircase. "We don't need to add me to the list of the dead."

Nick stopped, turned.

"Go on up," the man said, panting, hanging on to the banister. "I'll catch you in the bathroom."

The retired cop was sweating profusely and had to bend over, hands on knees, to catch his breath. Nick waited, back against the sink.

"Those were dark days for Tony," the man said, gulping air. "I'm Bob Mark." They shook hands. "Like I was saying, bad days. Drinking too much, boxing guys around. He was in the Seven-Eight and partnered with Johnny Sullivan. A real prick, Sullivan. He was a guy with his hands in everybody's pocket, if you catch my meaning."

"I do."

"Ah, fuck that guy. He got his, anyways."

"Sullivan?"

"Yeah, the stupid bastard was taking a selfie on a big rock up by where he retired upstate. The asshole slipped and broke his fucking neck." Mark was laughing, shaking his head. "Dumb prick. He was about as photogenic as a Gila monster. But people and selfies these days—it's a big thing."

"How long ago was this?"

"Let's see . . . I guess about a week—no, two weeks before . . . you know. I'll miss Tony. Sullivan, not so much."

"Strange coincidence, their deaths so close, huh?"

Mark shrugged. "Bad shit happens in threes. If you count Rosa, right?"

"I guess."

"But other than that time he was in the Seven-Eight and the time he spent on the rubber-gun squad after Nine-Eleven, he was the best."

"No argument from me. Thanks for saying that."

But Mark couldn't leave it there. "Your dad was a good cop too, but he shoulda just transferred out instead of making a stink. He shoulda done the right thing."

"Listen, Bob, transferring out—that's what a fucking coward would do. My da may be an asshole, but he's not a coward."

Nick brushed past Mark and went back down the stairs.

Back in the room, Annalise Puleo came over to Nick. They stood at the rear behind Rosa's family.

"Was my partner being a dick?" she asked.

"Only a little bit. For him, that's a rare accomplishment."

"You wanna go riding Sunday? The weather's supposed to be nice. I mean, I know that piece-a-shit Norton can't keep up with me, but—"

"You asking me out?"

"I liked being back in your place again and now I'm, you know, unattached." She touched her fingers to her neck.

Before Nick could answer, two things happened simultaneously. The priest got up and moved to the center of the room between the two coffins, and Shana made an entrance through the just-closed doors. The priest had no chance. Shana won. She always did. The woman knew how to make an entrance. Heads turned to the doorway. Annalise looked past Nick.

"That's her, isn't it? Shana?"

"It is."

"She's so fucking hot. How could you date me after—"

Nick put his finger across Puleo's lips. "Don't! Don't ever say that. I'll be back."

THIRTY-ONE

Shana tried hard to look as if she weren't trying hard to find Nick in the crowd. He got to her before she spotted him. It happened as it had happened the first time Nick held the door open for her at the memorial service for the employees of her father's investment firm. Chemistry wasn't a matter of will. The two of them proved as much every time they were in close proximity. Nick grabbed her arm and walked her out of the room, closing the doors behind him.

"What are you doing here?" He forced himself to be calm. He hated that Shana was his kryptonite.

"I loved Tony and Rosa. I have every right to be here."

"Who told you about this—Sean or my dad?"

"Your dad. I called him."

"Okay, you're right, but this isn't helping."

"Helping who with what? I love you. I want to be with you as a family."

"That isn't going to happen. It can't happen."

"There's that word again, can't."

"Jesus, Shana. It's because I love you and Becky that I can't, we can't."

"Explain it to me again."

"Today at the park, you were wearing a sheepskin coat and a long beige scarf over a black sweater."

Shana's eyes narrowed in anger. "I thought you weren't going to—"

"I wasn't. I didn't. I saw you and Becky from a drone camera—someone else's drone camera."

Shana's expression transformed itself from anger to confusion to fear in less than a second. "What do you mean, someone else's?"

"I can't let you and Becky become useful to people who might want to manipulate me."

"Nick, I don't understand."

He brushed his hand across her cheek. "For now, only one person besides you, Brad, and me knows the truth. That person won't hurt me or you guys. There are other people who, if they knew, wouldn't hesitate to use you or hurt you. You just have to believe me, Shana. You have to accept it."

"But you're just a street cop."

"And Tony was just a retired guy who wore a uniform and drove around in a patrol car, drinking free coffee." Nick pointed toward the doors. "Now he and his wife are in caskets in that room."

She grabbed Nick's wrists and placed his arms around her, threading herself between them. He could not help but hold her tight to him as she rested her head on his shoulder. "You're scaring me, Nick."

"I'm trying to." The feel of her, the warmth of her touch, the citrus-and-honey scent of her perfume, made it nearly impossible to concentrate.

"What about you?"

"I'll be fine. I'll always be fine."

She kissed him hard on the mouth. He tried and failed not to kiss her back. The doors opened and Annalise Puleo came out. Her face reddened as she stopped in her tracks. She made a throat-clearing sound.

"Nick—Detective Ryan—the priest is starting. I thought you'd wanna know."

Nick held Shana by the shoulders and pushed her away. "Thanks, Detective Puleo. I'll be in, in a minute."

Puleo went back inside.

"Who was that?" Shana asked. It sounded like an accusation. "And don't tell me just another detective."

"One of the detectives who caught the case."

"And someone you're fucking, right? Her expression gave her away."

Nick ignored that. "Go in and pay your respects, but you can't just pop up like this around me, Shana."

She fixed her lipstick, handing Nick a tissue. "Will you come in with me?"

"No. I'm serious." He wiped the lipstick off his mouth. Holding the door open for her, Nick whispered, "Forget about jealousy and think about why you're here."

She gave him a hard stare as she entered. Coming in behind her, he headed to the opposite corner of the room.

When the priest was done, Nick watched Shana with his family. The Ryans couldn't manage to embrace each other, but Shana—they loved her. Sean, his father, and Marie all hugged her tight, kissed her. Their faces lit up at the sight of her. No one understood that better than Nick.

"God, Nick, she is something." It was Annalise. "Beautiful and rich."

"And married."

"Someone should remind her."

"You?"

"Not me, Nick.

"It's complicated, AP."

She snorted. "Love usually is."

"Even when we were sixteen it wasn't simple with Shana and me."

"Two different worlds."

"Exactly. You're pretty perceptive."

"Firsthand experience, Nick. Imagine the look on his parents' faces when Ronnie Epstein brought a gang girl to Riverdale to meet his folks." She laughed. "*Horrified* don't quite describe it."

"The invitation to go riding still stand?"

"You think one kiss from a rich, gorgeous woman gonna change that? See you Sunday. I better go compare notes with Rosen or he'll bust my balls."

"Disappointed the killer didn't show?"

"Not like we expected him to, but we had to come just in case." Puleo walked away.

Nick left before Shana could ask the same question he would never be able to answer.

THIRTY-TWO

Nick waited for the headlight covers to flip back. He depressed the clutch, putting the Hurst T-handle shifter in first. Feathering the clutch and gas, he rolled into the thinned-out traffic on Coney Island Avenue. As much as he loved the old Pontiac, Joe's Malibu was a lot more powerful and handled like a modern machine. For all its beautifully restored qualities, the GTO, like all muscle cars of its era, was best at straight-line speed. Once you did any driving that involved a turn of the wheel, you didn't so much drive the GTO as contain it.

He was thinking about cars to not think about Shana. Cars were less complicated than love. The only thing as complicated was war, the reason the two were so often paired. Both heightened your emotions and drove you to take stupid chances. Both could damage you in ways that would haunt you to the grave. He was glad Lenny's hovel was less than five minutes away.

He moved into the left-turn lane at Avenue L. Turning, he did something that even he didn't understand as he did it: he checked his side-view mirror. Maybe it was the discordant roar of an engine, or the flicker of a streetlight shadow that didn't belong. Whatever caught his eye or ear, it was his willingness to pay attention to the little things that had kept him alive when other men were added to the body count.

In the mirror, he saw the grill of a lifted Silverado. The pickup was turning behind him, trying to cut the turn by taking a straighter line. Nick shifted quickly from first to second into third. He shot ahead just before the right edge of the Silverado's bumper could plow into the rear driver's-side wheel well of the GTO. The pickup didn't completely miss him. *Bang!* The back end of the GTO slid hard right from the force of the contact. Nick steered hard and downshifted to regain control, but there wasn't enough room or time. The right side of the GTO thumped into a parked car, scraping the metal as it went. The contact with the parked car helped cancel out the GTO's spin. The Silverado came alongside, urging the GTO into another line of parked cars, the pickup's high bumper caving in the GTO's curved sheet metal as it went. Nick put the gas pedal to the floor, rocketing away from the Silverado. After a brief bit of fishtailing, he had the car back under his control. In his rearview he saw the Silverado cutting across traffic, reversing direction.

Ahead of him, a blue Lexus pulled out directly in his path. Nick swerved around it and blew through the red light at East Tenth Street. Going way too fast, he turned left down East Ninth, the ass end of the GTO once again sliding in the opposite direction. East Ninth was a one-way street. With cars parked along both curbs, it would be impossible for anyone pursuing him to do anything but stay behind him. The blue Lexus appeared in his rearview mirror as it came around the corner at speed. When it passed beneath a streetlamp, Nick saw that the Lexus's driver had company. He could make out the silhouette of a man in the front passenger seat. The Lexus quickly made up the ground between them, getting to within fifty feet of Nick's rear bumper.

With the traffic light going yellow and before the Lexus could close the gap any more, Nick yanked the steering wheel left, turning onto Avenue M. Halfway through the turn, the GTO's rear windshield shattered, a stream of bullets whizzing past the back of Nick's head. Seemingly in slow motion, the front passenger window cracked, spiderwebbed in five spots, and crumbled into hundreds of little glass chunks. The wind hurled some of the shards Nick's way.

He didn't go for his gun to fire back. The odds of hitting anything or anyone other than an innocent bystander were next to zero. Only careless idiots tried to drive and shoot behind them at the same time. Besides, divided attention was what got you dead. Focusing on what mattered kept you alive. Nick had learned that lesson a long time ago. You had to pay attention to the magician's off hand, not the one he was trying to distract you with.

As he came through the turn onto Avenue M, his head snapping back around, Nick saw the Silverado turning off Coney Island Avenue, coming toward him. They were trying to pen him in. If he had kept his focus on the Lexus, he would have been trapped.

The Silverado driver would probably anticipate him making yet another left, down East Tenth toward Avenue L. But Nick was tired of playing defense, so he raced through the red light. He barreled straight at the Silverado.

"You wanna play chicken, motherfucker?" Nick screamed, his adrenaline pumping. "Here's your chance."

At the last second, the Silverado swerved right, crashing into the front quarter panel of a parked Mercedes. Nick tugged the steering wheel, barely missing the rear end of the pickup. It was all he could do to keep the GTO from spinning out. By the time he had corrected the fishtail, he was at the corner of Coney Island Avenue and Avenue M. Molloy's Funeral Home was across the street, directly ahead.

Sensing the Lexus closing in behind him, he winced in anticipation, running the red light. He turned right onto Coney Island Avenue doing forty plus, narrowly avoiding the flank of a B68 bus. Nick checked his rearview for the Lexus. There it was! He gradually let it gain on him. Also a good idea because he had felt a wobble in one of his front tires. When he felt the Lexus was close enough, Nick pulled into the right lane in front of a slower-moving car. As he did, he reached for the off-duty Glock. There were times the added control of a manual transmission was beneficial. This wasn't one of them. Even someone as resourceful as Nick

Ryan needed one hand to steer, one hand to shift, and one hand to use a gun. That left him one hand short. He dropped the Glock 26 in his lap.

The slower car behind Nick turned right onto Quentin Road. Nick moved his right hand off the shifter to the steering wheel and hit the window switch with his left hand. The noise from the wind through the shattered windows was already deafening. Now his hands were freezing up on him. In his side-view mirror, Nick spotted the man in the Lexus's passenger seat raising the unmistakable profile of an MP7. The blue Lexus sped forward. When it was nearly door-to-door with the GTO, Nick steadied the steering wheel with his knees. He held the Glock just below the windowsill until the last second. He didn't hesitate, raised the 26, squeezed the trigger, getting off three shots.

One bullet punctured the Lexus's door. One of the other two hit its mark, blood spurting from the neck of the guy in the passenger seat. He squeezed the MP7's trigger as he slumped into the driver. The bullets smashed the windshield and tore a ragged line of holes through its roof. The Lexus driver veered into oncoming traffic at Kings Highway, managing to evade a head-on collision. He grazed a lime-green cab as he turned onto Kings Highway. Nick followed, then slammed on his brakes to avoid skidding into a Denali turning off Kings Highway. He shifted into third gear, weaving through oncoming traffic to a chorus of blaring horns.

Nick was a block behind the Lexus, his right front tire wobble worsening. The car was hard enough to control when the front wheels were perfectly aligned. Now he also smelled burning motor oil. Worse, he smelled the telltale stench of antifreeze evaporating on hot metal. He had to get the Lexus soon or not at all.

Nick wasn't the type of man who talked to the dead, but he made a rare exception. "Sorry, Uncle Kenny, she's fucked anyway."

With that, he put the GTO in fourth, pressing the gas pedal down as far as it would go. On a summer Saturday afternoon, he'd be lucky to get to fifteen miles an hour on Kings Highway. On this late-fall evening, Nick stopped looking at the speedometer once he hit sixty. As he passed under the subway station, he was nearly on the Lexus. At

East Eighteenth, the Lexus turned right. Nick turned the steering wheel right to follow. The GTO had other plans.

The wobbly wheel collapsed, folding under the front suspension. Nick downshifted and stood on the brakes to no avail. He laid his arm on the horn as warning. Thirty-one hundred pounds of metal traveling at speed hitting a concrete curb was a recipe for ugly. The impact that Nick felt as the front end hit the curb and his chest hit the steering column was much like the shockwave from a roadside IED. The impact lifted the back end of the GTO up over the top. There was a second impact when the GTO hit the storefront window, finally coming to rest.

Nick lost track of time until he felt hands pulling at him, dragging him through the bits of glass and along the sidewalk. His chest felt stuck between the jaws of a vise. He moved his neck, his arms and legs, just to make sure the pain in them wasn't wishful thinking. He looked up at the stars, smiled, and closed his eyes. The last thing he remembered was hearing someone ask, "What's he smiling at?"

THIRTY-THREE

Nick's eyelids flickered as he emerged from the floaty netherworld between consciousness and sleep. His nose told him he was in a hospital. No mask covered his face. No tubes in his nose. There were no atomized hints of blood in the brew of chemical scents and human frailties. The room was dark, silent. That was good. He wasn't hooked up to any machines. A year ago, he'd twice woken up in hospitals. Once with a concussion from a bomb blast. Once after getting stabbed with six inches of sharp glass. This time, while that floaty sensation was dissipating, he couldn't rouse himself fully awake, not even with his eyes open.

He became aware of someone sitting by his bed, turned his head to look, and winced. "Joe?"

"No, Rumpelstiltskin. Who else?"

"This is getting to be a habit, you being here when I wake up in the hospital. Where am I?"

"Brookdale. You'll be here at least overnight." Joe stood and leaned over Nick. "You're the luckiest SOB I've ever encountered. I've seen your car. The hood scoops are the only things left intact. Remarkably, you're still in one piece."

Nick smiled. "Bet you're pleased. Now I have no choice but the Inspector Gadget car."

"Small mercies." Joe smiled in spite of himself. "I am anything but pleased. Your cowboy shit never pleases me. Would you like to explain to me what this evening's reenactment of the *French Connection* chase scene was about?"

Nick stalled for time. He couldn't be certain what it was about. He'd struck a nerve and pissed someone off. That much was clear. Problem was, he couldn't be sure whose nerve it was or what he'd done, exactly.

"The vehicles—the Lexus and the Silverado."

Joe cocked his head. "What about them?"

"That's what I'm asking. What about them?"

"The Silverado was abandoned on Avenue M, its front tires atop the hood of a Mercedes-Benz. The Lexus . . ." Joe shrugged. "A witness gave us the plate number of the Lexus. Stolen, like the Silverado. But you would have expected that."

"You find it?"

"Out in the swampland by the JFK cargo area. Someone used it to make a bonfire."

Nick sat up and swung his legs over the side of the bed, pain lighting him up like a red neon sign. He doubled over, catching his breath. "Holy shit. That hurts like a bastard!"

Joe laughed. "I said nothing was broken. I didn't say you weren't injured. Your car may be gone, but for the next few weeks you will be able to remember it fondly by the black-and-blue imprint of its steering wheel on your chest."

"Fucking lap belt." Nick gathered himself, sitting up slowly. "Was there a body in the Lexus?"

"In the front passenger seat, burned beyond recognition. No wallet." Joe wasn't laughing now. "Are you telling me you shot someone else?"

"Pretty sure I hit him in the carotid artery."

"Jesus Christ, Nick! You haven't even been cleared of the last shooting."

"Because you think I need incentive to do my job."

"Apparently, you don't need incentive to kill."

"Pardon me," Nick said, turning on the light. "Next time I'll let them kill me instead."

"No need for dramatics."

"I didn't supply the drama. All I did was leave Tony and Rosa's wake and go to my car. The men trying to drive me off the road. Your argument is with them."

"Why drive you off the road if they were going to shoot you anyway?"

Nick laughed, immediately regretting it. "Before they autopsy the guy, ask him."

"This is serious, Nick."

"No shit. To answer your question, I don't think they were trying to kill me, not to begin with. Once I went on offense, they felt they had no choice."

"Then what was their purpose?"

"Intimidation."

"Apparently, they don't know you very well, do they?"

"I guess not. When are they going to autopsy the body?"

"Why?"

"Morbid curiosity." Nick shook his head, grimacing in pain. "Because I'd like to have some idea who I'm dealing with and why they thought they needed to scare me off."

"So you have no idea?"

"None."

Nick lied. He lied because he wanted to be sure before he planned his next steps. He lied because his theory about who the men in the Lexus and the Silverado were didn't compute, not so far as he could figure. The men on South Fourth Street who had confronted Vicky Lansdale and him had been armed with MP7s, just like the man in the front seat of the Lexus. Nick didn't understand why they would still be bothering with him. He'd walked away from that, leaving the Lansdales and Carver's retired Secret Service crew to sort it out.

"You're sure?" Joe was skeptical. "It isn't like you to be caught flat-footed and unaware."

"If I were flat-footed, I'd be the one getting autopsied instead of Mr. Crispy in the Lexus."

"Point taken. Could this have anything to do with Markovic?" Joe couldn't hide his smile.

"I don't see how." That was another lie. The odds of Markovic having come from Serbia, the Serbs threatening Jonathan Lansdale's family, and Franjo Petrovic's Croatian roots all being coincidental were becoming less and less likely. Beyond the obvious, he still couldn't see the connection. If there was one, he would find it. Nick slowly swung his legs back into bed, rested his head against the pillow. "Joe, I'd love to keep talking, but . . ."

"Okay." Joe checked his watch. "You're right. It's late. I'll make sure you're cleared of the incident in Staten Island. This other thing . . ."

"I wouldn't sweat it. They swept the car before torching it. If my bullet was still in him, they dug it out."

Joe grimaced, picturing the bullet being dug out of the dead man's neck with a pocketknife. "How can you know any of that if you don't know who it was?"

"Experience. It may not have gone the way they planned it, but the message was delivered. I've been put on notice. Someone wants me to stay out of their business. That's all."

"And . . ."

"Given that I feel like I tripped in front of a steamroller and didn't get out of the way, lying low shouldn't be an issue. Whoever is trying to warn me off will think they succeeded. One more thing."

"Yes."

"Email me the autopsy report."

"Done. Take a few days, but no more. I—we—need results on Markovic. Good night."

"Night."

He rolled gently over onto his side, shut his eyes, and listened to the retreating sound of Joe's shoes. When he was sure Joe was gone and not coming back, he fished his cell out of the nightstand drawer.

THIRTY-FOUR

He hadn't woken up in Annalise Puleo's bed in four years. Now it was two days in a row. Back then, when her marriage was in midexplosion and Nick was desperately erasing Shana, morning smelled of sex, vodka sweat, and cigarettes. Not yesterday. Not today. Today it was coffee. Only coffee. Annalise had spent two nights on her futon. Good thing too. The pulsing pain was worse yesterday than the night of the accident. The ride on the back of her Ducati after she sneaked him out of the hospital hadn't exactly been therapeutic. The ice bath helped.

"Here," she said, placing a mug of coffee next to two Aleve tablets on the nightstand.

"Thanks." Nick girded himself, propping himself up against the pillows. The pain was duller, though his bare arms and thighs were an ugly shade of purple. He swallowed the tablets with a sip of coffee. "What time is it?"

"Seven." Annalise had changed, but she still dressed as she always had: cutoff Yankees T-shirt, gray sweats, bare feet. "I gotta shower and get downstairs. Rosen's picking me up in forty-five. I don't want him to come up. So far I haven't had to lie to my partner, 'cause he ain't asked nothin' about you. I don't wanna have to explain you being here." She sat on the edge of the bed. "The apartment and Ducati keys are on the kitchen counter, but are you sure you're up for this?"

"No choice."

"I haven't asked you to explain nothin' to me, Nick."

"Don't start now, okay, AP?" He reached out and brushed wisps of her black hair over her left ear.

She stiffened, stood up, brushing her hair back. "Whatever you say."

"I'll have your Duck back to you as soon as I can."

"I trust you, Nick." She turned.

"AP."

"What?" She looked back over her shoulder at him.

"Why'd you undo your hair like that?"

"This is hard for me, having you here like this. Jus' 'cause a how things shook out between us—forget it. I gotta get ready."

Nick took another gulp of coffee, watching her head for the bathroom.

Annalise was in the shower when Nick stepped in after her. She stiffened when he put his hand on her shoulder.

He said, "You want me to, I'll leave. I'm sorry if—"

She turned to face him, put a soapy finger across his lips. "It's okay. It's hard because I never stopped . . . you know."

"I know." He bent over, kissing her softly on the lips.

"You taste like coffee and soap."

He pulled back, wincing in pain.

"Did I say stop? I like coffee and soap when it's on your lips." She placed her hand on the back of his neck and gently urged his head toward hers. Pushing back, she said, "Well, at least one part of you ain't bruised."

They both laughed.

"Let's take it slow, AP."

"Is this about her?"

"Shana? No, this is about us."

She kissed him hard. "Now, get outta here or Rosen'll be at the door."

"That killed the mood."

"Don't disrespect my partner."

"No disrespect. He's just not who I want to think about when I'm standing in a shower with you."

———

Not even his wrecked face could mask Lenny Feld's shock at the sight of Nick Ryan standing at the synagogue's basement door.

Nick smiled. "Surprised to see me?"

"More surprised you're alive at all. You look like shit."

"Coming from you . . ."

Lenny laughed, placing his good hand on Nick's shoulder. "I guess I put that one on the tee for you, huh? Come in. Come in."

Nick had rarely seen this side of Lenny. He had only known Lenny PF—post fire. The tragic Lenny, scarred and grieving his wife and daughter. It was a pleasant change from the man who was always this close to suicide. But as soon as Nick stepped inside and the door slammed shut behind him, Lenny's good spirits turned in the opposite direction. Lenny didn't get ten feet before he began sobbing uncontrollably.

"Lenny, what is it?" Nick put his left arm around his friend's shoulder and held him tight.

"What is it? 'What is it?' he asks me!" Lenny wrenched himself out of Nick's grip. "You want to know? It's you, Nick Ryan. When you didn't show two nights ago, I knew something was wrong. The first reports of your accident didn't say whether you were alive or dead. Do you have any idea what would become of me without you? Do you ever think about that? Any hope I have in this world is tied to you." Lenny shoved his stubbed fingers into Nick's chest.

Nick bent over in pain. "For chrissakes!"

"I'm sorry."

"It's okay, Lenny. I get it, but you know better than anyone that what I do comes with risks."

"The undercover work, I understand. Even this other thing you do I'm not supposed to be aware of—I know it has inherent risks. But a car accident . . . It dawned on me as it never has before that I am a castaway on a tiny island and the only person who is there with me sometimes is you."

"If it makes you feel any better, pal, it wasn't an accident. Someone was trying to kill me."

"You have a peculiar method of reassuring people, Nick. You know that? After you retire, don't go into social work."

"I promise not to."

"Shut up and come in. Coffee?"

"No, thanks," Nick said, stepping into Lenny's odd little room. He sat, as always, in the metal folding chair. "I've had real coffee this morning and I don't want to ruin the memory." The memory was of the taste of coffee on AP's lips and of her body next to his.

"Should I ask you why you're smiling?" Lenny fussed with the kettle and instant coffee. "I'm having some. By the way, that rental car reservation number from Markovic . . ."

"What about it?"

"It was for September 11, 2001, at the LaGuardia office of Nifty Rent-a-Car on Ditmars."

"Nine-Eleven!"

"Can't get anything past you. Yes, Nick."

"His wife said he was on the phone all day trying to get a way to get to work. He was trying to get to Queens, but not for work. He was flaking out. He was running."

"Who from and why?"

"When I find out, I'll let you know." Nick placed his cell phone and a burner phone on the workbench. Lenny stopped fussing. Curiosity was Lenny's sole vice.

"Okay, Nick, you've got my attention."

"I'm going to disappear for a while. I need you to make my phone untraceable. For now, though, I know you've set this room up so that no one can locate it here. Let my calls go to voicemail. Read my emails. Then either relay them to me with the burner phone or call."

"I've always wanted to be a receptionist."

"Isn't one of your degrees from MIT in Receptionist Studies?"

"Fine." Lenny went back to making his coffee. "What else do I have to do with my time? By the way, who was trying to kill you? I mean, if you don't mind me asking."

"Long story."

"With you, it always is. I can tell you aren't ready to discuss it." He sipped his instant coffee, half-smiling. "You know that image you sent me the other day—the eagle, shield, and sword? Fascinating."

"How so?"

"It's the symbol for the Serb Volunteer Guard. Quite a colorful history, that bunch. Colorful as in blood red. It was a paramilitary group that evolved, I kid you not, from a Belgrade soccer team. They were also known as Arkan's Tigers. Arkan, Željko Ražnatović, was their leader. No military genius, he was more a mobster and thug."

Nick sat forward in his seat. "You mentioned blood."

"Arkan's Tigers and a few related splinter paramilitary groups were involved in ethnic cleansing in Croatia and in places like Banja Luka in Bosnia. For them it was a convenient opportunity to murder the local populations in the name of nationalism and patriotism while looting towns and villages. There were centuries of pent-up hatred. If you think New York is a pressure cooker of competing ethnic, racial, and religious grievances, the Balkans make us look like a Little League team.

"The Serbs still commemorate a battle they lost to the Ottoman Empire in 1389. In World War Two, the Croats sided with the Germans. Their Ustaše regime committed atrocities so brutal against the Serb population that it even gave the Nazis pause. The Serbs are Eastern Orthodox. The Croats are Roman Catholic, and the Bosnians are Sunni Muslims. The reality is rather more complex than this. There are plenty of scars, real and imagined, to go around. Suffice it to say, people in the Balkans have long memories and know how to hold a grudge. You take all that and force them to live together after the war and it's a recipe for future disaster. When Yugoslavia began to disintegrate, it didn't take much to rekindle the old hatreds that had been tamped down by the government."

"Trust me, the Afghans are pretty good at grudge holding too. But what happened to Arkan?"

"Arkan and his followers were charged with war crimes."

"In your research, did you come across the name Zmaj?"

"The Dragon." Lenny was impressed. "How do you know about him?"

"The key ring with the SVG symbol was on Vlado Markovic when he was murdered. Apparently, he served under Zmaj. He would only talk about it when he was drunk. Even then, not in great detail. That's what the wife says."

"Understandable. Zmaj was a lesser monster. He wasn't quite a match for Arkan in terms of brutality, but not for lack of trying. In one way, though, he excelled Arkan."

"How so?"

"Arkan was assassinated in a Belgrade hotel lobby over twenty years ago. Zmaj . . ." Lenny shrugged. "He disappeared, escaping assassination and trial. When, exactly, or how he managed it is unclear. There's speculation he came here with the help of some people in our military whom he bought off, or people in the intelligence community. Rumor is, he was willing to testify against his old mates in return for a new life. No one really knows and no one is talking. Does any of this help?"

It was Nick's turn to shrug. "Hard to know, but it opens a different door. Since the day after Nine-Eleven, everybody has assumed a singular scenario about the murder of Vlado Markovic. That he was the victim of bad luck, a man in the wrong place at the wrong time when he encountered an angry man or angry men mistaking him for something he was not. Until a few days ago, it was what I believed. It may still be the truth." As the word *truth* came out of his mouth, Nick's cell dinged on Lenny's workbench. "Email."

"Here." Lenny handed the phone back to Nick.

"The autopsy report."

"Autopsy report?"

"Remember I told you it wasn't an accident? That someone was trying to kill me? Well . . ."

"Another one! For goodness' sakes, Nick. Do you notch your gun grip?"

"That's not funny, Lenny."

Nick forwarded the email from his phone to Lenny's email. He asked Lenny to open the attachment. By the time Nick realized his mistake, it was already too late.

"Lenny, stop! Don't look."

Lenny stood frozen before one of his huge monitors. There on the screen, a photo array of the burnt, charred body of the man Nick had killed. He was on the ME's stainless-steel table. Nick got to Lenny just in time to catch him as he fainted. He hoisted Lenny over his shoulder and laid him down on his cot. In pain, Nick forced himself to go back to the computer. Nothing he saw in the autopsy report was of much use until he saw a notation about the victim's left Achilles tendon having been severed. It confirmed his suspicion that the dead man was one of the attackers from South Fourth Street. Nick deleted the file from Lenny's inbox.

"Is that what my wife and girl looked like after the fire?" Lenny asked as he came to, tears rolling over the sides of his cheeks. "I didn't identify their bodies because I was in the hospital."

"They used dental records and DNA."

"I wasn't even at their funerals. It haunts me, Nick, not saying goodbye."

"I was there."

Eyes wide, Lenny sat up as if he were spring-loaded. "You were at the cemetery?"

"I was."

"You never told me."

"What would I have said, Lenny? I just felt I should go. I got you out, but I couldn't save them."

Lenny patted Nick's cheek. "Thank you, Nick. You really are a mensch."

"I gotta go." Nick stood. "Remember about the calls and the—"

"I remember. Go."

Nick emerged from the dark, chilly basement into brilliant sunlight. Bright as it was, the sun felt a little bit farther away than it had less than an hour ago.

THIRTY-FIVE

Ninety minutes north of New York City, Old Rotterdam was a forgettable dot on a map in the Catskill Mountains. Once the home of second-rate hotels, it had become more Rust Belt than Borscht Belt. In the past several years, it had been making a comeback as a landing spot for retirees who wanted land and low property taxes. Retirees who didn't want to swelter under the Florida sun or be too far away from their downstate grandkids. Until a few weeks ago, it was also the home of a retired NYPD cop named Johnny Sullivan.

Nick parked Annalise's Ducati outside the town hall. The building was an ugly concrete pillbox as welcoming as a sarcophagus. The air outside was fresh, its pine scent coming from the surrounding trees, not from a bottle of detergent. Helmet off, Nick shook out his hair. He took in the mountain scenery. The ride up limited his appreciation of nature. He found the bathroom, swallowed more Aleve than any human should, and sat, resting his neck against the cold tile wall until the pain subsided. Fifteen minutes later, he filled a sink with cold water and plunged his head into it as far as it would go for as long as he could stand it. Looking into the mirror, finger-combing his hair, Nick realized he was coming up on the first week in a year that he wouldn't see Becky.

"You all right there?" A man's voice broke Nick's trance.

Nick turned, saw that the man was dressed in a khaki uniform. There was a bronze, star-shaped badge on the left side of the man's chest. SHER-IFF was written in block letters across the middle of the five-pointed star. *Barson* was written on his nameplate. The sheriff was as distinctive as the khaki of his uniform: medium height, medium build, brown eyes, brown hair, neither handsome nor ugly. The most outstanding thing about him was that he smelled of cherry pipe tobacco.

"I've been better, Sheriff Barson." Nick turned, showed the sheriff his detective shield. "I'm here to see you."

"Well, I'm here to do something else."

"I figured."

"My office is down the hall to the right. I'll be there presently."

Nick found the office easily enough. The deputy at the desk told him to sit at a bench across from his desk. He did and was glad for a seat that didn't vibrate or bounce or rumble. Nick would probably talk to the state police at some point. They would have been the agency to investigate Sullivan's death. But Nick trusted that the locals would know the dirt, if there was any, on Sullivan.

"Detective." Sheriff Barson offered his still-damp hand.

Nick shook it as he stood. "Nick Ryan."

Barson nodded to his right. "C'mon in."

The sheriff's office looked pretty much the way Nick imagined a small-town sheriff's office would look: flags, certificates, photographs—lots of photographs—mounted fish, a gun cabinet. Like his uniform, Barson's office smelled of cherry pipe tobacco.

"Pipe smoker?" Nick said.

The sheriff laughed. "Guess I don't hide it too well. Who's going to arrest me for smoking in my own office?"

"Not me."

"You smoke a pipe, Detective Ryan?"

"Not a smoker. My granddad smoked one. Made me try it once."

"No go?"

"One of those things that smells great and tastes, you know."

"Takes some getting used to." The pleasantries and small talk out of the way, the sheriff got to it. "What can we do for the NYPD, Detective?"

"Johnny Sullivan." Nick dropped the name like a grenade, waiting to see if it would explode.

Barson made a face, not a happy one. "A shame."

"Really? I hear he was kind of a dick."

"You didn't know him?"

"Nope."

"You working a case?"

"Not officially."

Barson stood up, came around, and sat on the edge of his desk to loom over Nick. It was an old technique used to intimidate. "You want to explain yourself to me? Seems I'm missing something."

Nick wasn't intimidated. "Yesterday they buried Sullivan's old patrol partner, Tony Angelo, and his wife."

"And . . ."

"They were murdered. Professional job." Nick leaned forward as if to take Barson into his confidence. He spoke in a hushed voice. "Interesting coincidence, the timing of Sullivan's slipping off a rock and the Angelo homicides. Me and the other detectives I know, we don't care much for coincidences."

Barson rubbed his clean-shaven cheek. "I'm not much of a fan either. You think Sullivan was murdered?"

"It's not important what I think. I'm interested in what you think."

"I didn't like it from the get-go, not for a second."

"Why?"

"Johnny Sullivan was a miserable prick, you want to know my opinion. Most folks around here barely tolerated him. A pain in the ass from the day he moved to Old Rotterdam. He was in my office or some other office in this building every other week. One week, it was neighbor's dog kept shitting on his property. Another neighbor's fence was six inches over his property line. Too many helicopters flew over his house on the way down to the city."

"So, he was a grumpy asshole, but—"

Barson waved and started for the door. "C'mon with me."

———

Johnny Sullivan's house was a cedar-shingled ranch with a detached garage on a five-acre plot. The sheriff's car spat gravel coming up the driveway. On the short trip from the town hall, Barson told Nick that the state police hadn't worked very hard at finding an alternate explanation for Sullivan's death.

"They made up their minds before they even got to the scene. Heart Rock is a popular place for climbers and lovers to take selfies because Sheldrake Falls is in the background. Beautiful spot. Two people before Sullivan died up there taking selfies. But Sullivan! You'll see."

Nick saw. Barson walked him around the house. It was neat as a marine's footlocker and just as warm and fuzzy.

The sheriff asked, "You notice anything?"

"Not a single photo on the wall."

"Bingo. There's only one photo album in the house and it's still in its cellophane wrapper. When we checked his phone, there were photos of suit filings, of complaints he filed with the town, of his old house down in the city, and a few of his grandkids. Not one selfie. Not one of his ex-wife or his own kids. Not one of him in uniform. Nothing."

"Maybe he was taking a photo for a dating site or something."

"Him! He was a bitter divorced guy who made no secret of his misogyny. We had to bring him in once for roughing up a local working girl. He paid her off and she refused to testify against him. Never got to court. He was a nasty bastard, but one thing I got to give him."

"What's that?"

"He had an eye for beautiful cars."

"Sorry."

"This way, Ryan."

Nick followed the sheriff to the garage. Barson lifted the door with some effort. Nick's nose was assaulted by an odd combination of mustiness, gasoline, and solvents. The metal shelves lining the walls were full of car waxes, car-wash soaps, cases of motor oil, antifreeze. There, beneath a dust-covered black vinyl tarp, was a car. The tarp couldn't hide the sleek shape beneath it.

Barson said, "Take a guess."

"A Corvette, every old man's dream. I know lots of cops who buy one when they retire."

"Not even close, Detective Ryan." Barson reached under the front end of the tarp and pulled it back. "Ta-da!"

"Holy shit!"

"That's right, Ryan. Holy shit indeed. A 2002 Ferrari Five-Fifty Maranello."

The sleek, slope-backed car looked fresh off the showroom floor. Its distinctive Ferrari red glistened in the ambient light. On the back edge of the front quarter panel, the iconic Ferrari badge—a prancing black horse against a yellow background. The Maranello's five-spoked silver wheels gleamed.

"There's barely any mileage on it. Look at the window sticker. Registration ran out in oh-three. Hadn't been driven in years, but it's meticulously maintained. Amazing, huh? Guy drove around in a Chrysler PT shitbox and had this in his garage."

"Maybe he was storing it for someone else."

"Nope. It was his. Clean title and everything."

"On a uniformed cop's salary and pension?"

Barson shrugged. "What can I tell you? Everybody's got their secrets."

Nick didn't like it, but it was clear the sheriff wouldn't be able to answer his questions.

As they reentered the house, Nick asked, "Did you check his computer?"

"You see a computer anywhere? There isn't one. Far as we can tell, he never owned one. No, Detective Ryan, I think someone brought him to Heart Rock or lured him there and then broke his neck and threw him over or just pushed him over the edge. Problem isn't what I think. It's what I can prove, and the state investigators aren't interested in proving it."

"Was his PT Cruiser found at Heart Rock?"

"It was."

"What did the tox screen show?"

"We haven't gotten it back yet. Well, the troopers haven't shared the results if they've gotten it back. But he smelled of alcohol. Nothing unusual in that." Barson pointed to a well-stocked dry bar at one corner of the den. "He could've run a nice little tavern, except he would've been his own best customer. That day, he paid for drinking at Molly's. Local bar about three blocks down Main Street from the town hall. You want to see where he died?"

Nick shook his head. "Maybe another time. Is there any CCTV from that day?"

"Some. Nothing particularly interesting."

"Can I see it? I'll buy us lunch on the way back."

"Deal."

————

Nick walked into Molly's Bar feeling half-dead. After lunch, Barson had stood over his shoulder as he watched the town's limited CCTV footage from the day Johnny Sullivan died. He hadn't found what he was looking for because he wasn't sure what he was looking for. It didn't mean there was nothing to see. It just meant there was nothing obvious.

"Sheriff, you think you could send this footage to me?"

"Sure. I'll do it right now. We'll call it cooperation between departments, and payback for a fine lunch."

Ten minutes had passed since he'd said so long to Barson.

Molly's was a run-down pub on the first floor of what was once a two-story house. There was a Piels sign in the window. That was the newest thing in the place and that was forty years old. The woman behind the bar was older than that by half and looked older still. Like Barson, she smelled of tobacco. The whole empty place smelled of cigarettes, old and new.

"You Molly?" Nick asked, sitting down at the bar.

"She was my mom. I'm Maxie. What'll you have?"

"Piels."

"Comedian, huh?"

"Detective." He showed her his shield. "I'll have a Maker's Mark. Were you working the day Johnny Sullivan died?"

She laughed and coughed at the same time the way only two-pack-a-day smokers could. "That douche? Yeah. He was pretty tanked up when he staggered out."

"Was he drinking with anyone else?"

Maxie put his bourbon on the chipped Formica bar top. "Just me, and I had no choice. I'm trapped back here."

"Was he talkative? Did he say anything about going out to Heart Rock?" Nick raised the glass to Maxie and sipped.

Maxie twisted up her mouth, put her elbow down on the bar. "I answered these questions twice already. Why's a city cop interested?"

"Sullivan was my dad's partner for a while," Nick lied.

"Your dad has my sympathies, Detective . . ."

"Nick Ryan."

"Sorry, Nick, but there's nothing to tell. He was in here a lot. Got drunk a lot. Was nasty all the time. He was nothing if not consistent."

"You have any security cameras?"

"Not out front, but got one on the parking lot in the back. Insurance company made us install it. Our regulars know not to fuck around in here, but we get lots of brawls out back, lots of smashed car windows and stuff."

"Is it digital, or old-style tape?"

"This place and me may be old, but the security system is digital."

Nick checked his watch. He figured he had just enough time to get to his next stop before sundown. "You got a pen?"

"You want my number?" She winked, putting a chewed golf pencil on the bar. "Best I can do."

He wrote his personal email address down on the back of his NYPD card. He put two twenties underneath it and slid it across the bar to her. "Do me a favor. Send the footage from the day Johnny died to that email address." He put another twenty down. "Do it as soon as I leave, okay?"

"Will do. Come again and I'll introduce you to my daughter. She's cute and about your age." Maxie made a sweeping gesture with both arms. "Best part. Someday, all this will be hers."

Maxie was still doing that laugh-cough thing as he left.

Outside, Nick dry-swallowed some more Aleve, started up the Ducati. In the bike's sleek side-view mirror, he noticed the fumes coming from the tailpipe of a black car idling in a corner of the parking lot behind Molly's. Sun glare off the car's windshield prevented him from seeing the driver. As he pulled out of the lot, Nick kept an eye on the mirror. The Ducati could outrun anything on four wheels, but it couldn't outrun bullets.

THIRTY-SIX

There it was. Nick caught sight of the black Ford Taurus in his mirror as the thruway toll scanner strobed above him. The Ford was made conspicuous by its popularity with law enforcement. Although Nick's shield would give him leeway to speed, he let the Taurus keep up. He would stretch out the distance between them and then let it shrink. The driver let Nick get ahead, almost out of sight.

Funny, Nick thought. There were so many ways to read the world if you knew the right alphabets. If the guy following him had planted a transponder on Annalise's Ducati, there would be no need for the car to expose itself. *No transponder.* If the Taurus was willing to let Nick get so far ahead that one burst of speed would lose it, then it was a multicar follow. There was probably a car or cars somewhere ahead and behind the Ford, waiting to take over. Nick would know the deal soon enough. The first exit off the thruway was coming up. If it was a multicar follow, the Taurus wouldn't turn off and a trail car would pick up the Ducati. Regardless of the method, there were two big questions to be answered: How did these people, whoever they were, know where he was to begin with? Why was he being followed?

The burner phone in his pocket buzzed. If Lenny was calling, it had to be important. *Change of plans.* Nick got low on the bike, taking the exit at ninety. He stopped checking the speedometer when its digital readout hit 120. Off the thruway, he turned onto a two-lane county road abutting a farm field. Feeling he had put enough distance between himself and his tail, he purposely stalled the engine and let the Ducati roll to a stop. That way his brake light wouldn't give him away. He carefully rolled the bike into a drainage ditch between the field and the road. He laid the bike down so that he could use the mirrors to check out oncoming traffic.

A car appeared in the distance, moving very slowly down the road in his direction. As it came toward his position, he could see that it was the black Taurus. Nick was confident the driver had lost his trail and was trying to pick it back up. That was what accounted for the Ford's moving at a snail's pace along the empty road. As it got closer, Nick could make out the movement of the driver's head. He was scanning, moving his gaze from side to side. As the Taurus got closer still, the outline of the driver's blurry silhouette sharpened into a face with definable features. When the Taurus got near enough for Nick to hear its tires rasping against the blacktop, those features went from definable to recognizable. *Willoughby.*

The driver was one of Carver's coterie of retired Secret Service men. As the Taurus rolled by, Nick lay perfectly still. Only the fading sounds of the tires, the dissipating heat, and the stink from the exhaust let him know it had passed. He kept motionless for several minutes, making sure he wasn't being baited into giving his position away.

Certain he was clear, Nick took off his black leather motorcycle gloves and fished the burner out of his pocket.

"You called, Lenny?"

"I did. You've gotten a few calls, some voicemails."

"From . . ."

"Your dad, your brother, and Martellus Sharp."

"About?"

"About why you weren't at the cemetery. Your dad and brother were pissed."

"Shocking."

"Sharp was concerned. Also curious, if I'm reading his voice correctly."

"Anyone else?"

There was an uncomfortable silence. Lenny cleared his throat. "Shana. That women can scream and sigh in a single sound. I'm not even going to try to interpret her message, but you should call her."

Nick kept his thoughts to himself. "And the last message?"

"Jonathan Lansdale. He said it was urgent that you get in touch. He left a number."

"He wasn't lying."

"What?"

"Never mind, Lenny. Is that it?"

"No, actually, none of that is why I called."

"I'm waiting."

"Better if I show you. Come here when you can."

"Might be late."

"Do I sleep? Besides, when has late ever stopped you?"

"Good point."

———

It had been a lot easier rolling the Ducati into the ditch. Pushing the motorcycle up the embankment, he felt the pain pulse through him. He mounted the bike, taking a few seconds to let the pain ease, and headed back toward the thruway. He was curious why Jonathan Lansdale had called him yet had his security men following him. As he revved the Ducati's engine, he looked down at the sleek red machine he was perched on. Nick knew how Annalise had managed to buy it. How, though, had a belligerent shithead like Johnny Sullivan purchased a two-hundred-thousand-dollar Italian sports car? Where had he gotten that kind of money? What had he done to earn it? For that matter, where had a mook like Jimmy Gabrelli gotten the money to buy a Porsche? With those questions swirling in his head and the sun setting off to his right, he got back on the thruway.

THIRTY-SEVEN

Donny Breen was a big man with a bigger rep. He was off the job before Nick came on, but everyone knew about Donny "No Bullshit" Breen and his legendary ability to "coax" confessions out of suspects. Nick had read Breen's and Harris's reports on Markovic. They caught the case and kept it until they put in their papers in '04. Harris was dead. One of those guys who lived for the job, then couldn't live without it. A year after his retirement, he drove to a Publix near his condo in Naples, Florida, and put one through his brain.

Nick could have called ahead. Didn't. He'd found he got better answers when people were unprepared, uncomfortable. Cops especially. They were too used to testifying, to giving one-word answers, to never giving more than what had been asked for. Often giving less and less than the truth. He wasn't even sure what he was looking for with Breen. He and Harris had been pretty thorough, as far as it went. Nick didn't love that the two detectives had so quickly settled on the "wrong place, wrong time" scenario, never wavering from it.

Breen lived in Rockland County, north of New York City. He had plenty of company. Rockland, like Nassau and Suffolk Counties on Long Island, was a popular landing spot for certain members of the NYPD.

White members. It was close enough to the city to take advantage of the museums, the music venues, the sports teams—the things cops would talk about in mixed company. The stuff they discussed over beers at backyard barbecues was that the city was far enough away to carve out a niche that let them pretend the world was white and Catholic.

It was just night when Nick rang the doorbell of Breen's two-story brick colonial on a woodsy cul-de-sac in West Nyack. He didn't have long to wait.

"I know you?" Breen said, giving him the death stare.

He held up his shield. "Nick Ryan."

Breen filled up the doorway. Besides being tall, he was wide through the hips and shoulders, thick around the neck and thighs. "I know that name."

"You know my father's name, not mine."

"Right!" Breen snapped his fingers. "The Argent Commission. Your old man's the rat motherfucka."

Before the retired detective could slam the door in his face, Nick stuck his motorcycle boot between the door and the jamb and pushed. He stepped inside. "Thanks for inviting me in."

Nick could see he had caught Breen off guard—just how he wanted him. He saw that Breen was thinking about how to react, whether it was worth throwing a punch, calling the local cops, or just stepping back and listening.

"All right, Ryan, what's this about?"

"Vlado Markovic."

There it was—the tell. Panic flashed across Breen's jowly face. Disappeared. Nick wondered whether anyone else would have seen it if they hadn't been looking for it. Didn't matter. *He* had seen it. Better still, Breen knew he had seen it.

"That shit again." Breen made a dismissive sound, squeezing a puff of air though his lips. "You kiddin' me or what?"

Nick didn't blame him for playing it down. He would have been disappointed if a guy with Breen's rep hadn't tried it. Eventually, he would get around to threats, violence, or both. Nick wasn't in the mood.

He was tired and the pain was making him impatient. That second of weakness from Breen, that brief moment of panic, was all the ammunition Nick needed.

"C'mon, Breen, you had to know it would come back to you someday. That someone would look hard at the case and find the holes."

"You must have me confused with an asshole, Ryan, 'cause I got no clue what bullshit you're peddling here."

"You really going to make me slow-walk you through this, Donny?" Nick used the name to piss him off. "A man like you, with your reputation, you're going to run and hide until I paint you into a corner? And then what, you going to take a swing at me?"

"Fuck you."

"Not me who's getting fucked here. You can make it hard or gentle. That's up to you. Or maybe you'll take your partner's way out, the easy way. We both know he couldn't take the wait, knowing the day would come when both of you were found out."

Before the last word was out of Nick's mouth, Breen's right fist was headed for his chin. Nick easily sidestepped it. Bowing under Breen's extended arm, he stepped forward so that his right hip was touching Breen's. He cupped his right arm around Breen's neck and swept his right leg hard across the back of Breen's calves. Breen went down with a terrific thump, his head bouncing off the floor. The air came out of him in an audible wheeze that smelled of beer and cigar smoke. It was Nick's day for smokers.

"Stay down. You're still big, Donny, but you're old, fat, and slow. If you try that shit again, I'll really hurt you. Now, I'm going to talk to you as you catch your breath. Nod your head if you get it." Breen nodded, gasping for air. "Good. I want you to hear this. I'm not here to jam you up. This isn't about you. It's about Markovic. He's who I'm interested in. The people who killed him—that's who I want."

Breen wheezed again as he tried to laugh. "Yeah, sure. You know how many times I said that same crap to mutts I had in the interview room? *I'm not interested in fuckin' with you. It's your partner we're interested in. Tell us everything, give his ass up, and we can do business.* So don't try it with me."

"I'm telling you the truth. Believing it or not is your responsibility." Nick put out his right arm. "Come on, get up."

Breen grabbed the arm and stood. Nick knew he wouldn't give up that easily. Almost before he was fully upright, Breen threw a looping haymaker with his left. Again Nick ducked. When he came up, the Glock 26 was in his hand, its muzzle buried in the loose flesh under Breen's chin.

"Enough!"

Breen put up his palms. "Okay."

"Wife?"

"Divorced."

"From a sweet guy like you? What a surprise. Kids?"

"Long gone."

Nick stepped back, keeping the Glock aimed at Breen. "We going to talk or you want to lose another round?"

"Let's go on the deck," Breen said, grabbing a lined hoodie off a coat peg.

Nick followed him through the house into the kitchen, reading Breen's body language as they went. What it told him was that Breen was relaxing. He wasn't slouching in defeat, nor was he girding for a fight. He was stalling, working out how to spin a story to put him in the best possible light. A guy like Breen would still think he could win. Nick knew the routine. Breen would try to turn him from enemy to ally.

They stepped outside, Nick closing the sliding door behind him. The deck was a well-lit teak wraparound with a full outdoor kitchen. There was a custom-made gas-fed metal fire pit in the center of the deck. The deck, covered in-ground pool, and back fence abutted a thickly wooded area. The temperature had dropped, so that they could see their breath.

"Put the piece away, for cryin' out loud, Ryan. I'll light the fire pit. It's freezin' out here."

Nick put the gun down by his thigh, not away. Breen fiddled with some knobs below the granite countertop, and flames shot up from the fire pit. Breen moved to the mini refrigerator. "Beer?"

"No, thanks."

"Sit." Breen lit a cigar. He carried a bottle of Blue Moon in his other hand. "My wife hated me smoking in the house. Even with her gone, I still only smoke out here. Want one? Cuban—it's good."

"No." Nick sat in a cushioned Adirondack chair, keeping the Glock in his hand on his lap. "Vlado Markovic. My guess, you have him to thank for all of this."

Breen sat opposite Nick, the fire pit between them. He made a sour face, blew out a mouthful of smoke and steam. "Markovic? Yeah, we hit the jackpot with that." He changed subjects. "Beautiful out here. I love it. All the houses on the cul-de-sac back up to a county park. The land can never be developed. Not like the city. Only animals out here are on four legs." He took a pull on his beer, put the bottle on the deck. "But there's no fuckin' escape, not really."

Nick had had enough. "Who bought you off?"

"Did you talk to Sullivan and Angelo yet? Was it one of those pricks who gave me up? Sullivan, probably. What an asshole."

"Angelo? *Tony* Angelo?"

Breen cocked his head. "Who you think I'm talking about? Him and Sullivan were the responding uniforms that night . . . sorta."

"That's not what your paperwork says."

Breen blew out another mouthful of smoke and chased it with a cynical laugh. "You never fudged paperwork, Ryan? Yeah, it was Sullivan and Angelo, but first on the scene depends on what you mean by *first on the scene*. Funny thing is, they made out like bandits and never had to answer nothing because it's two other uniforms who show up in the report."

"Miller and Rodriguez."

Breen applauded. "You can read and everything."

"I just came from Old Rotterdam. Johnny Sullivan retired up there."

"Catskills. Fucking Hasidic Jews up there. Now they're down here like a swarm of fucking ants."

"You really are a prick, aren't you?"

"I got no problem with regular Jews, but them freakin' Hasids . . ."

Nick got to the point. "Sullivan."

"What about him?"

"Dead. He conveniently fell off a rock and broke his neck."

"Boohoo."

"The sheriff doesn't buy that it was an accident. Me either."

"So what?"

"Oh, yeah, I almost forgot to mention, Tony Angelo's dead too. He and his wife were murdered last week. So let's see . . . Harris killed himself. Sullivan's dead, probably murdered. Angelo was murdered. I'm thinking the people behind the killings understand that Miller and Rodriguez either don't know anything or they're dead too. You good at math, Breen?"

The gas flames highlighted the fear on Breen's face. This time, the fear stuck. He shoved the cigar back in his mouth, nervously puffing out clouds of smoke. He rubbed a meaty hand across his face, failing to wipe the worry away.

"What happened that night? Who paid you guys off?"

Breen was close to breaking but wasn't there yet. "Why the fuck you even care?" He finished his beer, stood up. "I'm gettin' another. Sure you don't want one?"

"Stop stalling. Who paid you off?"

Breen took another Blue Moon out of the fridge but didn't sit. He paced back and forth in front of the fire pit. "You gotta remember what that night was like. People were scared, locked in their houses, the streets were pretty empty. Everyone in the city was focused on Ground Zero. Did we even call it Ground Zero then? Whatever. So I get a phone call from Sullivan for me and Harris to come over to Smith and Ninth Street station. We show up and it's me, my partner, Sullivan, Angelo, and the token booth clerk. Well . . . not quite."

"What does that mean, *not quite*?"

"The token clerk didn't like the looks of these three guys who came into the subway station together but went to different platforms. You gotta remember how jumpy everybody was that day. They were seeing terrorists in their soup. But the phone in her booth ain't workin', so she goes down to the street to flag down a unit."

"Sullivan and Angelo."

"Nothin' gets by you, huh?"

"I'm asking you one last time. Who—"

Breen shrugged. "Only did business with one of 'em. Didn't know his name then. Don't know it now. Some goombah. You know the type. Low-level mob guy thinks he's gonna be John Gotti someday. Thing is, he's got a duffel bag stuffed with enough money to choke a horse and with a promise of more to come. No bullshit. More came, a lot more. First of the month for a year."

"Describe him."

"Stocky, kinda squat, but good looking, I guess."

Nick didn't change his expression, but he remembered the photo he'd seen of Jimmy Gabrelli. "So, you guys covered up a homicide?"

"Any other day, Ryan, I think we all woulda told that guy to take his money and shove it up his ass, but that day . . . The rest was easy. I mean, the way the vic looked with the beard and everything and with that foreign name, he was tailor-made for a bullshit story. We went downstairs; Harris called nine-one-one anonymously. Dispatch sent Miller and Rodriguez. Me and Harris were next up on the board. We knew we'd get the call."

Nick opened his mouth but sensed something out beyond the back fence. Breen saw the look on his face and asked, "What is it?"

Nick stood up, raised his palm. "Quiet." He heard a twig snap, scanned the woods behind the house. "Shut off the pit and the lights and get in the house!"

"You ordering me around in my own—"

"Forget the pit." Nick raised his Glock, aiming it blindly out at the woods. "Just get in the house. Do it! Do it now!"

Breen turned. Too late. The flash in the woods and the explosion of Breen's skull felt as if they happened in the same instant. The muted report of the rifle seemed to lag behind. Breen's big lifeless body fell atop the fire pit. Nick hit the deck, the next shot whistling over him into the house's back wall. Brick splinters careened off the teak planks. Nick combat-crawled behind the fire pit, keeping it and Breen's body between himself and the woods. He waited for the flare-up from Breen's clothes catching fire. A flare-up would distort the shooter's night-vision scope just long enough for him to make it into the house.

There! The night brightened as Breen's hoodie burst into flames. Not as much of a flare-up as Nick had hoped for, but he had to move. Just as he got through the slider, the glass blew apart and a large hole appeared in a cabinet door across the kitchen. Covered in glass, he rolled to his left, putting the brick wall and sink cabinet between himself and the shooter. The kitchen window glass above him shattered into the sink. This time there was a new hole in the stainless-steel refrigerator door. Nick could wait out the shooter. Someone would take notice of the flames or would hear the shots. The shooter would know it too.

Nick raised his hand, still gloved, above the sink to bait the shooter. *No shot.* He waited a few seconds. Did it again. *No shot.* Nick was unconvinced. He found a short-handled broom in the cabinet beneath the sink. He removed his jacket and, using the broom, hoisted up the jacket. The force of the bullet wrenched the broom handle out of his grip. He hadn't wanted to do it. Now he had no choice. He reached for the Glock on the floor at his side. He took a few deep breaths. As he let out the third breath, he rolled back to the shattered sliding door, aimed at where he thought the shooter might be, and fired a few shots. The Glock, as accurate as it was at close range, was unlikely to hit anything but a maple tree at that distance. No shots were returned. He waited until he heard the sirens. When he did, he scooped up his shell casings and jacket and moved.

THIRTY-EIGHT

The disappointment was manifest on Lenny Feld's face. He grabbed Nick with his good hand and pulled him into the synagogue basement. He swung around Nick, closing the heavy steel door. He shoved the old-fashioned dead bolts at the top and bottom of the door into the jamb—something Nick had never seen him do before. He turned back to Nick.

"Who was it this time?"

Nick was confused. "What are you talking about?"

Lenny put the stub of a finger through the quarter-size hole on the right side of Nick's motorcycle jacket. "Come." He pulled Nick into his room, shoved him in front of the small mirror on the wall. "Look!"

Nick understood. He'd been in such a rush to get away from Breen's house before the cops showed that he hadn't considered what he must look like. Never mind the bullet hole through his jacket's chest and back. There were streaks of dried blood—Breen's blood—on his gloves and across the worn black leather of his jacket.

"Took me fifteen years to break this jacket in." Nick shook his head, put his hand on his friend's shoulder. "It's not what you think, Lenny."

"Well, you explain it to me, then. That's a bullet hole in your jacket and that's somebody's blood, even if it isn't yours. So, yes, what am I thinking?"

The adrenaline that Nick had been feeding on for the past few hours was wearing off. He took off his jacket and gloves. He plopped down on the metal folding chair. "It's someone else's blood."

"I got that, but you won't be surprised if I find that less than comforting."

Nick raised his hands. "If it makes you feel any better, I was a bystander, and the shooter took a few tries at me."

"Whose blood is it?"

"Donny Breen. He was—"

"One of the two original detectives on the Markovic case."

Nick was impressed. "You remember that?"

"When I do research for you, I retain a good deal of what I read. I didn't get those degrees and patents on my good looks alone."

"Cops don't like coincidences, Lenny."

"That's an abrupt change of subject even for you."

"Not really. We're trained not to believe in them—coincidences, I mean. Experience backs that up."

"But . . ."

"Would you think I was losing my mind if I said that I believe Tony Angelo's murder, the shooting on Staten Island last week, and Vlado Markovic's murder two decades ago aren't three distinct cases but one?"

Lenny didn't answer with words. Instead, that impish half-smile appeared on his face. Nick had long ago gotten past Lenny's disfigurement. That smile was like a bucket of ice water poured down Nick's back, bringing Lenny's fire-ravaged appearance back into focus. Nick watched Lenny turn and go over to his workbench.

"What are you smiling about?"

"Whatever it is, you won't be able to see it from there. Come, Nick, stand by me."

Nick obliged. The screen of Lenny's largest monitor was divided into three. Each of the three sections had a frozen image of a different location. Each had a white date-and-time stamp in the upper right-hand corner.

Lenny said, "This is what I wanted to show you, why I called earlier."

"I recognize all of these." Nick pointed to the top left image. "That's the Ocean Parkway exit from the Belt Parkway, less than a block from Tony Angelo's house."

"Indeed. Look at the time stamp."

"Two ten on the day he and Rosa were killed." Then Nick pointed to the top right image. "That's the parking lot in back of Molly's Bar in Old Rotterdam. Time stamp says that's from the date Johnny Sullivan died."

"Really?" Lenny nodded. "That makes this even more interesting. I was wondering why someone had sent you this footage."

Nick pointed at the bottom image. "That's the county road leading to Heart Rock. It's also on the day Sullivan died."

"Very good."

Lenny tapped some keys and advanced all three video images frame by frame using the oversize ball on his mouse. "There!"

On the screen, in all three boxes, was what appeared to be the same white Volvo S60.

"Jesus. I watched the video of the road by Heart Rock, but . . ."

"Don't be too hard on yourself, Nick. There's no reason you would have ascribed more importance to a passing Volvo than any other car."

"So how—"

"If one can design something as complex as facial-recognition software, vehicle-recognition software is, to be cliché, child's play."

"You designed FRS?"

"Yes, but I have never shared it and I never will. Because I designed it, I could teach you how to defeat what's out there on the market now. In the wrong hands, my programs would be too dangerous and invasive." Lenny hung his head. "Scientists like Szilard, who helped design the atomic bomb, realized too late that once the technology is available, even to a select few, you can't control it. The only way to control it is to keep it to myself."

"Do you have a piece of paper? I need to take the tag number."

"Please. I already ran the plate. It's a rental from Euro-Car in Manhattan." Lenny tapped a key. The printer came on. A few seconds later, three sheets of paper fell into the tray. "There's what you need."

Nick collected the sheets, studying the information. "The timing works. The name is probably an alias. Lenny, can you manipulate the images so I can get a look at the driver?"

"I'm a computer wizard, not an actual magician, but let's see . . . Give me a few minutes."

Nick stepped out of the room into the cold hallway. He had some calls to make. He knew that Shana would get back to him. It was her nature. His father and Sean would ignore him. Martellus would be patient and wait. As for Jonathan Lansdale, Nick had other ideas. What Breen had told him gave him only one choice who to call.

Louie Randazzo picked up on the third ring. "I don't hear from you for years and now you're like a freakin' deer tick I can't get off me."

"I love you too, Louie."

"Yeah, sure. What is it?"

"Jimmy Gabrelli."

"Mother of Christ, him again! I told you what I know."

"One last thing and then I can owe you *two* favors."

"That's like sayin' you can get me two unicorns. Okay, what?"

"Simple. Just find out for me who the guys were he was closest to in his crew."

"That's it?"

"That's it."

"I'll call you."

As Louie hung up, Lenny stepped out into the hallway to fetch Nick. "Come."

Again Nick stood at the workbench.

"This is the best I can do." Lenny pointed at the screen. "This is from the camera in the bar's parking lot. I filtered out sun glare, filtered out the shadows, compensated for the reflective nature of the windshield. Still, the image isn't sharp enough to run software on."

Nick studied the image. The shape of the head was right. The face was blurred, but he thought the man in the photo might be Franjo Petrovic. He'd have a better idea soon enough. Right at that moment, all he wanted to do was to crawl into Annalise Puleo's bed and sleep forever.

THIRTY-NINE

Annalise Puleo's reaction wasn't disappointment, but shock. That changed when she saw that Nick wasn't actually bleeding from the hole in his jacket. Shock turned immediately to suspicion. With Lenny Feld, it was more a kind of academic curiosity. With Annalise, it was professional.

"Whose blood, Nick?"

He handed her the keys to her Ducati. "Better not to ask."

"Sorry, it don't work that way, not even for you, Nick. Hiding you for a few days, lending you my Duck, okay. But you can't walk into my apartment with a fucking bullet hole through your blood-covered jacket and tell me don't ask."

"You're right. Look, AP, can we do this in the morning? I'm beat."

"Don't bullshit me, Nick. The other stuff didn't risk my job. This is different. You still mean a lot to me, but I overcame too much shit to throw away my career."

"Before, when we were together, did I lie to you?"

Her rich medium-brown skin flushed red. "No, it was me who lied."

Nick reached out and stroked her cheek. "I promise. Right now I need a shower and sleep."

———

Nick knew where he was, and when. He had been there many times. The Afghan mountains had a distinct smell to them—a rich, earthy smell of horses, human sweat, gunpowder smoke, and wild grasses fed by centuries of blood: Macedonian, Mongol, Persian, British, German, Russian, American. Mostly, overwhelmingly, Afghan blood. Invaders came and went. They always went. Always. He would leave too. A bloody-handed hero. The mountains had a stark, foreboding allure. For Nick, the beauty was always subsumed by their danger.

He was in the mountain village and there she was. *The girl.* He knew her name, but it would not come to him. Thirteen, innocently beautiful, but the weight of war rounding her shoulders beneath the shawl with blue, black, and red bands that covered her head and upper body. She turned away. He stepped around to catch the gaze of her prismatic hazel eyes like mood rings—sometimes an impossible light brown, sometimes almost pale blue. She turned away. He stepped around her. She turned away. It was a familiar dance, an unchanging ritual. The earth chasing the moon, one face always turned away. He stepped, she turned. He stepped, she turned. On it went. On and on and on until he grabbed her shoulder, stopping her turns.

Instead of him capturing her gaze, *the girl's* gaze captured him, her stare an accusation. She lifted her arm, her index finger pointed at him. The finger a dagger. He was pinned, stone-still but for his mouth.

"I'm sorry."

She said nothing. The accusation pressed down on him.

"I'm sorry."

She said nothing.

"I'm sorry."

Her mouth remained still, but he heard her. "I begged you to help us. I begged you to help. I begged you. I begged you."

"I'm sorry."

Her anger filled in the crevices and cracks in the brown dirt street. He reached for her, but she slid backward as if on rails, her finger still pointing at him. "I begged you to help us. I begged you." As she slid away, her face caved in, blood pouring from the corners of where her eyes had been, from where her nose had been, from her mouth. Her shawl soaked through and turned the crimson red of the dress she wore beneath. "I begged you."

"I'm sorry."

"Nick. Nick!"

The ground shook. His body shook.

"Nick!"

He opened his eyes. The girl was gone. She was always gone, even when the ground didn't shake.

"AP," he whispered, smiling up at her.

"What are you sorry about?"

He was confused. "What are you talking about?"

"You were screaming, 'I'm sorry.' It was pretty loud."

"Bad dream."

"No shit. About what?"

He didn't discuss it with anyone. Not Shana, not his family, not anyone. Joe knew about it only because he had accessed his military records, but very few others had any idea.

"Afghanistan," he said. For some reason, he wanted to tell Annalise. "A lot of guys I served with came back fucked up or in pieces. I came home intact, but there's this one thing . . ."

She put her finger across his lips. She replaced her finger with her lips and pressed them hard to his. Their mouths opened at the same time; their tongues slid across each other. It was a little awkward at first. Four years of hard feelings and longing weren't so easily overcome. As she leaned forward, Nick rolled her over him onto the mattress. He laced his fingers through her thick hair. He stopped the kiss, pushed away.

"Look, AP, I want you, but—"

"Shut up, Nick." She clenched his T-shirt in her hands and pulled him down to her.

He didn't argue, putting his lips back to hers. As he did, he slid his left hand beneath the waistband of her sweats. Her body tensed, then relaxed, tensed again. She grabbed his wrist and moved his hand down.

"Like that, Nick. Like the way you used to."

After only a few seconds, she sighed, her back arching. He moved down along her body, sliding her sweats off her, then gently urged her legs apart. He put his mouth to her, the scent and taste of her filling up his head. He sighed as he lost himself in the dark, giving himself over to her, the moment, and her shudders.

Later, her head on his bruised chest, him staring through the darkness at the ceiling, Annalise said, "You wanna tell me now about what happened?"

"There was a girl, Osman, in a village in the mountains near our firebase. Her father worked for us. Nothing official. He would translate, do errands, all sorts of small things. The local Taliban leader put him on a death list as a collaborator. The girl came to me and begged me to help her father. I went to our commanding officer, who basically told me to mind my own business. That because the relationship wasn't official, we couldn't protect the father or offer the family asylum."

"So the father was killed."

"No. They kidnapped and raped Osman. Then they stoned her to death on video and put it out as a warning."

"Oh, my God! What did you do?"

"That part I can't talk about."

Five minutes later, Annalise got on top of him, put him inside her, and rocked both of them sore.

FORTY

Annalise was still sleeping when Nick eased himself out of bed and into the shower. He regretted washing her scent away, but this second shower in less than eight hours was necessary. He had a lot of places to be. He was close. The answers felt paradoxically just out of his reach and just within it. He was pretty certain he knew who had killed Markovic, but not who was behind it, not exactly why. It was an execution having nothing to do with Vlado Markovic being mistaken for something he wasn't, or a killer's misplaced rage. The larger motive was the same reason a lot of people were murdered: money. Money and murder were more than high school sweethearts.

He knew where the blood was. The blood had names: Vlado Markovic, Johnny Sullivan, Tom Harris, Donny Breen, Jimmy and Carmine Gabrelli, Tony and Rosa Angelo. Nick had only to follow its trail. That was the easy part of the equation. This wasn't $E = mc^2$, a simple, elegant equation explaining the universe. This was uglier, more complicated than that, as any equation hoping to explain human behavior would have to be. Wherever the money came from, there had to be a lot of it. Between Sullivan's Ferrari, Harris's Naples condo, Breen's house, and Markovic's safe-deposit box, it was already a pile, but not enough to account for all the bodies dropping. He was still missing the biggest piece of the puzzle.

Before leaving Annalise's apartment, Nick kept his promise—to a point. He left a note about how he had witnessed Breen's execution. That the blood on his jacket was Breen's. He didn't have the time or inclination to explain the bullet hole. There was a lot he wasn't inclined to explain. He knew Annalise would begin putting some of the pieces together herself, but that like him, she wouldn't have enough material to make it all fit together. He didn't ask her to keep his name out of it if her Ducati had been spotted near the murder scene. He would come forward if he had to. Only if he had to. Then, or when he had made sense of it all. He reasoned that the answers at his first stop would go a long way toward making things fall into place.

He held his shield out to the woman in the blue business suit at the counter. The circle of gold stars of the European Union was embroidered on the left chest and cuffs of her jacket. She was petite, raven-haired, with a sharp nose and thin lips pulled tightly over her teeth. She was unimpressed by Nick's shield, smirking and shrugging her little shoulders.

"Yes, Detective . . ."

"Ryan."

"*D'accord*, Detective Ryan. I am Claudette. How may I assist you?"

Once he heard her French accent, Nick understood. Being unimpressed by Americans was as French as foie gras. He placed two things on the counter: the rental agreement Lenny had printed for him, and the photo of Franjo Petrovic. The photo from the file Tuva had forwarded to him. He turned both so that they properly faced Claudette.

"Were you on duty when this Volvo was rented?"

She barely glanced at them. "I was, yes."

Nick tapped Petrovic's photo. "Was this the man who rented the vehicle?"

"It was him. He was a little thinner in the face, maybe, but yes."

"The name he gave you was Dasho Gharibyan? His driver's license was from Armenia. Was his passport also Armenian?"

"If you already have this information, why—"

"I ask the questions, Claudette."

"It was Armenian, but he was no more Armenian than you."

"Why do you say that?"

"I rent cars to people from all over the world—Arabs, Europeans from all corners, Africans, sometimes Americans." She tapped her nose. "Like a detective, one gets a sense of people. That is one reason."

"The other reason?"

"My name is Claudette Hakobyan. My mother is from Dijon. My father is Armenian."

Nick laughed. Claudette too. The laugh transformed her attitude.

"Do you have his passport information? It isn't on the rental agreement."

"One moment. *Ne quittez pas.*" She looked away from Nick and tapped her keypad, and he heard the whine of a printer coming on. "Here you are, Detective Ryan."

On the first sheet was a colored photo of the blue passport with gold lettering and a stylized image of a bird of prey and a lion facing in opposite directions. The words *Republic of Armenia Passport* in English were beneath the birds. There was beautiful Armenian script in gold both above and below the image. On the next sheet was a page much like a page in an American passport. Photo, name, date of birth . . .

"Merci beaucoup, Claudette." Nick placed his card on the counter. "If this man returns the car, please call me immediately. But after he leaves. No heroics. It's not that urgent. Please have anyone else working here do the same if you are not on duty."

"Now, may I ask what this man has done that you are looking for him?"

"Money laundering," Nick lied, knowing the truth would be a mistake. He couldn't risk her or any other employees acting too nervous in front of Petrovic. A man as violent as he would not hesitate to kill if he felt cornered. Nick tapped his temple. "*Souviens-toi, après son départ.*"

"Yes, Detective Ryan, after he leaves. Your French and your accent are excellent."

"For an American."

"For anyone." She clapped. "*Très, très bien.*"

"Thank you for your help, Claudette. May I use your fax machine?"

Claudette didn't respond. She gestured for Nick to come around behind the counter. On top of the sheet with the passport photo page, he wrote:

Attn: Det. Annalise Puleo
    This is the name Petrovic is traveling under.
    Driving 2019 Volvo S60 White NY Reg as per attached.
Will update if I come across anything else.
                                  Nick

When he had confirmation that the fax went through, he thanked Claudette.

"I am off for lunch at noon," she said. "Why not meet me at the Rive Gauche Bistro around the corner?"

Nick winked, putting his hand over his heart. "If only I could. *Je suis désolé.*"

She smiled, turned up her delicate little hands. "Au revoir, Nick Ryan."

———

In the mirror that morning, he had noticed that his bruises were beginning to turn from the deep, ugly purple to lighter shades of red and yellow. It didn't make them hurt any less, just let him know he was healing. He had tried everything in Joe's Malibu but the radio. As he made his way toward the Ed Koch–Fifty-Ninth Street Bridge into Queens, he risked it by tuning in to a news radio channel. After a weather-and-traffic update, the lead story was the murder of a retired NYPD detective at his home in Rockland County. The reporter mentioned Breen's reputation and his connection to the Markovic case. But it was the end of the report that Nick focused on.

While there are no suspects in custody at this time, a witness, neighbor Maryanne Schaffer, says she saw a man on a motor-cycle pulling away from the victim's home within minutes of hearing the shots. Unfortunately, she did not see the license plate number nor could she describe the man. "It was dark and he was dressed in black with a dark-colored helmet." West Nyack Police are asking anyone with information to please call. All tips will be confidential.

Nick wasn't concerned that he would be a suspect. The police would know that the shots had come from the woods and that the bullet that had killed Breen was from a high-powered rifle. They would find his 9mm bullets in the woods too. They were unlikely to trace them back to him. What Nick wanted was to be able to finish his work with a free hand. Once he showed up on police radar, that would be impossible.

On the bridge, Nick reflexively took a quick peek over his shoulder to the right and behind him. Shana's building was down there on Sutton Place. He turned back, Manhattan quickly disappearing behind him. He had never been able to leave Shana fully behind him, not even when he was seven thousand miles away in Afghanistan or in Annalise Puleo's bed. Shana couldn't seem to let it go either. They were afflicted with each other, but the stakes were higher now. He had to find the cure, for Shana's sake. More importantly, for Becky's. Shana had called. He would not return the call. He hoped that would be a start.

FORTY-ONE

With its narrow, tree-lined streets of single-family houses and little local shops on the boulevard, College Point seemed like a small town somehow wrongly grafted onto Queens. The ass end of the point stuck out into the East River, giving residents less-than-scenic views of Rikers Island. And with its proximity to LaGuardia, the air smelled of spent jet fuel. The roar of turbofan engines had lullabied generations of its babies to bed.

Petar Stankovic lived in a tired-looking asphalt-shingled house near the wastewater treatment plant. From what Carla Ruvolo had told Nick, Stankovic had worked with Vlado Markovic and was his only friend who wasn't her friend first. The blood trail was one thing. The money trail was another matter. If anyone could shed some light on the money trail leading to Vlado's murder, Nick thought it would be Stankovic. He might be able to pick up the trail without Stankovic's help, but it would be easier if Stankovic could point him in the right direction.

Stankovic was a big-bellied man in his sixties with a head of thick steel-gray hair. Faded blue eyes stared out of a face with broad cheeks, a flat nose, and a gap-toothed smile. The smile remained even after Nick introduced himself. He raised his fleshy right hand to Nick. His shake was like a hydraulic press.

"Years of kneading bread makes a man strong," he said, seeing the look on Nick's face. "Come in, please."

The little living room was crowded with fussy old furniture and an incongruous flat-screen. The house smelled of cabbage and stewing meat. Everything was clean and tidy. Stankovic gestured for Nick to sit on a grandma sofa as he sat in a corduroy-covered recliner.

"It has been a long time since someone comes to me about Vlado."

"Why would you assume that?"

"There is no other reason policemen have ever spoken to me. Would you like something to drink—a soda, a beer?" His Serbian accent persisted but was softened by his decades in America. "I have Jelen beer from home. It's very good."

"No, thank you."

"What I can say to you I have not told the others? Understand, Detective Ryan, I mean not to be rude."

Nick didn't answer. Instead, he handed Stankovic a piece of paper that bore an image Nick had downloaded and printed before leaving his condo this morning. Given that the human links between the money and Vlado Markovic were disappearing at an alarming rate, Nick had decided to take a direct approach.

Stankovic's ever-present smile disappeared. "You know about Vlado?"

"That he was part of the Serb Volunteer Guard? I know."

"Such ugliness then in our homeland. Such things our countrymen and others did to one another." Stankovic hung his head. "Vlado wanted only to forget things he had done. When he was killed, I thought those things had not forgotten him. Then the police say he was murdered because the killers thought he was an Arab. It is sad, Detective Ryan, but I was . . . relieved. Relieved that our ugliness was not the reason. I felt ashamed for this."

"Vlado had a burn mark on his—"

"It was a tattoo of this." Stankovic held up the image of the Serb Volunteer Guard logo. "He had it burned off before he comes to America."

"Carla told me Vlado was drinking a lot, that he was more nervous than normal in the month before his death. Do you know why?"

He shrugged. "Carla, the wife, is right." Stankovic pushed himself up out of the recliner. "Please to come with me."

He followed as Stankovic struggled up the stairs. He turned back to Nick. "Years of standing for many hours kneading. Strong hands. Ruined knees. I almost never come up here anymore since my wife has passed."

At the top of the stairs, Stankovic turned right, leading Nick into an empty spare bedroom. Its walls and floor were bare. Stankovic wasn't lying. The upstairs, while just as tidy as the first floor, was a bit dusty and smelled of mold. The retired baker pointed to a square outline in the ceiling, from which a cord dangled. He pulled the cord. A wooden ladder unfolded.

"Please, you will go. My knees . . ." Stankovic pointed to the corner of the ceiling near the outside wall. "There you will find a black leather bag. Not a suitcase. I don't know the word in English for it, but it is in that corner. Bring it."

Nick climbed the ladder. The only light in the attic streamed through a small south-facing oval window. Things in the attic, like everywhere else in the house, were neatly arranged. Nick moved to where Stankovic had indicated. The joists beneath the old plywood creaked and complained with each step. The dusty, cobwebby black leather bag was right where Stankovic had said it would be.

"It's called a Gladstone bag," Nick said, placing it on the floor after he climbed down from the attic.

Stankovic made a face. "Why is it called this?"

"No idea."

"That August before he was killed, Vlado came to me during a coffee break. He gives me a key and a paper with an address in Astoria. He says if anything happens to him, I should get this bag and what is inside I should keep for my own."

"What's inside?"

"I have never looked. I think probably money, but it is dirty money. I never needed it. My wife and me"—he crossed himself—"we were happy as we were. I did not want the blood from our homeland to touch us. I did not look, but also I did not know what to do with the bag. I did not want to give it to the police."

Nick patted Stankovic's shoulder. "I understand."

"For most of the time, I forget it is here. But when you show me the picture and I see you know about the bad things Vlado has done . . . I want it gone."

Nick knelt down, brushed the dust off the bag's clasp, and unzipped it. Once he saw inside, he knew immediately what it was. "His bugout bag."

"What is a bugout bag?"

"It means if he had to leave in a hurry, he could grab the bag and go."

Nick went through the contents: ten thousand dollars cash in a banded stack of hundreds, an Italian passport with Markovic's photo but under the name Giovanni Romello, a long-expired American Express card for Giovanni Romello, road maps of New England and Canada, a six-inch folding knife, an old Czech-made 9mm handgun with a full magazine, a change of clothes, a small medic kit, a travel toiletries and razor kit.

"Is this what you thought, a bugout bag?" Stankovic asked.

Nick nodded. "None of this is relevant anymore. Do you want the money? He wanted you to have it?"

"No. I am going downstairs."

Nick replaced the contents of the bag. When he got back down to the living room, bag in hand, Stankovic was in his recliner. There was a beer bottle in his hand and tears in his eyes.

"Did Vlado tell you why he was nervous, why he gave you the key?"

Stankovic didn't answer immediately. Nick read the old baker's face and could tell he was weighing his options. Nick pushed him.

"You haven't lied to me yet, Mr. Stankovic. Now isn't the time to start. I can walk out that door with this bag and let you remember your friend happily or—"

"He said that someone was coming."

Nick repeated, "Someone was coming. That's it? Not who?"

"Only this."

"Do you have any ideas?"

"From the way he acted, I can only think it was someone from the Guard. Someone who knew of the bad things. Someone I think he was afraid of."

Nick placed his card on the table next to the recliner. He left with the bag and without another word.

Pulling away from the tired little house, Nick decided to take a detour into the past. Less than two minutes later, he was parked in front of a well-kept vinyl-sided split ranch on a street a few blocks from the river. Pete Moretti, Nick's first detective partner and best friend, had once lived here. After his divorce, Pete's first wife and kids had lived here. No one Nick knew lived here anymore. A few months after Pete's suicide, his family had moved south. Nick, who rarely looked back, wasn't sure why he was here. All he knew was that Pete's planting evidence was the first domino in a line of dominoes leading to Nick's job as the city's invisible fixer.

His burner phone rang, snapping him back into the moment. "Yeah."

"I got those names for ya." It was Louie. "Two ain't gonna do you much good and if you don't hurry, none of 'em will."

"Dead?"

"One got clipped about ten years ago. The other guy had a heart attack. You want their names?"

"Skip those two."

"Vincent Gardi."

"What's his story?"

"Not the brightest bulb, but Jimmy Gabrelli's running mate in the crew. Dyin' of lung cancer. He's in . . . whatyamacallit these days . . . palliative care. Whatever happened to fuckin' hospice care or just takin' it until you croak?"

"Where is he?"

"Someplace on the island. I'll text you the address. This gonna help?"

"I'll let you know. Thanks, Louie. Now maybe I can get you that second unicorn."

Louie hung up.

Nick turned to see a woman coming out the front door of the old Moretti house. She held her young daughter by the hand. He watched them walk down the street and disappear around the corner. He was no longer thinking about Pete Moretti. One sadness erasing another.

FORTY-TWO

St. Teresa's Palliative Care facility was on Jericho Turnpike in Commack, Suffolk County. Nice as the building was, it wasn't where Nick would have chosen to spend his last days. Choked with traffic and strip malls, Jericho Turnpike was as picturesque as a spiral fracture.

"Vincent Gardi," Nick said, flashing his shield at the duty nurse.

"You do realize what this place is, Detective."

"I do. That's why I'm here. It's urgent I speak to Mr. Gardi."

"Is he expecting you?"

Nick opened his mouth to answer, then realized the answer he was going to give was wrong. "Not me, but someone like me, yeah. He's been expecting that person for a long time."

The nurse was confused. "What does that mean?"

"It means, let's ask Mr. Gardi and see what he says."

She stood up. "Wait here, please."

When she returned, her expression was full of contempt, but she told Nick that Gardi was waiting for him in room 113. "Try not to upset him."

"I think he'll be relieved to see me. Listen . . ."

"Anna."

"Anna, I may need someone to witness Mr. Gardi's statement."

"I can do that. There's a call button next to his bed. Ring it and I will be right in."

"Thank you."

They tried hard to beat the hospital atmosphere out of the place, but no one had any illusions that it was anything but the train's last stop. The *113* might have fooled someone into thinking that it was a room in a motel, but for the oxygen tubes in the nose and the IV stuck into the arm of the skeletal man in the hospital bed. Skeleton was watching Fox News and cursing under his breath. Noticing Nick, he turned the TV off.

"You the detective?" Gardi coughed. Stopped. Coughed some more.

"I'm not the priest."

"Been there, done that. Already got last rites. You figure they'd let me smoke, right? Nah, not even dyin' gets you a freakin' pass in this place."

"Priest forgive you for killing Vlado Markovic?"

"Fuckin' cops." He coughed up phlegm and blood into a towel. When he was finished, he said, "I been lookin' over my shoulder almost twenty years for one a you pricks to show up."

"Here I am. Name's Nick Ryan."

Gardi nodded. "How'd you find me?"

"We can talk about that afterwards. You have my word. First, I need you to tell me about Markovic. Press the call button. We need a witness."

Thirty seconds later, Anna Foley stepped into the room. Nick took out his cell, put it on video. He identified himself, gave the location, the date. He explained that he was here to take the statement of confession from Vincent Gardi concerning the homicide of Vlado Markovic in Brooklyn on September 11, 2001. He tapped pause, aimed the cell at Anna Foley. "Please identify yourself. Give your full name and your title, please." She did as Nick asked. Nick paused it again, turning to Gardi. "You ready for this?"

"Yeah, yeah, let me get this shit off my chest."

"Okay, when I point to you, identify yourself, then wait for my questions." Nick focused on Gardi, counting down with his fingers from three, and pointed. When the preliminaries were done, he gave Gardi the go-ahead to tell it his way.

"So Jimmy Gabrelli promised me and Allie a shit ton a money."

"Who's Allie?"

"Alfonso Lima. The t'ree of us was tight, grew up together. We was our own little crew within the Malzones' crew. You know how it is. So Jimmy come out of the air force and he says he got a sweet setup that'll make us all a mint, but that we gotta do whatever. You know what I mean?"

"Wet work? Killing?"

"Killing. Yeah, like that."

Nick already had a pretty good notion of what Gardi would say. He wanted the details, the steps of the dance. Gardi gave it to him. They were as fresh to the dying man as if he, Gabrelli, and Lima had killed Vlado Markovic last night.

"Yeah, I was on the platform with him, the Vlado guy, and then he bends over to look at somethin' on the tracks as I'm squeezin' the trigger. My shots missed him. I wasn't supposed to shoot the guy, but I figured, fuck it, right? Dead is dead. He rolls onto the tracks, runs over to the Brooklyn platform where Jimmy's waitin' for him. He sees Jimmy and takes off runnin'. Allie's waitin' for him on the tracks and the guy trips into Allie's freakin' arms like special delivery. It was easy from there. Allie stuck him a lot to make it look like he was pissed at the guy. Shit, me and Allie didn't even know who the fuck he was. We just did what Jimmy said to do. We carried him onto the platform and watched him bleed out. We shouldn't a waited. That ruined the deal 'cause it gave the token clerk time to flag down the cops."

"Did Jimmy explain why you had to do the guy like that?"

"Not really. That fuckin' token clerk! She screwed it all up." Agitated, he had a long coughing fit. Even after he calmed, he struggled to breathe. "Anyways, she don't flag them cops down, the money Johnny used to pay the fuckers off for keepin' quiet woulda been *ours*."

Gardi went on a little longer, giving answers to the questions Nick asked him. No, he didn't remember the names of the cops who showed up. No, he had no idea what happened to Gabrelli.

"C'mon, Ryan, you know better. You do what we do, you don't ask those kinda questions. You figure either the boss got his reasons or someone from another crew got permission."

Nick looked at Anna Foley. She was horrified. "Why don't you go back to the desk, Anna? I'll call you if I need you. Mr. Gardi and I have things to talk about."

She didn't need to be asked twice.

"Civilians!" Gardi said, shaking his head. "Don't they read the papers or nothin'? They think shit gets done by magic or something?"

"People know there are waste pipes in their houses, Gardi, but they don't think about them until the toilet backs up."

"Yeah, I guess."

Nick got up. "Okay, Gardi, I hope you feel a little relief and that the pain isn't too bad. I don't think the DA is going to have time to do anything with this."

"I ain't worried. I hear the clock tickin' real loud. I'm a little surprised, I gotta say."

"Why's that?"

"Don't you wanna hear about the other guy?"

"The other guy? You did two?"

"I just said so, didn't I?"

Nick sat back down.

FORTY-THREE

So he had Joe's answer: Vincent Gardi, Jimmy Gabrelli, and Alfonso
Lima killed Vlado Markovic. Joe might be satisfied with it. Nick wasn't.
Sometimes an answer wasn't *the* answer even if it satisfied the question.
Sometimes the answer was a fragmentation grenade. Each piece of shrap-
nel another question. Gardi's confession was like that. Nick knew who
killed Markovic. Not why. That wasn't even the biggest question to come
from his visit with Gardi. It was the other killing, the one Gardi told
him about as he was leaving, that went around and around in his head.

Sitting in his living room, watching the sun scurry behind the rim
of the earth, he listened to the soon-to-be-dead Gardi cough his way
through the details of the other murder.

That guy on the train platform [laughing/coughing] *was after
we done the first guy. We picked him up at the . . . what the fuck's
it called? The International Arrivals Building at JFK last week in
August. Big, ugly foreign motherfucka. I mean I ain't no beauty,
but this guy, Christ, he was a* faccia brutta. *Asshole.* [coughing]
*He don't say much but he's all chesty, actin' like we should kiss his
freakin' ring or somethin', kinda like the way Old Man Malzone*

used to act. I'm thinkin', he can kiss my ass, you know. Fuckin'
guy waited for Jimmy to open the back door for him like he's a
king or somethin'. Jimmy gets in next to him. Allie's the wheel-
man. I'm shotgun. [laughing/coughing]

We had the prick's tour all mapped out. You know how much
of America he got to see? [laughing/coughing] *Rockaway fuckin'*
Boulevard. Jimmy put two in his ear as we're goin' out the back
of the airport t'rough the cargo area. Funny as shit, 'cause as we're
leavin', Jimmy points out the Lufthansa building where the big
heist was. Then we drive down Rockaway Boulevard to the south
shore. I don't know exactly where we was, maybe Hewlett Harbor,
but Jimmy had a boat tied up in a little isolated place off a dead-
end street. We haul the big guy onto the boat. Allie goes to ditch
the car. Me and Jimmy got on plastic suits, and we cut the guy up.
T'rew the weighted pieces overboard as we went. With the torso,
we made sure to put lotsa holes in it so he wouldn't float back up.

[Nick asks] *Where'd you go?*

Fuck if I know. Some little island in Jamaica Bay I'm thinkin',
'cause I can see the lights on the Gil Hodges Bridge. At least, that's
what I think. I hate boats and I never go on the water unless
I gotta go. [coughing] *So we pull up to this tiny little island.*
Fuckin' dark. No lights or nothin'. Just lotsa sand and brush and
shit. I mean, you can see lights in the distance on another island or
maybe it's Breezy Point. I don't know, but this place is dark, man.
Jimmy hops off and tells me to stay put. I can hear another boat
pulling up, but I can't see it. When Jimmy comes back like ten
minutes later, he got the duffel bag. You know, the one with the
money we used to buy off the cops. [agitated] *That was supposed*
to be our fuckin' money. Fuckin' token clerk! [long coughing jag]

Anyways, as Jimmy shoves us off and we pull away, I see the
ass end of the other boat. It's a big freakin' yacht.

[Nick asks] *Did you see the name of the yacht?*

It didn't have its lights on and it was dark out there, but
I caught part of the name on the back of the boat. It was Vic

something. I'm guessing Victory, *'cause if you could afford somethin' that big, you won. Anyways, it was a good thing Jimmy knew
where the fuck we was goin'. A few days later, Jimmy shows up
with a Porsche at the club. You gotta love the guy. You know he
took, like, seventy, eighty grand outta the duffel bag and bought
the thing with it. I miss that prick. What a set a brass balls on him!*

[Nick asks] *You ever hear the name Jonathan Lansdale?*

[silence] *Who's that?*

[Nick] *Never mind.*

*I heard Jimmy's brother, Carmine, got killed out on Staten
Island and his brother-in-law got shot in the head.* [coughing]
You think that had somethin' to do with this shit?

Nick reached over to the coffee table, hit Stop, and swiped the phone
back to its normal screen. After he poured himself a big glass of bourbon, he reached for the Joe phone.

"Ryan?"

"Who else calls you on this phone, Joe?"

"Don't be an ass. What is it?"

"I have an answer for you."

"About . . ."

"Are you actively trying to piss me off?"

"Markovic." Joe packed a lot of relief and excitement into those
three syllables.

"Yeah."

The excitement waned. "You said *an* answer."

"Glad to see you're paying attention."

"Care to explain?"

"When I see you."

"Place and time?"

Nick checked his watch, thought about the traffic between his apartment and the South Bronx. "The tire shop in an hour and a half. We
need it to be a place where we can talk without anyone around."

"Very mysterious."

"Ninety minutes."

Before he could get off the line, Joe said, "Nick, watch your back."

Nick's radar popped on. "I always do, but what's wrong?"

"Nothing. Nothing." Joe cleared his throat. "It's just that . . . it's that the answer about the Markovic case is more important than you know."

Nick already knew it was important, but there was something about how Joe said what he said that rang hollow. Joe was a lot of things, but he had never been insincere. "Joe, what's up? Is there something you want to tell me?"

"See you in ninety minutes." The line went dead.

As Nick stood to leave, the lobby buzzer rang before he grabbed the phone.

"Who is it?"

"Shana. I'm coming up."

"No, you're not. I'm on my way out."

"One way or the other, Nick Ryan, we're going to talk now."

"I'll buzz you in. Take the stairs to the garage and meet me by the silver Malibu parked in my spot."

"Nick!"

He pressed the buzzer long enough to ensure she would get in. He wasn't in the mood for a confrontation with Shana. He never was. But he admitted to himself that his heart beat a little bit harder at the thought of being near her again, furious or not.

FORTY-FOUR

Stepping out of the elevator, Nick noticed an uncomfortable stillness in the garage. He sensed trouble the way animals know when a tornado or earthquake is coming. He pressed himself to the square concrete pillar that stood between the elevator and his parking spot. When he peeked around the corner and saw that Shana wasn't there, he knew his instincts were right.

He slipped out of his Adidas for silent movement, pulled the 19 from his hip. He stepped away from the pillar, back past the elevator. He circled the internal perimeter of the garage to come at the Malibu from the opposite direction. At the farthest point from his spot, Nick slowly racked the 19's slide. As he got within a hundred feet, he saw a shadow moving between the rear bumper of the Malibu and the old Norton motorcycle parked behind it. He heard a heel scraping against the concrete, a muffled voice.

Nick needed whoever was behind the Malibu to show himself. Ducking behind a Camry, he put the 19 in his left hand. He removed the hawkbill knife from his waistband, tossing it so that it would skitter past the Malibu. The ploy worked. Shea Flannery stepped out from behind the Malibu. He wasn't alone. Flannery had his left arm around Shana's throat, holding a gun to her right ear. Nick stepped out from behind the Camry, his Glock aimed at Flannery's head.

"You looking for me?"

Flannery swung around, dragging Shana with him. There was fear in her eyes, anger too. *Good*, Nick thought, *I can work with that.* Anger would help stop her from giving in to the fear.

Before Flannery could say a word, Shana asked, voice cracking, "Nick, what's this about?"

"Nick! So that's your real name, Marty. Well, fuck you, Nick." Flannery pressed the muzzle hard against Shana's head.

"Marty?" Shana was confused. "Who's Marty?"

Nick raised his left hand, pointed the Glock up at the garage ceiling. "Take it easy, Shana. Stay quiet. Just do what the man tells you to do."

Flannery snorted, smiled, squeezed her neck. "Yeah, Shana, do what the man tells you."

Shana's eyes bulged; she gasped for air.

Nick kept his voice calm. "This is between us, Flannery. Let her go."

"You didn't hear me the first time, huh? Must be the acoustics in here. Fuck you! You ruined my life, you piece of shit! Your bosses got me by the balls. They want me to talk about people—the kind of people who won't stop after they kill me. Some of the men I've done deals with will torture my wife and kids in front of me. They'd go back in time and kill my fucking ancestors if they could."

Nick didn't think this was the time to tell Flannery the fault for that was not in his stars but in his own greed. Flannery dressed well, drank good scotch, and talked the talk, but he was like most criminals. When they got tangled in their own webs, it was always someone else's fault. Nick put the Glock down on the garage floor and kicked it over to Flannery.

"You a cop?" Flannery asked, smiling at Nick's gesture. "Yeah, you're a cop. I shoulda known. Now do the same with your off-duty piece and don't fucking lie to me. You lie to me and I'll blow the nose off her beautiful face. A reverse Pinocchio." He moved the muzzle from her temple to her nose, ran his tongue over her cheek. "Yummy. I wonder how you really taste. Tell me, Nick, what's she taste like? I bet she's sweet and creamy."

Shana's eyes filled with disgust. Nick slid the 26 toward Flannery. Flannery kicked it and the 19 under other parked cars.

Flannery asked, "The Malibu yours?"

"It is."

"You come out of your pocket with anything besides keys and—"

"I get it." Nick took the key fob out of his pocket.

"Who is she, anyway?" Flannery said, then asked Shana, "Who are you to him?"

Nick answered, "An old girlfriend who doesn't know how to let go."

"I'm going to make her wish come true. You're going to spend the rest of your lives together. Marty—Nick—you drive. Shana and me, we're getting in the back seat."

Nick hit the key fob; the doors clicked open. He got in the driver's seat and adjusted the rearview mirror to watch Flannery shove Shana into the back seat. Flannery sat directly behind Nick, not bothering with his shoulder belt. He seemed amused by Shana belting herself in.

"That's right, Shana, we wouldn't want you to get hurt."

"Where're we going?" Nick asked, starting the car.

Flannery made a quizzical face at the throaty rumble of the engine. "You put a new motor in here, or something?"

Nick shrugged. "Ask my friend Louie. I borrowed it from him. My car's in the shop."

Shana played along. "I was curious about that."

"Shut up, bitch!" Flannery pressed the gun hard into her ribs. "Don't open your mouth again or I'll shut it permanently." With his left hand, he tapped Nick on the shoulder. "Just drive. Make a left out of here, turn left on Shore Parkway, and get on the Belt going east."

Nick did as he was told. He'd gone through the hostage-negotiating classes, but this wasn't a classroom. This was a unique situation. The guy in the back seat wasn't some random stranger with a gun. His hostage wasn't just any woman. She was *the one*, the mother of his little girl. Nick knew in his marrow that Flannery wasn't lying. The people he had done deals with—cartel men, Russian mobsters, and the like—would torture and kill his family in front of him. Nick was sure Flannery would take Shana and him to a quiet place somewhere in the marshland along the Belt Parkway, kill them, then kill himself to save his family.

Flannery seemed unnerved by Nick's silence. "You're supposed to be begging for her life, for yours. Why aren't you bargaining? I want you to squirm."

Nick shook his head slowly from side to side to make sure Flannery noticed. "Remember what you said to me back in the garage?"

"Refresh my memory, Nick."

"Fuck you! I'm not begging. You're going to kill us. Kill us, you fucking coward."

"You trying to piss me off?" Flannery said just before he punched Shana in the abdomen with the gun butt.

She doubled over so quickly, the shoulder restraint stopped her. She gasped, choked; saliva poured out of her mouth. Flannery could not help but watch the effects of the punch. Nick took the opportunity to hit the cruise control button twice. The grill covering what should have been the door speaker popped down.

"Keep it up, Nick, and they're going to find your ex's body here with broken ribs and no nose."

Nick had a plan that might cause Shana more pain, but one that might also save their lives. "I call you a coward and you prove my point, asshole. Brave guy to hit a woman you're holding a gun on. She could probably kick your ass. Point that thing at me and give her a chance."

Flannery's face turned bright red in anger. "You think so?" He reached over and slapped Shana's face, splitting her lip. Blood leaked down her chin. "Come on, bitch. Catch your breath and then take a swing."

Nick saw Flannery switch the gun from his right hand to his left. Sensed him push the muzzle against the back of the driver's seat. That was exactly what Nick wanted. He tried hard to catch Shana's eyes in the mirror. When he did, Nick very subtly nodded. He mouthed, "Swing!"

As Shana lifted her right arm, Nick yanked the wheel left. Shana's punch grazed Flannery's chin.

Flannery reflexively squeezed the trigger. The gun went off with a flash and a deafening bang. The Malibu grazed the center median, then skidded across all three lanes, barely missing two other cars, and bounded onto the shoulder. As it rumbled along the shoulder, Nick grabbed the Kel-Tec P50 from the speaker cavity. He slammed on the brakes, throwing Flannery's head into the back of the driver's seat, stunning him.

That was all Nick needed. In one motion, he released his seatbelt, spun, and shot Shea Flannery in the left shoulder then the right. Blood sprayed onto Shana's face as Flannery's gun fell to the floor of the back seat.

"Shana!" he yelled so she could hear him above the ringing in her ears. "Get his gun and come sit by me. Now!" He barked at her so she wouldn't go fully into shock.

She did as he said. She dropped Flannery's gun on the mat and sat in front. She seemed to be staring a million miles away. Flannery screamed in pain and slumped down.

"I'm not going to kill you, motherfucker, because that would be too easy. No easy outs for you, not after this. Not after you hurt her. Now, pay close attention. I'm going to ask you one question. You lie or don't answer, it won't be your nose that gets shot off. Nod if you understand."

Flannery nodded. "Okay, just get me to a fucking hospital. Help me!"

"Here's the question. How did you find me?"

"Christ, get me some help, please! Oh, fuck, this hurts."

"You won't pitch in the majors or throw any touchdown passes, but you're not going to die." Nick fired a shot into the seat, between Flannery's legs. "Now, answer the fucking question."

"A call."

"From who?"

"I don't know. I swear I don't know. I didn't recognize the voice."

"Man or woman?"

"Man."

"What did he say?"

"Gave me your address and your parking spot number. It said Marty lives there." Nick raised the P50 again. "I'm not lying. I swear."

Nick drove the Malibu into the reeds. He pulled Flannery out of the car. The sharp stones poked through Nick's socks. The traffic noise blotted out the screams as Nick cuffed Flannery's hands behind his back. He put a plastic zip tie around Flannery's legs, threw him in the trunk. Slammed it shut.

He fished the Joe phone out of his pocket.

Joe asked, "Traffic? Are you going to be late?"

"Change of plans."

"What are—"

"I'll be home in fifteen minutes. Send a crew to get my Malibu. It needs some bodywork and interior cleaning. You'll find Shea Flannery in the trunk and his gun in the front seat."

"Dead?"

"Fucked up, not dead. He's going to need surgery and lots of occupational therapy. Don't come up to my apartment. Understood?"

"No, but I'll do as you ask."

"Joe, just so you know, the car saved my life." He didn't mention Shana.

"You're welcome."

"Fifteen minutes." He hung up.

When he got back in the car, Shana was sobbing uncontrollably. Her chest heaving, choking on her tears.

He stroked her hair, felt the sticky, drying blood. The car had the strong scent of urine. He said, "I can explain."

"No, Nick, you can't."

She was right.

FORTY-FIVE

When they got back to the garage under his building, Nick collected his guns from under the cars where Flannery had kicked them. He found his knife under the tire of a minivan. His Adidas were nowhere to be found.

"You're bleeding," Shana said, pointing at the red seeping through his white socks.

"It looks worse than it is."

These were the first words she'd spoken in ten minutes. Shana had gone silent and still on the way back to Nick's condo. People handled trauma differently, but they all had to process it or fight processing it. He let her be. They were halfway up to his apartment before she spoke again.

"Are you just going to let that man bleed to death in the trunk?"

"No."

"No. That's all you're going to say?"

"It's all I can say."

"Nick, I just realized . . ."

"What?"

"He shot you through the back of your seat, but—"

"He missed." He wasn't going to tell her about the Kevlar seat linings and ceramic inserts. "Bullet must've hit a spring or something and got deflected. I'm lucky like that."

"The gun you shot him with—"

"I lied to him. It's a car I use sometimes when I go undercover. I keep a gun under the seat."

"But . . ."

The elevator car jolted as Nick pressed the stop button on the panel. He turned, stepped in front of Shana, stroked her reddened cheek, brushed his thumb over the cut on her lip.

"I love you. I have always loved you, but you need to finally hear me when we get upstairs."

The tears began again, this time without a sound. Nick wiped them away. He kissed her forehead, stepped back, undid the stop button.

Inside his apartment, Shana ran into the bedroom and closed the door. Nick didn't follow. He poured her a large glass of Laphroaig and waited.

Twenty minutes later, she reappeared in an old, faded pair of Nick's blue-and-gold Xaverian High sweatpants and a Knicks T-shirt. Her hair was wet, her cheek was swollen, her lip was fat and her eyes red, and she was still the most beautiful woman he had ever seen. She was carrying the jeans and panties she had worn, bundled under her arm. Before Nick could move, she walked out the door. He heard the garbage chute open and close. She came back in, clothes no longer under her arm, and shut the door behind her. She leaned against it for support.

"Don't look at me," she said, but was the one to turn away.

He handed her the peaty single malt. "I'm going to clean up. I'll be back in a few minutes."

———

Nick came out to find Shana on his couch, staring out the window at the bridge. That view was why his uncle Kenny had bought the place. There were sights, like the Grand Canyon, the Chrysler Building, the Verrazzano Bridge encased in fog, that never got old. He hated thinking it but hoped this would be Shana's last time looking at the bridge through his window.

"More Scotch?" he asked, moving to the bar.

She didn't answer nor did she turn away from the window. "Tonight wasn't about undercover work, was it? Not your normal UC work. That man, Flannery—I heard what he said about the people who would be after him and about your bosses. I've been around you and your family long enough to know when people are speaking cop shoptalk." She turned, holding her empty glass out to Nick. "He wasn't talking about cop work."

"Remember our arguments about *won't* and *can't*?" He tilted the green bottle over the rim of her glass. "Do you understand now?"

"Yes and no." She took the Laphroaig in a single swallow. "I still don't understand what you're doing, but I see the danger."

He sat next to her on the couch. "Tonight you walked into it by chance. That was bad luck. Things like that happen, but like Flannery, there are people who would do the things he talked about to you and Becky. I can't let that happen."

"But why would—"

He grabbed her free hand and squeezed it. "I can't tell you. By telling you, I would put you in more danger than you were in tonight."

"You're hurting me, Nick."

He let go of her hand, kissed her palm. "I'm sorry."

"I'm sorry too. I have tried not to love you. I have tried to ignore you, to pretend you were a silly infatuation. In the brief periods we broke up before you went away, I tried fucking you out of my life. That only ever made it worse. I married Brad to punish you and punished myself instead. But I won't let Becky ever get near anything like what happened to me tonight."

"Good."

"Good!" Shana bolted up from the couch. "Becky's your daughter. Why don't you give this up, what you're doing, and make us a family?"

"It's already too late."

"How can that be?"

"I've done things that can't be taken back."

"Like . . ."

"Stop it!"

"No. Tell me or I will never let you be. And you know me, Nick. You are the only person who has ever really known me."

He hesitated, but she was right. He had to tell her something. "I've killed."

"In Afghanistan, I know, but—"

"In New York, last year. And *killed* is the wrong word. Murdered."

That got her attention. "Who?"

He shook his head. "No. It wasn't someone who fired first, not with bullets anyway."

"What does that mean?"

"He deserved it."

"Said who?"

"Said me."

Shana looked more horrified than she had when Flannery pressed the gun to her temple. She repeated, "Who was it?"

Nick knew she was looking for a way to give him an out, to rationalize it. If he gave her the name, she would forgive him. The man he had killed had earned the bullet Nick fired through his aorta. Problem was, Shana was never easily dissuaded. Her love for him was chronic.

"I don't care. If you say he deserved it—"

"Christ, Shana, stop it. Killing that man wasn't even the worst thing I've done."

"I don't care. I'm tired of fighting a battle I'll never win. Give it up, Nick. I have enough money for us and Becky to live anywhere forever. We'll go away somewhere none of this can touch us."

He stepped close to her. "There is no such place. If I've learned anything, it's that. You know me, Shana. I can't run. It's not in me."

Nick leaned over and kissed her softly. She took him by the hand and led him to the bed they had shared once a month for the past year. They wrapped themselves in darkness like the vampires they were. He took a moment to breathe her in, to be fully aware of her scent, the feel of her skin and hair. He needed to remember. The memory would have to last him the rest of his life.

FORTY-SIX

Shana's side of the bed was cool to the touch. She was gone. The tell-tale signs of her presence were not. The pillow was still damp from her wet hair and hollowed from where she had rested her head. The sheets where she had slept were ridged like a linen mountain range. Her scent lingered as a goodbye refrain. There would be no paper note. No text. No email. The last time he left her apartment before Afghanistan was the last time he had heard from her until the day, four years later, *he* walked back into *her* life. When she shut a door, she locked it. She would be safe. Becky would be safe. It wasn't all that mattered, but it was the most crucial thing.

Out of the shower, shaved, and dressed, he reached for the Joe phone. It buzzed in his hand before he could dial.

"I think you owe me an explanation." There was an unfamiliar edge in Joe's voice.

"I agree. How's Flannery?"

"Alive."

"You sound almost disappointed."

Joe hemmed and hawed. "Don't be ridiculous."

"Any details more than *he's alive*?"

"When you get here."

"Tire shop?"

"Yes. In an hour."

"I'll get there as soon as I can. With Ace out of action and both my cars out of commission, I've only got the Norton. Have some empanadas or arepas for me. I haven't eaten."

"I can do that."

Nick put his hand on the door, stopped. So much had happened in the past twenty-four hours that he hadn't had time to really consider who had made the phone call to Flannery about him. He knew that Flannery was well connected up and down the hierarchy of the city's rich and powerful, but Flannery had no reason to believe Marty Berg wasn't who he claimed to be. Besides, there were only a very few people in the entire city who knew about Nick's second job. Nick suspected United States Senator Renata Maduro knew. There were Ace and Mack, of course. He was aware that NYPD Chief of Detectives Joon and Martellus Sharp had their suspicions. None of them would have ratted him out even if their lives depended on it. That left a solitary candidate.

Nick turned, went into his spare bedroom office. He retrieved three pieces of paper: the one sheet from Flannery that he had held on to as leverage after the fake shooting outside L'Autobus, the one Mack had given to him at the Black Harp the night he went there with Victoria Lansdale, and the one with the phone number Lenny had culled from Flannery's cell phone. He spread the sheets out on his desk. His suspicions were confirmed. Just to make sure, he put a new SIM card in his phone and punched in the number. It rang three times before a man with a familiar voice answered. Nick hung up, replaced the new SIM card with the old. That done, he called to check on Vincent Gardi.

———

The noses of delivery trucks stuck out of loading bays all along the street. The smells from the body shop were strong in the air as he rolled the Norton slowly to the curb. There was an old Accord on a pneumatic jack in front of the shop. Nick nudged down the Norton's kickstand with the metal-lined toe of his Dainese boot.

Nick walked around the fat guy at the tire shop desk. He wasn't in a polite, ask-for-permission kind of mood. He knew that the men in Joe's little private NYPD army had orders not to fuck with him.

"Whatchu think you doin'?"

He ignored the man, looking under the counter at the closed-circuit monitor. One quadrant of the screen showed Joe where he always was: seated on a green plastic chair in the middle of the shop. Nick reached behind the screen and yanked the power cord out of the monitor, then got down on the floor and pulled the plug out of the socket. He stood up, taking the power cord with him. He turned to the desk man. "I'll bring this back when I'm done. Trust me, he doesn't want this on camera."

Inside, Nick threw the cord on the floor at Joe's feet. There was a round foil container with a clear top on Nick's plastic chair. Inside he saw two empanadas, a container of dipping sauce, and sour cream. He took the container off the chair, placed it on the floor. He turned the empty plastic chair next to Joe to face him, sat.

Joe looked at the cord, then back up at Nick. "Should I ask what the dramatics are about?"

"You won't have to."

"I ordered you pork and beef." Joe frowned when Nick put the food on the floor. "I thought you were hungry."

"But first . . ." Nick took out his cell phone, got to where Vincent Gardi's video confessions were stored, and hit Play. He handed the phone to Joe. "Watch and listen."

As Nick ate the empanadas, he watched Joe watching. He had gotten the answer, fulfilled the assignment, but it felt empty because there were only questions behind the answer. He knew who had killed Vlado Markovic. So what? He had only a vague notion why. *Why* mattered to him. Always had. Always would. Nick was curious whether Joe would be satisfied or if he would want to know why as well.

Joe looked over at Nick. "Do you believe this Gardi?"

"Hundred percent."

Joe didn't look pleased, hadn't looked pleased all through the viewing.

Nick said, "You were expecting a different result? Maybe one that didn't involve police corruption and another murder that's not even on the books?"

"Honestly, yes. But you did your job. Where is Gardi now?"

"Somewhere you can't touch him."

Joe smirked. "Come, now, Nick. You of all people should know how far our reach extends."

"Not far enough."

"Very well, you've got my attention. Where is Gardi that he can't be reached?"

"Hell is my best guess. He died last night. You heard him coughing. He had stage four lung cancer. Smoked three packs a day up until they put him in the hospice. Look at the fingers and nails on his right hand. Yellow."

"Shit!"

"No one says you have to tell the truth, right? Everyone believes the narrative that's already out there, that Markovic's murder was a matter of his being in the wrong place at the wrong time. Just go with that. You've been known to do it before."

"Not my decision to make," Joe said. "And what is that crack supposed to mean?"

"What *is* up to you? Who decides the things above your pay grade? Who knows about me, anyway?" Joe was caught off guard by that. He opened his mouth to answer, but Nick interrupted. "Hold that thought. Sorry, but there's a call I have to make first." Nick grabbed his cell phone from Joe's hand.

"Would you like me to leave?" Joe stood.

"No, no, stay." Nick waved him back down in his seat. "It's fine. This'll be quick."

Nick called a number he had called earlier that morning. A few seconds later, a phone rang in Joe's pocket. Joe ignored it, squirming in his seat. Nick's call went to voicemail. Nick stared directly at Joe.

"Joe, or should I say, William T. Patterson, attorney-at-law, this is Detective Nick Ryan Jr. Don't bother calling me back, because if you don't explain to me why you told Shea Flannery where to find me, I'm going to kill you." Nick clicked off, slipped the phone into his jacket pocket, and pulled the Glock off his hip. "Now do you understand the dramatics?"

"From the monitor at the front desk."

"Very good, Bill."

"You realize you won't get out of here alive if you harm me."

"That the best you can do?" Nick laughed. "You forget who you're talking to? There's a reason I have the job you gave me. They need me a lot more than they need you. If it came down to it, would they choose me or you? Now, make it good."

"Why should I bother?"

"Because you didn't only set me up to kill Flannery or have him kill me, but you nearly got someone I love killed. The first part, I can live with." Nick racked the slide of his 19. "The second part, not so much."

"Shana Carlyle?"

Nick shoved the Glock under Joe's chin. "Say her name again and those will be your last words."

"She wasn't meant to be there."

"How can you be so smart and so ignorant at the same time?" Nick shoved the gun harder into Joe's flesh. "I wasn't meant to spot those cars heading to Staten Island, but I did. There's no such thing as *meant to be*. If things went as they were meant to, the world wouldn't be half as fucked up as it is. Because it is, I have this job."

The man tried hard to be cool about it. Failed. Beads of sweat formed on his brow.

Nick pulled the gun away, tapped his watch crystal. "Joe, you want to die in silence, that's your choice."

He wiped his face with the sleeve of his six-thousand-dollar suit. "Joe? But you know who I am."

"I know you drive a Gullwing Mercedes and where you live and lots of stuff, but I'll always think of you as Joe. It's like when you go back to an old school to visit a teacher and she says to call her by her first name.

You can't do it. But while I can't bring myself to think of you as Bill, I *will* shoot you. Don't doubt it."

"How did you know?"

"Stalling won't help."

"I'm not stalling. I'm curious."

"Everyone gives themselves away. That warning about watching my back . . . that was a mistake. You've been acting hinky lately, distracted. You came to the meeting on Valentino Pier without backup. I knew something was going on."

"I'm sorry about Flannery."

"Apologies are empty things at best. When I had my gun to Ricky Corliss's head, he had the good grace not to try apologizing. That fucking guy, he told me how proud he was of doing what he did to those little boys. Told me he had made his mark in the world. That the world would forget his victims' names, forget my name, but not his."

Joe laughed. "He was right, though."

"Being right has its limitations. And you, Joe—will anyone remember you?"

"I suppose not. I have always been a facilitator, more the grease between the gears than the gears."

"Nice metaphor. I'll put it on your headstone."

Joe raised his palms in surrender. "Flannery was blackmailing me."

"I didn't figure it was a lovers' quarrel. Be careful, Joe. I know you and the truth have an interesting relationship, but everything you say now will determine your lifespan."

"Several years back, I did work for Flannery's union. Shea and I became . . . friendly. You know the man. Charm is his gift. Right after the financial meltdown, I was hurting."

Nick laughed. "*Hurting* means not being able to feed your family or heat your house, or losing your home. The wealthy people I knew back then said they were hurting too. They defined *hurting* as having to give up leasing their Gulfstream jet and flying commercial. I wasn't shedding any tears."

"Then you won't shed any for me. I'm not asking for your sympathy, but you asked for an explanation."

"You're not dead, right?"

"Flannery knew I was hurting and got me involved in a deal. The details aren't important, but a man like you can figure it out."

"Money laundering."

Joe looked sick. "For a Colombian cartel."

"You did well by it."

"Very. Numbers-matching Gullwing Mercedeses were expensive at auction even during Obama's first term. That was a toy. The money I made was serious money—solid-gold toilet, champagne, and truffle money."

"But . . ."

"Seven months ago, Flannery came back to me with a deal even I couldn't be part of. It would have destroyed whole neighborhoods in the city."

"I guess sometimes even the devil says no."

"He was going to give me up. I couldn't let that happen."

"You sent him my way figuring either I would kill him or he'd kill me. If I killed him, no problem. You could make that go away, even make me feel like I owed you. If he killed me, he'd be finished. He wouldn't live long in jail. Maybe someone would arrange for him to do a Jeffrey Epstein. Lawyer like you would have connections to make that happen. Maybe he'd actually kill himself after he killed me, to protect his family. Any way it would've worked out except the way it did. See what I mean by 'there's no such thing as *meant to be*'?"

"You've made your point."

"Now you won't be able to shut him up. The minute he gets into the system, you're screwed."

"*Screwed* seems a polite understatement for my situation."

"So all the work I did over the last few months setting Flannery up—that was for you?"

Now Joe looked even more uncomfortable than before. He bowed his head and whispered, "Yes."

"The money in the bank accounts—that was your own money, not the city's?"

Joe nodded.

Nick laughed.

That pissed Joe off. "What do you find so amusing?"

"Never mind. What are you going to do about Flannery?"

Joe shrugged. "You've put me in an untenable situation."

"I think you might want to rephrase that, Counselor. You put yourself there."

"I'm in it regardless."

"If I get you out of it, I'll own you," Nick said, holstering the 19. "You realize that?"

"You already have me at quite a disadvantage. Don't toy with me, Ryan."

"Not my style."

"It's not money you want," Joe said. "You have your own and you despise real wealth. It's not power either, is it?"

"Control."

"Of what?"

"I'm going to keep doing my job, but my way. You and me—no more secrets between us. No more you acting like I'm your poodle. When I get an assignment, I want to know why."

Joe looked sick. "I will try, but there are limits. I often don't know why exactly, or who is the beneficiary."

"A list of names of everyone who knows about me and what they know about me."

"Done."

"Ace is gone."

Joe smiled. "He was gone anyway. His shoulder is never going to heal right and he had run his course."

"No harm comes to him. Anything bad happens to him will happen to you."

"Understood."

"Vlado Markovic."

"What about him?"

"You don't go to the bosses until I know all the answers. Gardi, Lima, and Gabrelli aren't the answers I want."

"I can stall the bosses for a little while longer. How are you going to deal with Flannery?"

"I will need more money put into the bank accounts I used to set him up."

"How much?"

"I'll let you know and I need Flannery's location."

"Are you going to kill him?"

"You don't get to ask that question."

"Anything else?"

"It's a start."

Joe stood up. "Are we done?"

"For now."

"Nick, I am truly sorry about last evening. I was desperate."

"You should have just come to me. I would've helped you."

"For a price?"

"No. But even if it had been, it would have been cheaper than what you're paying now."

"All the should-haves in the world stacked one atop the other are worthless."

"I disagree. Should-haves are worth thinking about because there are always next-times."

Nick picked up the power cord and left.

FORTY-SEVEN

He rode over to the new Yankee Stadium. Stopped, swallowed some more Aleve. He hadn't let Joe see that he was still in a fair bit of pain from the crash and from his confrontation with Flannery. The ride to the Bronx on a finicky '70s-era motorcycle didn't do much to relieve the soreness. Events had taken on a momentum of their own, so that he hadn't had time to mourn the loss of the GTO. As a rule, Nick didn't invest himself in things. Things were replaceable. People were not. The GTO was different. Its loss was the loss of a connection to his uncle Kenny. That left only his condo and the damned Norton.

As he waited for the drugs to kick in, Nick looked at the empty stadium. He didn't much like it because it looked like the old stadium. As Joe had said to him last year, the Yankees—the richest, most successful franchise in baseball history—could never do something new. They were victims of their own legacy, forever tethered to the past. Nick understood there was a lesson in that for him. He just wasn't sure yet what it was. He'd ponder it some other time. Now he punched another newly memorized number into his cell phone.

"Hello, how may I be of assistance?" the electronically distorted voice answered.

"I don't know that you can be, Tuva."

"Nick Ryan." The distortion was replaced by her familiar flat, unaccented voice. "I was not expecting to hear from you so soon."

"I am glad to be able to surprise you."

"Small, pleasant surprises, yes. Never delude yourself that I will not see others coming."

"A threat?"

"A friendly warning." The small talk came to an abrupt end. "I believe the American expression is *the meter is running*. As much as I enjoy our chats, business is business."

Nick doubted the strict truth of that. He was sure Tuva's interest in him extended beyond money for services provided. This call, though, *was* about business.

"Can you disappear someone without . . ."

"The implication is clear to me. A rendering can be arranged, certainly. I would advise against it."

"Why?"

"Don't disappoint me, Nick. You know the reasons."

"Anyone who is still drawing breath is never truly disappeared."

"That is, perhaps, the most fundamental reason of all. There are others."

"Anything that involves more than one person increases the possibility of error or extortion or leakage."

"There is one other reason—a very basic one."

"It's more expensive."

She clapped her hands together loud enough for him to hear. "Nick, you see things so brutally clearly. Please stop pretending you are who you are not. Fully embrace your skills."

"Why does this matter to you?"

"My reasons are my own. One day, possibly, I will share them with you. Not yet."

"I need a fee structure for—"

"I will disappear the man permanently for no fee."

"That's not what I want. Why would you do that?"

"You still believe in choices and that you are, to use a quaint phrase, on the side of the angels. You are not. There are no angels and you were ferried across the River Styx long ago. Osman, the Afghani girl, knows that to be true. There are choices, indeed, but people like us know immediately which is the only real option. Because you still pretend and cling to your conscience, I will tell you that death is a better outcome than a rendering. This is true not only for you or who you represent, but for the target. What do you imagine this man or woman's life will be like in their new country? At best, it would be a transient life. At worst, and far more likely, it would mean rotting to death in a Mexican or Bulgarian prison, not cruising the Mediterranean."

Nick heard all of what she said, but was focused on one thing. "How do you know about the girl?"

"Someday, Nick, all will be revealed."

"I want a price."

"As you wish. Later today, look at your inbox."

He hung up. He was furious not because she was wrong, but because much of what she said was exactly right. He got on the bike and pointed it toward Long Island.

———

As he rode along the walls and fencing of the Lansdale estate, Nick thought it was more impressive in daylight than in the dark. Problem was, he was immune to being awed by wealth. His time with Shana had been an education in myriad ways. People in Nick's world aspired to wealth because they'd been sold the proposition that money was both an invulnerable fortress and a magic pill to salve all wounds. There was some truth in both notions, just not enough to make it worth Nick's while. Money by itself didn't make you detestable. Money was an amplifier. It exaggerated the good and bad in people. When a rich man's wife died, his tears were no less real than a poor man's.

Turning the Norton off Route 107 toward the imposing stone-and-wrought-iron entrance, Nick knew something was wrong even before he saw it. The right gate had been blown off two of its three hinges. Twisted and broken, it clung to verticality by habit. The left gate lay flat on the driveway surface. Nick looked up at the stone columns the gates had been mounted to. The lens on a CCTV camera atop the left column had been painted black.

Nick rolled the Norton between the neatly trimmed hedges and the perimeter wall. He took the 19 off his hip, racked the slide. He held the Glock in two hands as he moved slowly forward onto the grounds of the estate. He wasn't thirty feet in when he came across the first body. *Willoughby.* The retired Secret Service man's throat was a syrupy red gash. The blood spray farthest away from the body had already dried to rust on the trimmed grass alongside the driveway.

Nick knelt down. Didn't bother checking for a pulse. Willoughby's bloody gloved hands were up by his throat. They were stiff but not completely rigid, so rigor was either setting in or easing up. The wound to the dead man's throat was one long, very deep cut: arteries, veins, larynx, trachea taken care of quietly, efficiently, professionally. He checked the back of Willoughby's neck. No Petrovic slit. The retired Secret Service agent's P90 was slung over his shoulder. Nick sniffed the muzzle. The submachine gun hadn't been fired. The way he figured it, Willoughby must have been sent down to check out why the CCTV camera had malfunctioned. When he came down the driveway, the assailant came up on him from behind.

Nick stood. He ran up the long sloping driveway to the house. Whatever violence had taken place here was done with hours ago. As he got closer to the house, he came across two more bodies. Another of Carver's men—the man at the wheel of the Suburban who had driven Nick to the estate the first time—and a man dressed in matte black and a balaclava.

"Those guys in Williamsburg weren't fucking around," Nick said to himself aloud.

That was all the time he would take for reflection. He moved to the grand front entrance. At the open front door, he once again looked up at the glass-coffin light fixture overhead. It now seemed so much more appropriate than the first time he'd noticed it. At the base of the sweeping staircase, Nick found Carver and two more of his men. The eyes from the family portrait stared down at him as he checked all three for a pulse. Only Carver was still alive.

"What happened?" Nick asked, checking the lead security man's wounds. There were several. Carver's clothes were wet with blood.

"Early this morning. Team assault. Well planned. Gone. My men?"

"Willoughby's dead. The guy who drove me from Brooklyn and these two, also dead. One of theirs is dead. Where are the Lansdales?"

Carver said, "I'm cold."

"Where are the Lansdales?"

"The kids are safe. Out of town." Then Carver, choking on blood, said something that sounded like "Russel Bar."

"Who's Russel Bar?"

"Where, not who." Carver girded himself, straining. He shook his head furiously. "Ruffle Bar. Ruffle . . ." He coughed up blood, his body clenching. "Ruffle . . . like . . . feathers."

Before Nick could ask him another question, Carver went utterly limp. Nick ripped off the blood-wet clothing and began CPR. It was useless. Carver's heart had finished pumping forever.

Nick found a towel. With most of the blood off his hands, he called Lenny Feld, then 911.

FORTY-EIGHT

The Nassau PD detectives were less than pleased with Nick's narra-tive. He didn't blame them. His tale was sketchy at best and downright bullshit at worst. He didn't know Jonathan Lansdale. He had no idea who might have done this. The dead man by the driveway was named Willoughby. The dead guy in the entrance hall was named Carver. He didn't know the identities of the other dead men. He didn't know why the dead men were so heavily armed or where they had gotten their weapons.

"Is there anything or anyone you do know in this whole fucked-up mess, Ryan?" asked O'Mara, the lead detective.

"Look, I know you know about the son's kidnapping. I was one of the detectives at the scene of the rescue on Staten Island. The wife wanted to thank me, so I've been here once. The husband was away. He called the other day to ask to see me. My guess, he wanted to thank me in person. I know the husband was in finance. Maybe that's why he felt he had to have armed security guards."

O'Mara snorted. "Security guards, my ass. The dead guys weren't square badges or retired cops."

Nick shrugged, feigning ignorance. "What were they, ex–Special Forces, Blackwater types?"

"Try retired Secret Service."

"You're shitting me."

"Nope. The minute we called in the identities of Carver and Willoughby, we got warned by the brass to keep this quiet. The FBI and Secret Service jokers will be here soon. Let's see if they believe that crock of shit you tried feeding us."

"Whatever."

Nick knew he had to get out of there. Once the feds arrived, he would be trapped, maybe for days. He didn't have days.

"Hey, O'Mara, I've got to hit the head."

O'Mara gave him a dismissive wave. "Use one of the bathrooms downstairs. Forensics hasn't cleared the upstairs yet. Wait a second."

"What?"

"You didn't stumble across any bodies up there, did you?"

"You being funny?"

"Christ, Ryan. Look how big this place is."

"No. No other bodies."

"You gave your comparison prints to the forensics people?"

"Yes. Can I go now?"

Nick had two options for escape, neither very appealing. He could try to get to the Norton, which was pretty well hidden behind the hedge near the front gate. The alternative was to get off the property and Uber it back to Brooklyn. The Norton was closer, but the front of the estate was swarming with official vehicles and uniforms. The estate was at least five acres and surrounded by six-foot-high walls. Even if he got over the wall, he'd be trespassing on another five-acre estate. He was sure to show up on that estate's security cameras.

Nick walked past the bathroom door, turned right, and found his way out the back onto the three-tiered deck. Scanning the stone patio below, the pool area, riding stables, corral, and the two acres of rolling hills, he decided to try to get to the Norton. Off the deck, he walked along the perimeter wall. Out of sight, at the far right corner of the property, he had another choice to make. He could climb the wall, work his way between the hedge and the outside of the wall until he got to the motorcycle. He thought he could probably make it to the Norton but didn't like his chances from there. He wasn't up for a high-speed chase. No, he had to give himself a good head start.

Nick strode right up to the gate. The uniform manning the crime scene tape wasn't one of the guys who were first on the scene. He wouldn't recognize Nick. The responding officer was still up at the house, being debriefed by a detective.

"Detective Ryan, NYPD," Nick said, showing his shield to the uniform at the tape.

The young cop looked a bit confused. *What was the NYPD doing here?* It didn't hurt Nick's cause that there was a distracting flurry of activity in close proximity. The crime scene unit and bomb squad were working on the gate. A crowd had formed and a local news truck was just pulling up. The uniform kept alternating his gaze between the crowd, the other cops, and Nick.

"Listen, O'Mara told me to tell you the FBI and some other feds would be here soon and not to give them any grief. Just make them give you their names, shield numbers, and let them pass." Nick put a reassuring hand on the uniform's shoulder. "I've got to get back to the city. My bike's over here. Do me a favor and clear some of these people back."

"Sure, no problem."

Nick walked past him, rolled the Norton out of the hedges, and started it up.

"Thanks, Officer," Nick said before slipping on his helmet. Helmet on, he saluted the kid and took off.

Nick didn't doubt that the young cop would get reamed for letting him leave, but the kid would survive and learn. Nick made a mental note of the kid's name. He'd make it up to him somehow. In that moment, he thought of Shana. How she understood everything about him except his instinct for the little guy and the lost. He fought hard against the desire to be with her again. He didn't bother fighting thoughts of her. That was a battle he could never hope to win. He wasn't even sure he wanted to.

FORTY-NINE

It was startling even to Nick how he could read a face as wrecked as Lenny Feld's. But one look at Lenny as he came through the basement door of the synagogue told Nick there was serious trouble ahead.

Lenny gave it voice. "What have you gotten yourself into this time?"

Nick closed the black steel door behind him, shutting out the remaining daylight. "I was hoping you could help me with that."

"Come."

He followed Lenny into his high-tech monk hovel, sat on the metal chair as always. Lenny walked back and forth in front of him.

"You going to stop pacing? You're making *me* nervous."

"You should be nervous."

Nick shrugged. "Nassau PD's looking for me. I know. Big deal."

"They're the least of your worries. There's a federal warrant for you."

"That's not good. They'll just get in the way."

Lenny Feld shook his head. "When I think I am getting a handle on who you are, you prove it is impossible to actually know anyone. You kill a man—men—and show up here the next day as if nothing had happened. Now I tell you the federal government is after you and you act as if I told you the teacher gave you an A instead of A-plus."

"We've talked about this. It's how I'm built, Lenny. How would my acting guilty or frightened change anything? When I pulled you out of the fire, I was scared, sure, but I couldn't give in to it. If you give in to your feelings, it paralyzes you. It doesn't mean I don't feel things. It means I won't surrender to them."

Lenny twisted up his mouth, gave a last skeptical shake of his head. "When you called you asked about Ruffle Bar."

"I did. What the hell is it?"

"Interestingly, it's part of Brooklyn."

"Lenny, I've lived in Brooklyn my whole life. I know every neighborhood from Vinegar Hill to Sea Gate and—"

"Well, I should have said part of Brooklyn and *apart* from it. It's a tiny one-hundred-and-forty-acre island in Jamaica Bay. I don't know why it should be of any interest. No one lives there any longer."

Nick dug out his cell phone and got to Vincent Gardi's confessions. He played it so that Lenny Feld could see and hear it.

Some little island in Jamaica Bay I'm thinkin', 'cause I can see the lights on the Gil Hodges Bridge.

Lenny nodded when Nick hit Pause. "I'd say that would be quite a coincidence if he was speaking of *another* of those islands in Jamaica Bay."

Nick said, "What about Lansdale?"

"Even more interesting."

"How's that?"

"I think he used to work for the government."

"Work?"

"Intelligence work."

"Based on what? Intuition?"

"Let's say intuition plus experience." Lenny winked with his good eye. "When my hobby was disproving conspiracy theories, especially those involving government figures, I would come across certain pro forma backstories in my research. They were bios that seemed detailed, but when I delved into those details, I would hit a wall. Behind the wall, a series of facts that wouldn't stand up to careful scrutiny. The problem being, it fed the fires of conspiracy theorists."

"How's that?"

"Because if you're prone to believe in conspiracies and you distrust the government . . ."

"I get it, Lenny. They discover those phony cover backstories and it allows them to weave whatever convoluted narrative suits their predetermined conclusion."

"Exactly."

"Lansdale."

"In the nineties, his business activities seemed to coincide directly with the conflicts involving our troops. In 'ninety to 'ninety-two, he was in Turkey. His firm was allegedly helping to privately finance a dam very near the Iraqi and Syrian borders. Mysteriously, the dam was never built. From 'ninety-five to two thousand, he moved around—Italy, Greece, and Romania. All countries close to the Balkans. Again, inexplicably, none of the projects his company was considering financing got built. In 2001, when you would have thought his service would be highly valued, his shadowy government activities seemed to come to an end."

"Interesting, but—"

"Let me finish, Nick. It was after Nine-Eleven that Lansdale's wealth took an exponential leap. He formed a new firm, of which he was president and CEO. Suddenly, those projects and businesses his new firm financed got built and prospered. The man now has nearly a billion dollars in assets."

"His wife said he came from money."

"Not that kind of money. To be old-fashioned about it, his family was well-to-do, not wealthy. He had the classic intelligence background. Brilliant, a facility for languages. Yale undergrad. Skull and Bones. Kennedy School at Harvard, MBA from Wharton . . ."

Nick half-whispered, "I was right."

"About?"

"Money. This is about money. Somehow there is a confluence between Vlado Markovic's wartime activities, Jimmy Gabrelli's air force service, their subsequent murders, and Jonathan Lansdale's bank account. All of it, all the violence, and Franjo Petrovic—it's all one thing."

"I'd like to see you sew that string of beads together."

"Watch me."

Lenny Feld's face lit up with excitement. It didn't go unnoticed.

"No, Lenny, you can't come." Nick stood, put his hand on his friend's shoulder. "This is going to be dangerous. It already is. Besides, you know what happens to you when you get worked up. You can barely breathe."

Lenny bowed his head, the excitement gone. "I know, Nick. I know."

"I've got to go."

Smiling, Feld wagged his stumped fingers at Nick. "If you get killed, don't come back here."

Nick laughed. "Believe me, pal, your anger scares me more than Franjo Petrovic."

"Good. Now, get out of here and string those beads together."

Nick left and didn't look back. He had a lot of calls to make, a lot of juggling to do. No matter how skillfully he managed to keep the balls in the air, he knew there would be blood. He was trying to make sure it wouldn't be his.

———

Mack met Nick on the corner of Ocean Avenue and Emmons Avenue in Sheepshead Bay. Sheepshead Bay was where the Atlantic Ocean sneaked around the back of Manhattan Beach. Across the avenue, the fishing boats that hadn't yet headed south bobbed gently on the oil-sheened water. Although the bay was cleaner than it used to be, it stank of gutted fish and dirty water in Nick's memory. Tony Angelo used to take him and Sean fishing for porgies and blues when they were kids. When the boat came back in, the crew would sell the catch from the dock. As an added bit of irony, Vicky Lansdale had grown up less than a mile from where they stood.

Mack, a good thirty pounds overweight and twenty years past his prime, bounced on the balls of his feet as Nick approached. He seemed less like a performer than when he was dispensing bourbon and blarney across a bar top. He had always protested to Nick that he hadn't realized what he was getting into working for the Brits in the North all those years ago.

"Them fookers were full of promises about what the job would encompass. When it came to the skin of it, I was already wading bollocks deep in the shite. On a one-way street I was, with no hope of turning me arse about. To use the quaint Mafia phrase, after I made me bones, they had me. So when they gave me the order, I said yes, sir, may I have another."

As with much of what Mack said, Nick ran it through his bullshit machine. In the same way he could see the trouble in Lenny's face, he could read the excitement in Mack's body language. Last year, Mack had the chance to run, to start another new life, one that would have left Nick dead. With Nick dead, Mack's trail would have gone ice cold. But Mack had stayed, helping save Nick's life in the process. The truth was, Mack was addicted to the action, the adrenaline rush. He may not have loved what his old job entailed, but even if it meant killing, it made him feel alive.

When Mack extended his hand for a shake, Nick put a .40 Beretta in it.

"Is it to be that sort of evening?" The excitement in Mack's voice was palpable.

"That's backup," Nick said. "If the delivery goes as promised, there'll be heavier equipment waiting for us. Come on across the street."

Both men scanned the area as they crossed Emmons Avenue to where the boats were docked at angles to the sidewalk. Though he could see no one, Nick could not escape the feeling they were being followed.

"Do you see anyone?" he asked Mack.

"You sense it too? Aye, there's someone out there in the shadows. Have you an idea who it might be?"

Nick lied, "Not a clue. Just know we've got to watch our backs."

Mack might not quite believe him, but he was too juiced to care.

They walked about fifty yards toward the mouth of the bay, stopping at the rear of a fishing boat. Dubbed *Merry Mermaid III*, she was painted white with black striping circling the upper deck. She was sturdy looking but a decade past her prime. Her engines were idling and the smell of exhaust fumes filled the air. If Nick had had the luxury of time, he might have chosen differently.

He urged Mack ahead. "Let's go."

At an opening in the railing, a metal gangway extended from the boat to the pier. Above them, on the upper deck above the gangway, stood a gnarled man, his face covered in gray stubble.

"That you, Ryan?" the man called down to him.

Nick skipped the banter. "Permission to come aboard."

"Permission granted."

Nick and Mack walked up the gangway. A crewman pulled the gangway up, replaced the railing.

"Captain says to go up to the bridge. He says to tell you your cargo is aboard. In there." The crewman nodded to the lower-deck cabin.

Nick was acquainted with Captain Railsback from the Quarterdeck, a dive bar in Gerritsen Beach that catered to the crews of the local fishing boats. The "Deck" was the place Nick's brother, Sean, would turn up after one of his inevitable falls off the wagon.

Railsback, a chewed cigar stuck in the corner of his mouth, turned to Nick and Mack when they got to the bridge. "The job is that I take you within paddling distance of Ruffle Bar. From there you're on your own. All I do is anchor and wait."

Nick nodded. "Those are the terms of the charter. Half the money's already in your account."

"Ruffle Bar—why the fuck you wanna go there? Nobody's lived there since the forties."

Nick never felt the need to explain himself. "Just do what you've been paid to do."

"Your funeral."

"Jesus wept. You're a cheery bastard, ain't ya?"

Railsback spat at Mack's feet. "Your equipment's down below."

"Remember, running lights and engines off when we get in the vicinity of the island." Nick signaled for Mack to go ahead. When Mack was out of earshot, Nick stuck his hawkbill knife under Railsback's neck. "Don't fuck up or the funeral will be yours."

FIFTY

Nick and Mack slipped into their night camo, black-and-gray tactical pants and shells. Put on their body armor. Laced up their waterproof LaCrosse boots. Covered their faces in black-and-green camo paint. Nick handed Mack his night-vision goggles.

"Know how to use these?"

Mack was annoyed at the question. "What do ya think?"

Nick took a long look at Mack and failed to stifle a laugh.

"What do ya find so amusing, Ryan? I mean, if ya don't mind me asking."

"You make a fine camouflaged bearded bowling ball."

"Well, boyo, you just watch me when the shite hits the fan and ya'll see what this bearded bowling ball is capable of. And, Christ, Ryan, why a *fishing* boat? The stink of a year's catch in here is enough to make a man gag."

"That's my cologne."

They both laughed too loudly. This banter was an unfortunately familiar ritual to them both. It was a pattern that reached as far back in history as the first time men went into battle. Humor to release tension, a final check of equipment, then the silence of warriors alone with their thoughts.

They loaded high-capacity mags into their M4s, slipped them into plastic bags to protect the rifles from the salt water when they paddled over to Ruffle Bar from the *Merry Mermaid III*. They checked their sidearms and marine combat knives.

Mack asked, "How'd ya manage all this?"

"Joe."

"The lawyer in the Gullwing?"

"Let's say he's very amenable to my requests these days."

"Whatever."

The engines slowed. They were passing directly beneath the Gil Hodges Memorial Bridge that connected Brooklyn to the Rockaways. They heard traffic noise from above as they glided beneath the center section of the vertical-lift bridge. To Nick, the bridge had always looked like a large-scale model of a kid's metal Erector Set creation—a mass of towers, girders, and rivets. They heard the rush of air from the canisters the crewman was using to inflate their small Zodiac boat. Then a splash as the Zodiac hit the water.

Captain Railsback's voice came over the speaker. "We're only a few minutes out."

Nick pointed to the mic strapped to Mack's shoulder. They tested the system. Nick checked the power light on the handheld he would give to Railsback. When they were sure the system worked, they looked at each other, nodded, gave each other the thumbs-up.

The rumble of the engines stilled as they left the bridge behind them. They were drifting, and the only noise came from a jet passing overhead on the glide path to JFK. The *Merry Mermaid III* went completely dark.

Railsback's voice filled the lower-deck cabin. "I can make out another vessel anchored just inside the island's only small inlet. The aft extends out into the bay. Looks to be a private yacht. She's a beaut too—big, a top-of-the-line—but that's all I can tell from here."

Nick pressed the intercom button. "Can you read the name?"

"*Victoria Four*, in gilded roman numerals."

Nick remembered Gardi's mention of the boat he saw when he and

Gabrelli were at Ruffle Bar two decades back. He'd mentioned being able to make out part of the name of the boat. *Vic something.*

I'm guessing Victory . . .

"No, Vincent," Nick whispered, "it was *Victoria*." Then he was back on the intercom. "Scan the island. Let me know if you can make out any activity."

"What was that, Ryan?" Mack cocked his head.

"Nothing. Just a message to a dead man."

If Mack thought about asking Nick to explain, he needn't have. The captain's voice filled the cabin.

"I see one man. I think he's carrying a rifle, but it's impossible to be sure."

Nick said, "That's it?"

"All I can see."

"I'm going to give your crewman a handheld to give you after we shove off for the island, so you can communicate with us. Once I tell you to end communication, don't come back on no matter what. Can't let you give our position away. Understood?"

"Yeah, yeah. You guys better get going. You got some paddling to do. No activity there. The dark and topography should give you cover."

"Thanks."

On the aft deck, Nick gave the crewman the handheld and instructed him to bring it to Railsback. The crewman hung a small ladder off the port side of the *Merry Mermaid III*.

"I'll pull the Zodiac's line so that you can climb down onto her," said the crewman. "I'll hand down the oars and your equipment."

Nick and Mack flipped down their night-vision goggles, adjusted them, then climbed down into the Zodiac. The crewman handed them their rifles and two oars. When he was sure they had what they needed, Nick cut the nylon line that tethered the little rigid assault craft to the fishing boat. He pushed away with the oar.

———

The smell of the ocean and rotting marsh vegetation was strong in the air as they approached Ruffle Bar. Mack was breathing heavily, black-and-green camo sweat dripping down his cheeks, straining as they paddled close to the shore.

Nick turned back, said, "What was that you said about showing me your stuff when the shit hit the fan?"

"If I could feckin' breathe, I'd have a witty retort for ya."

Nick raised his hand, signaling for Mack to stop rowing. "Do you hear that?"

"All I can hear is me heart about to explode."

"What's that sound?"

"I don't hear anything."

Nick didn't like it, but they were committed. He leaped out of the Zodiac as they got close to the shore, and tugged on what was left of the nylon tether. Mack got out as well. They pulled the black Zodiac up onto shore, dragging it inland above the high-tide mark.

Mack lay on his back, catching his breath. Nick combat-crawled over the rocky ground, up a low dune. Peering through grass and brown fescue, he saw the *Victoria IV* rocking in the water. Light came through a sleek cabin window on her port side. He recognized the man doing guard duty on the shore as one of Carver's men who had shown up outside Nick's apartment the night he and Vicky Lansdale were attacked in Williamsburg. He figured there was probably another of the retired Secret Service men on board. Given what had gone down in Old Brookville, Nick supposed these guys were either extremely well paid or loyal to a fault. Although he thought they could handle the situation, Nick could not escape the feeling there was something at the very outer bounds of his senses alerting him to trouble.

He turned, scanned across the water at Breezy Point, at the tip of Rockaway. There was light coming from the houses there, but not much noise. Looking behind him, he saw the *Merry Mermaid III* sitting still in the Jamaica Bay waters. Focused beyond the *Victoria IV*, he saw Howard Beach and the many-colored lights at JFK. Unable to shake his sense that there was unseen danger waiting out there in the dark, he crawled back down the dune to Mack.

Nick said, "You ready to show me your stuff?"

"Lead on, Macduff."

"It's '*Lay* on, Macduff.'"

"Are you seriously giving me a fookin' literature lesson here, now?"

They'd discussed their plan of attack while rowing to the island, had worked out what to do if things didn't go as expected. A ragged diamond in shape, Ruffle Bar was relatively flat with only a gradual rise at the center of the island. Its shoreline was sandy and rocky in places, covered in grasses and fescue elsewhere. None of it afforded a man much cover. Mack got to his knees, crouched, ready to head into the fescue and come at the *Victoria IV* from the opposite direction as Nick. Just as Mack put one foot forward, Nick grabbed his arm.

"Remember, don't kill him. He's just doing his job."

"And if the bastard starts blasting away?"

"You'll make sure that doesn't happen." Nick let go of Mack's arm.

Waiting for Mack to get into position, Nick thought he heard that distant sound again. Louder now, it was still indistinct. Two minutes later, Mack keyed his mic twice. That was Nick's signal to move. He didn't hesitate, combat-crawling along the shore toward the inlet where the *Victoria IV* was anchored. When he was about fifty yards from where Carver's man stood guard, Nick rolled out of sight into the grasses and called out, "Help me!"

The guard looked up, raised his weapon. That was all the distraction Mack needed. By the time Nick got there, the guard was disarmed, unconscious, with his hands and feet zip-tied behind him.

Nick gave Mack the thumbs-up. "How'd you manage it?"

"When he comes to, he'll have a wee bruise on the back of his head."

Nick pointed at the yacht, using his hands to indicate how they would board the vessel from opposite sides. Mack nodded. As Nick had anticipated, there was another of Carver's men aboard the *Victoria IV*. When he stepped out on deck, P90 raised, things went to shit all at once.

FIFTY-ONE

Before Nick could speak, before Mack could move, a gun barked in the darkness behind them. A stream of bullets whistled over their heads. All hit their target. Carver's man bounced back against the cabin, caromed forward, and toppled over the railing into the shallows with a faint splash. A faint splash, Nick thought, was no way for a man to die. Night-vision goggles didn't show crimson, but he was certain the waters of Jamaica Bay were redder than they had been only seconds before. As Nick turned behind him to locate the shooter, Railsback keyed the mic.

"Shit, Ryan, there's a Zodiac approaching from the east. It's still distant, but I'm pretty sure she's coming your way. Over."

"Roger that. Stay in position. Over and out."

Turning back to Mack, Nick saw that he wouldn't have to work hard to locate the shooter. The shooter had located him. Nick raised his night goggles.

The man stood six feet behind them. His HK417 assault rifle was equipped with a nightscope and sound suppressor. The muzzle was aimed at Mack. He was outfitted much like Mack and Nick, body armor included. He too had on night-vision goggles, now raised. His face was painted green and black. Despite it all, Nick recognized him immediately.

"Franjo Petrovic."

Petrovic's smile was cold as the night air. "Very good, Nick Ryan." Without a second's hesitation, he pointed the HK away from Mack and fired a three-round burst into the zip-tied man, one of the bullets to the head. "Do I need to explain anything to you and your man?" Petrovic's accent was distinct, but his English was perfect.

In war, Nick had seen too many innocent people killed for nothing. He wanted to rip Petrovic's heart out for killing a helpless man, to say nothing of what he had done to the Angelos. But Nick knew he had to remain as cool as Petrovic's smile.

"My partner's name is Mack." As he said it, he wondered how Petrovic had found them. Before he could ask, Mack spoke.

"*Dobra večer.*"

Petrovic's smile broadened. "Good evening to you, Irishman. You speak a little of many languages, I suspect. As do I. But these techniques to humanize yourselves for me are a waste of our time. What I have just done to the guard should prove to you as much."

"What you did to my uncle Tony and his wife proved that to me."

"Like the others, he was scum who took money to cover up a murder." Petrovic's voice shook with anger. "They all knew their time would come to pay. For the wife—for her death, I am sorry. She left me no choice by coming to look for the husband."

"Why should you care about the murder of a little man like Vlado Markovic?"

"Because he was a connection to the things that happened in my village. This *little man*, as you call him, killed my family. They tortured my father in front of them. Then they killed them all." Petrovic leaned over and spat. "Murdering pigs!"

Nick was finally beginning to see how this might all fit together.

Captain Railsback keyed the mic again. "Ryan, the Zodiac is getting closer. Four men, armed. Over."

"Over and out." Nick turned back to Petrovic. "You heard?"

"These men are former SDB, Serbian State Security. They are here for the money. Yes, let them come. Maybe then, after, you will live."

Petrovic was using the cruelest of human weapons—hope. Nick knew he was lying. Liar or not, Petrovic had given him time to play it out. He couldn't just give in. He had to act as expected.

"Fuck you. You're going to kill us, kill us. Then those assholes on the Zodiac can kill you."

But instead of losing his temper, Petrovic laughed, spoke over his left shoulder. "Come out of the night, my new friend."

Another man Nick recognized stepped forward. "Hi, Nick."

"Lenny!"

"I'm sorry, Nick. You didn't want me here, but this gentleman had other ideas."

Petrovic pointed the HK away from Mack, putting the suppressor to Lenny's stub of an ear. His voice again went cold. "He was very brave, this man. I can be persuasive. You will help now?"

Nick nodded. "What do you need?"

"You, Irishman, get Lansdale and the wife off the boat and bring them to cover. In the middle of this island is what remains of an old house. Do it now!" Mack took a step. "Stop. Put your M4 down. You may keep your sidearm."

"Are you feckin' mad? How's one man going to protect anyone against an assault team with a sidearm, forty caliber or not?"

"You are resourceful, no? In any case, if these men get past us, it won't much matter. Now, go!" Mack didn't hesitate and climbed aboard the yacht with surprising agility. "Lenny, you will please pick up the weapon and give it to me."

Lenny looked to Nick. Nick nodded. Lenny picked up the M4, handed it to Petrovic. Petrovic slung it over his shoulder.

Thirty seconds later, a visibly shaken Vicky Lansdale and her smug-looking husband appeared on deck, Mack holding the Beretta to Jonathan Lansdale's back. Vicky Lansdale peered over the railing and gasped at the sight of the dead man lying face down in the shallows. She looked up. "Nick!"

"Go with Mack and do what he says."

"Yes," Petrovic said. "Do what the man says and you, at least, will live." He pointed the HK at Jonathan Lansdale. "You have much to answer for. I should kill you now, but that would be too easy. Go!"

Railsback keyed the mic. "They're coming ashore."

Lenny started wheezing, his breathing labored.

Nick said, "Let him go with Mack or you might as well kill us both here. Let him go, give him Mack's M4, and I'll do what you ask. I give you my word."

Nick knew that Petrovic knew he wasn't bluffing. He handed the M4 to Lenny. "Go! Go with them." As Lenny struggled to catch up, Petrovic said to Nick. "If you think that killing me will solve your problem, you are wrong. Those men want Lansdale and will leave no witnesses."

FIFTY-TWO

Petrovic flipped down his goggles, knelt by the dead guard, and cut the zip ties. "Put him in prone shooting position. I will do the same with the other one."

Nick didn't hesitate. He rolled the dead man over, put a piece of driftwood under his chin to prop up his wrecked head, and used wet sand and stones to hold the P90 upright in front of the body. He looked over his shoulder to see that Petrovic had done much the same with the other dead guard, only nearer the yacht.

"Ryan." It was Railsback. "They came around the island and are heading your way. They're getting close to where you landed. They'll be on you soon. Over." Nick noticed Petrovic listening intently.

"Okay, when you see them approaching the yacht, key the mic and scream my name into it. Over."

"Are you fucking crazy? Over."

"Roger that. Just do it! Over and out."

Nick removed the mic from his shoulder and placed the rig on the dead guard he had fixed up in shooting position.

"You are good, Ryan," Petrovic said with admiration in his voice. "You could be quite good at my profession."

"Seems to be the prevailing view." Nick pointed at a spot on the opposite side of the inlet. "I'll go there. You go—"

"Understood, Ryan. We set up a killing zone between us. We can fire at will without shooting at one another." Petrovic's voice became very grave. "These are skilled men. Look for two to circle around. Maybe they too come at us from the water. But I will finish them."

"Why are you so sure?"

"They come for money. I come for blood."

With that, Petrovic took off past the prow of the *Victoria IV*. Nick headed into the water. Anyone coming near the perimeter of the yacht would be caught in their crossfire.

Though he had felt the chill of the water as he and Mack pulled their boat ashore on Ruffle Bar, it was something different to submerge his legs and part of his abdomen in it. The burning and numbness set in after only a few seconds. It could get incredibly cold in the Afghan mountains, the winds cutting right through him. This was a whole other level of freezing. Waiting for the battle to begin was always the worst part. Once he was in it, he was in it. As he explained to Shana one night a few months back, "You don't know the meaning of being in the moment until you've been in battle."

Nick calmed himself, slowing his breathing, ignoring the cold. Like a sound engineer canceling background noise, he took in the rhythm of the lapping water, the rush of the wind, the hum and whine of passing jets, until they vanished from his consciousness. With them filtered out, he became aware of the soft shushing sound of a body crawling along wet sand. He moved his finger away from the trigger guard onto the trigger. All the sounds he heard previously were the types of calming sounds to put someone to sleep for the night. Soon, Nick knew, the sounds would change to those that would put someone to sleep forever.

Railsback keyed the mic. "Ryan! Ryan!" he screamed and kept screaming, "Ryan! Ryan!"

The night exploded in a cacophony of coughs of muted gunfire and muzzle flashes. Ten yards in front of Nick a man stood up out of the darkness and fired a short burst into the body of the propped-up guard. Nick fired four rounds into him: two high, two low. The man gasped, falling back on his heels.

Two broken strings of bullets came out of the night from different directions, both aimed at where Petrovic had gone into the water. Night-vision goggles lent a sense of unreality to things. In a firefight, hot rounds looked like streams of shooting stars against a grainy green background. Nick pulled himself out of the water, located one of the two remaining shooters. Fired. Petrovic fired too. So many rounds filled up the air, it was impossible to be certain who had put down the two men firing at them. What was certain was that after fifteen seconds, the firing had ceased, and no more shooting stars came from where the attackers had stood. They weren't all dead, though. The sounds of gunfire had been replaced by moaning and pleas for help. Nick didn't have to speak their language to understand.

Nick watched Franjo Petrovic crawl out of the water from a spot several yards away from where he had initially entered. Petrovic got to his knees behind a low grass-covered dune, scanned the night, stood. One by one, he paid visits to the three downed shooters. Petrovic's voice carried on the wind as he knelt by the wounded Serbs. Nick didn't understand the words, but he knew Petrovic was interrogating them. Questions answered or unanswered, Nick understood what Petrovic did next. With cruel, cold efficiency, he stuck his combat knife into the first two wounded men. When he was done with them, the night was quiet once again. Petrovic dropped to his knees by the shooter Nick had taken down, felt for a pulse. Apparently finding none, he wiped the blade on the man's sleeve and put the knife back in its sheath on his belt.

"This one is dead. Come out, Ryan."

Nick emerged from the water, his legs stiff and slow to respond. "What now?"

"I'm afraid we have been outmaneuvered. Their commander used them to draw our fire and distract us while he tracked the others."

"The B Team."

"What is the B Team?"

"If their commander is the man I think he is, he was happy to sacrifice these men. You can count. Four men on the Zodiac. Three dead here."

"I can count." Petrovic wasn't smiling now. "You heard the screaming?"

"I heard."

"What I did to them—it produces the truth better than a talk to God. No man wants to go into the next life or the grave less than a man."

Nick mumbled, "You do like playing with your prey."

"What?"

"Never mind. Okay, we've been outmaneuvered. What next?"

"You disappoint me, Ryan."

"Fuck you."

"Much better," Petrovic said. "What do we do? We wait."

"You said this was about money for them. What money?"

Petrovic laughed. "Do you think what went on in our countries in the nineties was only about the dissolution of Yugoslavia, about old hatreds and grudges? That is like saying the Crusades were only about religion. Hatred, yes, but plunder too. There is a long, sad history of resentment and rivalry in our part of the world that over the centuries has taken on a life of its own. Momentum, Ryan. History is about momentum as much as anything."

"Like World War One."

"Exactly. The match might have been lit in Sarajevo, but the mass of history pushed the world into war. Once it began, it took the weight of forty million bodies to stop it, and not even then. It slowed it, but momentum pushed the world into a second war."

"You're pretty philosophical for a professional killer."

"What has one to do with the other? All of us have done things to be ashamed of. All of us have blood beneath our fingernails."

"The money," Nick prompted.

"In the case of my village, gold."

"Gold?"

"You know about Croatia during the Second World War?"

"The Ustaše. I've heard."

"Ugly things, terrible things were done to the Jews and Roma, of course, but mostly to the Serbs. Even more than the Hungarians, the fascists in my country were eager to please their Nazi masters and to— what is the American phrase?—settle old scores. After the war, there were wild rumors in all the occupied and Axis countries about where the Germans had hidden their stolen gold. On sunken barges in mountain lakes. In railroad cars hidden in caves. In hollow V-Two rockets buried in farmers' fields."

"Some did turn up."

"In Swiss banks eventually. Where was the rest of it? How much was there? No one I knew believed these rumors. I know my family didn't. But when Zmaj and the others looked to bury the dead of my village—"

"They found gold."

"Ironic, no? They found enough to make a few men rich, but it did not come without problems. Gold is not like diamonds. It is heavy and not so easily crossed over borders and oceans."

"They needed help."

"A special type of help."

Suddenly, it all made a perverse kind of sense to Nick. "Help, as in someone with diplomatic privileges and someone who could get cargo on an air force transport."

"You are forgetting the most important element of all: the catalyst. A little man with a guilty conscience who wanted to forget his past and make a new life in America."

"Vlado Markovic."

"Just so."

"I don't know why I should tell you this, but Zmaj has been dead since September 2001. He was killed by the same men who murdered Markovic. They picked him up at the airport." Nick pointed toward the maze of colored lights of JFK in the distance. "Murdered him when he got off his flight, then cut him in pieces and made him fish food."

Petrovic hung his head, gut-punched at having been robbed of his revenge. "You lie."

"You know I'm not."

After that, there were several minutes of uncomfortable silence. The silence was broken by the sound of four loud, distinct gunshots.

Petrovic smiled and said, "Our waiting is over."

FIFTY-THREE

Nick took off running in the direction of the gunshots. As he ran, he heard the crackle of the mic rigged to the dead guard. Railsback's voice was recognizable, his words indistinct. Petrovic called after Nick.

"Don't be so foolish, Ryan. Stop!"

It was moot. Nick liked Vicky Lansdale well enough. Didn't give a shit about her husband. Mack and Lenny were his responsibility. They were in this because of him. He would get them out or die trying. When the night began, he had been confident that his planning would allow for variations on the theme. Battle was jazz, not Beethoven. There was a score to play, but you had to be flexible, had to be able to adjust to the unexpected.

After his initial sprint, Nick slowed, stopped, returning to his calm self. Crouching, flipping his goggles back down, scanning, he let his mind work through the scenarios of who might have been on the receiving end of those four gunshots. Lenny's death would be a kind of deliverance, a release from the physical pain and disfigurement he suffered through with every labored breath. Lenny wouldn't see it that way. For him, the worst pain was not knowing who had torched his house and killed his wife and daughter. Nick had selfish reasons too for not wanting Lenny to die. Nick had learned some of Lenny's tricks, but Lenny was the sorcerer, Nick the apprentice.

He spotted Vicky Lansdale on her knees, a tall man standing behind her, the sound suppressor of an MP7 pressed to the back of her head. He couldn't see the others. It was evident to Nick that this man, whatever he was, operative or mercenary, was unafraid of standing out in the open this way. He was risking death because he had collateral that both Nick and Petrovic valued. Nick decided he could approach straight on. He understood that no matter what either this man or Petrovic might promise, they both meant to leave Ruffle Bar without witnesses to their crimes. For the time being, Nick would play his part.

He approached Vicky Lansdale and her captor with his fingers intertwined above the bracing for his night-vision goggles.

"Come ahead," the man said. This was definitely the man from South Fourth Street. "Very sensible of you, Detective Ryan. Drop your weapons behind you. All of them. Goggles too. Afterwards, you will please put your hands back on your head."

"I liked you better in your balaclava."

"I would have preferred never to see you again, Detective. I am sure you feel much the same."

"Nick . . ." Vicky said as she had before. No other words came out of her mouth. Her beautiful face blank, she was far beyond frightened. He had seen this expression before.

Nick nodded at her. "Can I?"

"Nothing foolish, Ryan. But yes."

He did as the man asked, tossing his M4, Glock, and combat knife behind him. Then, replacing his hands on his head, Nick knelt in front of her. "Vicky! Vicky! I need you to snap out of this. He doesn't want to hurt you. He doesn't even want to hurt Jonathan. He just needs your husband to tell him what he wants to know."

Some life returned to Victoria Lansdale's ashen face. There it was again: hope, cruel hope.

Nick dared to put his hand on Vicky's arm and pulled her upright. Her captor didn't object.

"She knows all about her husband," said the man in his cultured Serbian-accented English.

"Nick . . ." Vicky swallowed hard, her face going from scared to angry. "He threatened to kill me if Jonathan wouldn't tell them what he wanted to know."

"He didn't tell him, did he?"

The Serb put his gloved hand under Vicky Lansdale's chin. "No, he did not. He would have had me destroy such beauty. I'm afraid Mr. Lansdale will do whatever it takes, sacrifice whomever, to preserve his own life."

Not wanting to upset Vicky any more than she already was, Nick changed subjects. "What do I call you? If we're going to negotiate, I need a name."

"Call me Ishmael." The man laughed at his own joke.

"Nothing like a well-read assassin."

"No need for that, Detective. We are all looking out for our own best interests."

"Where are the others? Which one did you shoot?"

"None of them. Ask the woman. It was simply a way to move things along. We don't have many more hours of darkness, and this needs to come to a resolution."

Nick asked, "Vicky, is he telling the truth?"

She stared into Nick's eyes, shaking her head. "No—I mean, yes. He just fired into the air."

Ishmael said, "And, Ryan, I said *all* your weapons. I recall there was a hawkbill knife you used to cut my man's Achilles tendon. Now, please."

Nick removed the knife from under his belt and tossed it behind him. He turned back to Ishmael. "I had to try."

"I would have been disappointed had you not. Now, if you and Mrs. Lansdale will step this way. Mrs. Lansdale, please lead Nick in the proper direction."

When the three of them got to the side of the island that faced Canarsie, Nick understood why Ishmael could afford to be so confident in his behavior. From left to right, Mack, Jonathan Lansdale, and Lenny sat on their haunches. On either side of them stood two MP7-armed men in matte-black body armor and camouflage face paint.

Lenny looked frightened. Mack looked resigned. Only Jonathan Lansdale, smug as ever, seemed unperturbed. He knew he was the one with leverage. Nick knew all about that. These men wanted the money and they needed him to get it.

Nick nodded. "Your A team."

"Very good, Ryan." Ishmael let go of his weapon, letting it dangle from its strap, and clapped. "You remember our encounter in Brooklyn. Always have a secondary plan. These two launched their craft not from a boat, but from the edge of the Canarsie Pier." He pointed across the water at the Rockaway Parkway exit on the Belt Parkway, and the Canarsie Pier. "It is a pity that you care about these three, Mrs. Lansdale and your two friends, while Petrovic and I care only about Mr. Lansdale. Petrovic wants him dead. I want his money. Now, everyone, please lie face down for your own protection. You too, Ryan, next to your friends. We don't want any of you caught in the crossfire. Petrovic will no doubt come soon for Mr. Lansdale, and the shooting will begin. As I say, the only one Petrovic cares about is Mr. Lansdale, whom he intends to murder quite slowly and painfully. If I had the money, I would hand him over to Petrovic. I might even watch."

Lenny, Victoria, and Lansdale did as they were told. Lansdale knew he was safe, regardless. Nick and Mack understood that once they lay face down on the cold, damp soil, they would be executed. It was a fact of war: prisoners and hostages were usually more trouble than they were worth.

"What kinda shite is this, son?" Mack stalled. "No last cigarette? No blindfold?"

Ishmael's good humor seemed to seep through his boots into the moist sand. Vicky, now aware that she was about to be murdered, lost it. Screaming, cursing, she clawed her husband's face, pulled his hair.

Ishmael kicked her hard in the ribs, raised his MP7. "Enough."

Nick launched himself into Ishmael. They went down hard. The man closest to Mack turned his weapon on Nick. Before he could fire, his right hand exploded. Black fabric, bone fragments, skin, and blood landed on Nick and Ishmael. The wounded man howled. His pain was quenched as a second shot ripped his neck apart, spraying blood in the air as he spun a perfect 360 on his way to earth. Ishmael's other man emptied his clip into the night. There was a moan, Petrovic crying out, "*Sranje!*"

Ishmael pushed Nick off him, scrambling into a prone shooting position. "Good, you hit him." Then he spoke Serbian to his man.

"*Ne, ne.*"

Nick supposed Ishmael asked if his man could see Petrovic. *Ne* sounded enough like no, leading Nick to guess that he couldn't see the man he had wounded. Night-vision goggles were science, not magic. They didn't allow you to see *through* things. Nick wondered whether Petrovic was wounded or playing possum. He'd know soon enough. Ishmael's man dropped the spent clip out of his weapon. Just as he locked a fresh magazine in place, a bullet hit him in the left thigh. A second or two later, another round hit him square in his face.

"Then there was one," Nick whispered to Ishmael. "Kill us, and it's you versus him. Wounded or not, I'll bet on blood over money any day of the week."

"Why choose to help me over him?"

"Did *you* kill my uncle Tony and his wife? No. That was Petrovic. I've got blood in this game too. You want Lansdale's money. Take him. Take it. I don't give a shit. I just want my friends and the wife to come out of this alive."

"Okay."

Nick crawled over to the others. "Lenny and Vicky, stay low. Go to the shoreline and turn left toward the lights of the bridge. You'll find a small inflated raft there with oars. Row towards the bridge. There's a fishing boat anchored offshore, the *Merry Mermaid Three*. They'll take you aboard." Nick grabbed one of the dead men's MP7, handed it to Lenny. "Just in case."

Vicky hesitated. "We can't leave—"

"Mack and I will be fine, and your husband's the safest one here. He still has what both men want. Go!"

Nick watched them disappear behind a dune, listened for gunfire. Hearing none, he turned to Mack. "Grab the other MP and watch the left flank. Take Lansdale with you. Don't fire unless you have to. Let's see how this plays out."

"Are you mad, boyo? Why not let these bastards resolve this for their own selves?"

"You want out, go. I understand. I've got to see this through."

"Ah, fuck it, Ryan. Between working the sticks and risking me life for things I've not a bit of skin in, I'll choose the latter."

Mack turned to Jonathan Lansdale. "Come on. Apparently, I've got to keep you safe." He pushed Lansdale ahead of him. He snatched the remaining submachine gun, took the dead man's night-vision equipment too. They disappeared behind scrubby bushes.

Ishmael removed his .40-caliber Smith & Wesson sidearm from its holster and tossed it to Nick. Nick racked the slide to make sure it was loaded. It was.

"What was Petrovic armed with, Ryan? Those rounds that hit my men were very accurate. How do you think he will approach?"

Nick laughed, pointed the handgun at Ishmael. "Drop your weapon. Do it now. I think you know I would be able to end you before you could blink."

Ishmael slowly removed his left hand from the thick metal of the sound suppressor. He kept his hand near the trigger and quickly turned it in Nick's direction. Nick squeezed the S&W's trigger. The round kicked up dirt into Ishmael's face.

Nick said, "The next thing to hit your face won't be dirt."

Ishmael dropped the MP7, pushed it toward Nick with his foot.

"Petrovic, come on. This is over."

"No, Ryan. Not yet."

There, standing ten feet in front of them with the M4 in one hand, a knife to Lenny Feld's throat, stood Franjo Petrovic. He smiled at Nick, then fired.

FIFTY-FOUR

Ishmael was a bloody mess—a dead one.

"Ryan, tell the Irishman and Lansdale to come out."

Nick did as Petrovic demanded. "Mack, toss your weapon and come out with Lansdale."

"I've got a shot, Ryan," Mack said. "Let me take him."

Petrovic laughed, sticking the tip of the blade into Lenny's throat so that a stream of blood leaked down his neck. "If you had a shot, Irishman, you would have taken it. Now, come out of there or I will paralyze this man and you can watch him struggle to breathe his last breaths."

Mack stood up about twenty yards to Petrovic's right.

"Remove the magazine and throw it away. Then toss the weapon to me."

Mack flung the magazine behind him, then threw the MP7 at Petrovic's feet. Lansdale bolted. With Ishmael dead, his leverage was gone. Mack caught him before he got very far.

"No, please, he's going to kill me," Lansdale pleaded with Mack. "I have money, lots of money. Get me out of here and—"

Mack slapped Lansdale loud enough that Petrovic winced hearing it. "Be a man, arsehole. Take comfort in that ya won't be dying alone. He means to kill us all."

Mack had Lansdale by the collar of his coat. For his part, Lansdale kicked and clawed and kept begging as he was dragged. Mack let go of Lansdale, went and stood next to Nick.

"Here, go with your friends," Petrovic said, moving the knife away from Lenny's throat, nudging him forward.

Lenny, his breathing loud and labored, fell to his knees. Mack moved to help him. Nick thrust out his arm to stop him. Mack seemed to understand. Lenny needed to do for himself even if he was going to be killed. Maybe especially because of that. Lenny pushed himself to his feet. He no longer looked frightened.

Nick asked, "Where's Mrs. Lansdale?"

Petrovic didn't answer. He kicked Lansdale in the jaw, sending him sprawling. He spat on him. "This man, a stranger—he asks about your wife. You piece of shit. Do *you* ask after your wife? No. You care only for yourself."

Nick asked again, "Where's—"

"She should be near the fishing boat by now."

"Why let her go?"

"As a gesture to you, Ryan, for Angelo's wife."

"Thank you."

"*Molim.*"

"Can I ask you one last thing before—"

"Ask."

"*The Swede.* Why do they call you that?"

Petrovic smiled. "*This* is what you ask now?"

"Does it matter what I would ask?"

Before Petrovic could answer, Jonathan Lansdale scrambled to his feet and ran. Petrovic turned, shot him in the back of the right knee. Lansdale screamed and kept screaming. Petrovic said, "Don't worry, Lansdale, your encounter with pain has only just begun." Petrovic returned his attention to the others. "He is worse than the men who killed my family. Those men believed they were fighting for something. This Lansdale—he protected them. For what? For money. Now, Ryan, you and your friends will please turn around."

"Not until you tell me why they call you the Swede."

Petrovic shrugged. "In the next life, we will discuss it."

Nick and Mack turned to face away from Petrovic. Lenny did not. He said, "I want to see the face of the man that kills me. I need to know."

Petrovic raised his M4. The night got very quiet. Quiet never lasts.

The bullet shattered Petrovic's right femur, blowing out his femoral artery. The impact bent him backward. As he fell to the ground, he squeezed the trigger of his rifle. The rounds were just more impotent shooting stars sent into the night sky.

Unlike Lansdale, Petrovic did not scream. He stared up at Nick, his expression quizzical.

Nick pressed both hands down hard on the exit wound. Petrovic furiously shook his head no. He raised his left index finger and waggled it for Nick to come near. Nick put his ear close to the dying man's lips.

Mack and Lenny were working on Lansdale, binding a tourniquet above his knee.

By the time Santo Contreras reached them, Petrovic had bled out.

Nick looked up and back at the sniper, who was dressed in a shaggy green-and-brown suit that blended perfectly with the Ruffle Bar vegetation. He held a Barrett MRAD, muzzle down, by his side. "Christ, Santo, you look ridiculous in that outfit."

"Fuck you, Ryan. No one noticed me, did they?"

"Not until you shot the shit out of them."

"Not even then." Santo shook his head at the carnage. "Man, Ryan, how you gonna clean up a mess like this?"

"You let me worry about that," Nick said, the sound of thwapping helicopter blades in the distance. "Get out of here. Your money's in the bank. Leave the rifle."

"Too bad. This thing's a beauty. How'd you even get hold of one?"

Nick ignored the question. "So long, Santo."

"Adios."

Mack came over to Nick as Contreras disappeared. "Should I ask?"

"No. How's Lansdale?"

"Alive. At least the smug prick is in a shiteload a pain."

"I'll weep for him some other time."

"Nick, I saw Petrovic whisper something to you there at the end. What was it?"

"'Volvos and Saabs.' He whispered, 'Volvos and Saabs.'"

Mack walked away shaking his head as the spotlight from the helicopter lit up the tiny island covered in the casualties of a war ended two decades past.

EPILOGUE

On a Thursday night in mid-December, Nick had a date to meet Ace for dinner at Hometown Bar-b-que in Red Hook. As it was wont to do at this time of year, darkness had taken the day by the throat and squeezed the light and warmth out of it. It wasn't the dark, but the heavily falling snow that would let them have the restaurant to themselves. Everything for a square block, even the snowflakes, smelled like smoke, of beef and pork drippings. Before he walked inside, Nick stopped, listened. It seemed quiet. Snowfall in the city did that. *No*, he thought, hearing the clink of chains on bus tires against the cracked pavement, the mournful wail of a boat horn from the harbor. *Snow only muffles things. It can fool you.* What he knew was that you could be fooled only if you let yourself be fooled.

Shana, it appeared, was desperate to be fooled. Only a few weeks after Shea Flannery had come close to killing her, she showed up at Nick's building. She pressed the buzzer on and off for fifteen minutes.

"I know you're there, Nick. Please, can we talk?"

He watched her on the security screen as she became increasingly agitated. By the time she walked away, she had been screaming into the microphone, crying in front of the camera. He let her go, never raising his finger anywhere near the button to let her in. He could never let her in again. The line had been drawn, not in sand but in blood. Wind and water could easily erase lines in sand. Blood wasn't so easily dispatched. Shea Flannery and that night on Ruffle Bar had dissolved any illusions Nick might have had about there being a way for Shana, Becky, and him to live happily ever after.

It was something Franjo Petrovic had done and said that cemented it for him.

As a gesture to you, for Angelo's wife.

He had let Victoria Lansdale leave the island and thought that such a gesture somehow balanced out killing a woman whose only crime that day was going to see why her husband hadn't come upstairs for dinner. The gesture didn't square shit, didn't make a bit of difference to Rosa Angelo. Dead was dead was dead.

There had been a lot of that going around. The body count since the day he had gone to the used-tire shop in the Bronx was like something out of the Tet Offensive. *The Angelos, the security guard at Fresh Kills, Carmine Gabrelli, Sullivan, Breen, Petrovic, Carver, Willoughby, the other retired Secret Service agents, Ishmael and his men . . .* On the police boat going back to the mainland from Ruffle Bar, Nick had noted to Mack that he would have needed an abacus or a calculator to tot them up.

Mack had been resigned as always. Leaning over the rail, the cold wind blowing back his gray-and-ginger ponytail and beard, he said, "You're in it now, boyo. First lesson I learned when I stepped in this shite with the Brits was that this shadowy work is a horse that rides you. The very idea of control is a myth. Events are like a mighty force a man can only understand after the wind has blown the door shut on them."

"Petrovic said almost the same thing to me back on the island."

"He would."

"How's that?"

"Ask anyone from the Falls Road or Shankill, from Israel or the Gaza Strip; ask a Turk or a Kurd. It's all the Jets and the Sharks, Ryan."

"I didn't figure you for musical theater."

"I'm like one of them Mexican piñatas. Open me up and I'm just full of surprises. How do ya suppose all them bodies on the island will be explained away?"

"Not to worry. It will be managed."

The answer to what people on Breezy Point were told about all that gunfire on Ruffle Bar was simple. The NYPD, along with elements of the FBI, had carried out a counterterrorism exercise. So the papers and TV news said. For readers and viewers who lived in the rest of the city, it would be the first and last time they would hear of the little island in Jamaica Bay.

The complex answer to what had happened took months to play out and was unearthed by the kind of digging only Lenny Feld was capable of. It seemed, as Lenny had explained to Nick over a cup of instant coffee, that Ishmael and his men were an unfortunate diplomatic albatross for Serbia. One the American government was apparently willing to exploit in a subtle way.

"Air Serbia's jet fleet is exclusively Airbus," Lenny said, boiling water for a second cup.

"So?"

"So it seems they have suddenly taken an interest in Boeing products."

"Curious."

"Not really, Nick. You have said it yourself. It's always about the money."

Before Nick left that night, Lenny grabbed him by the arm with his good hand and said, "I'm sorry."

"For what?"

"When you came to me after shooting Gabrelli and his brother-in-law, when you killed the man who caused your GTO crash, I questioned who you were and what kind of man you were who could be so calm afterwards."

"Forget it. I have."

"I can't. I saw you in action. I saw the kinds of people you're up against. That, and you saved my life again."

Nick smiled, cocking his head. "Funny you should bring up aircraft."

"What's that got to do with—"

"Let me finish. I knew an airline pilot from when I worked in uniform in Queens. One day I asked him if he ever worried about all those people back there in the cabin. You know what he said to me?"

"No clue."

"He said that pilots were always the first people at the scene of a crash. That he worried about keeping himself alive and if he did that, the passengers would be safe too. Now do you understand?"

"That you were busy saving your own life and that if saving mine, the Irishman's, Lansdale's, and his wife's was a byproduct of that, you were happy to do it."

"For a smart man, you're sometimes slow on the uptake. But that's essentially it."

Nick turned to go.

Lenny called after him.

"Christ, Lenny, what?"

"I'm sorry just the same."

Jonathan Lansdale was a problem. Though he had once been a valuable figure in the intelligence community, he had used his position to pilfer and transport stolen gold, protect wanted war criminals, and collude with known crime figures. Since the CIA and FBI wanted to debrief Nick, they "invited" him to Langley. He accepted the invite with one stipulation: that he be permitted to view Lansdale's interrogations. They had accepted the offer, too easily for Nick's liking. Before he could witness the proceedings, however, Nick had to sign a security waiver that meant he could be tried for treason if he disclosed any aspect of what he would hear.

Nick already knew the big picture. The details were both fascinating and horrifying. Vlado Markovic was one of Lansdale's assets inside the unofficial militias operating in Serbia and Croatia. After the raid on Petrovic's village and the discovery of the gold, Markovic went to Lansdale, and from there the deal was made. He would supply Zmaj and Vlado with new Serbian passports and false identities. He would get them to Italy and eventually to the USA. Lansdale had identified Jimmy Gabrelli, stationed at Aviano, as easy prey and instructed Markovic to "befriend" him. As Lansdale had anticipated, for the right price, Gabrelli was only too happy to make sure the contraband got to the states and to "do what needed doin'," as Lansdale recounted.

When it came to the fates of Jimmy Gabrelli, Zmaj, and Markovic, Lansdale feigned ignorance.

Although his knee would never heal properly, Lansdale's smugness had made a full recovery. He said, "I've admitted that I supplied the two men with new identities and brought them over, but I cannot account for what Jimmy Gabrelli had in mind for them. As far as I know, it was one of Gabrelli's own associates who murdered him in hopes of getting access to the money. Gabrelli had a rather grandiose sense of himself. I can't imagine that worked in his favor. And frankly, the world is a better place without him, Zmaj, and Markovic."

He wouldn't budge from that position regardless of how, or how often, his interrogator asked. The remainder of the sessions were all rather dry. He gave details about how he had exchanged the gold for properties, businesses, and cash, and how he had grown those funds into vast wealth. And what price would he pay for what he had done? Nick would never know—at least, not directly. He did have a sense that once the bulk of Lansdale's assets were redistributed, there would be a bullet or a hit-and-run accident in the man's future.

They had a single brief exchange in passing during the two days Nick was at Langley.

Nick asked, "Did you care that the gold came from the teeth and jewelry of Holocaust victims or was stolen from the countries the Nazis ravaged?"

"Do you ask who touched your money when the clerk gives you change?"

After that, Nick would have happily volunteered to deliver the bullet or drive the car to end Lansdale's life.

A week after the bloodbath on Ruffle Bar, Vicky Lansdale met Nick at the Black Harp in Williamsburg. Before they asked, Mack put two Irish coffees, heavy on the Irish, in front of them. He didn't stick around to listen.

"I left him," Vicky said, sipping the coffee. "I've already filed for divorce."

"It would be fair to say I am unsurprised."

"I can't get one thing out of my head."

"Vicky, you're wondering why Petrovic let you go. Right?"

She choked on the coffee. "How could you know that?"

"A good guess."

"I call bullshit on that, Nick Ryan."

"Survivor's guilt. Why did you live while so many others on the island died? You must've thought Lenny and the rest of us were as good as dead when Petrovic got to you."

She hung her head, tears dripping into her coffee. "I rowed away as fast as I could without looking back."

"Your parents raised a smart woman." Nick cupped Vicky's chin in his hand. "You couldn't have done anything to help, and your presence would only have complicated things. I know about survivor's guilt. Anyone who's been in battle does. Why the guy next to me and not me? If it still bothers you, go see someone."

"Let's finish these and go back to your—"

Nick put his finger across her lips, shook his head. "No, not tonight. Not while you're in the middle of all this." He changed subjects. "If they take your husband's assets, what will you do?"

"I still have money of my own from when I was working. I'm a poor Irish girl from Sheepshead Bay, raised to do for herself. You're Irish, Nick. You know. For us, it's not that there might be rainy days ahead. It's a matter of when the rain will come and how long it will last."

Nick raised his cup of coffee and clinked it to Vicky's. "Sláinte."

Two days after Ruffle Bar, Nick finally sat down at his computer and opened the email from Tuva. He wrote down the numbers and shook his head at the cost. She hadn't lied. Killing Flannery would certainly be more cost effective than a rendering. The ghost email disappeared as he knew it would.

Walking into the living room, Nick flipped on the flat-screen to catch up with what was going on. He'd slept through most of yesterday. During the parts he hadn't slept through, he made sure to avoid any electronic devices. For the past year, the world had been too much with him. For twenty-four hours, he didn't want any part of it, nor for it to have any of him.

He was barely paying attention as he reached for the Joe phone. Then came this:

Again, our top story, laborers' union head Shea Flannery was gunned down in a hail of bullets outside a downtown after-hours club . . .

Nick didn't need to hear the details. They would be lies regardless of what they were said to be.

He called Joe.

"Good morning, Nick."

"For you, I imagine it is. Breathing a little more easily today, Bill."

"I've always detested that name, but yes, much easier. I much prefer Joe. I take it you've heard the news about poor Shea Flannery."

"How'd you manage it?"

"I called some of the other people named on those sheets of paper Flannery gave to you. As you might suspect, they were even less anxious to be exposed as frauds and cheats than I. All I had to do after that was sit back and wait."

"Maybe you should have my job."

"I think not. I could never have gotten off Ruffle Bar alive. Speaking of that, take some time off. You've more than earned it. By the way, that list of names you demanded—it won't be coming. Anything you imagined you could hold over my head died with Flannery."

Nick still had some cards to play with Joe, but now wasn't the time to use them. "Back to square one, then."

"That was too easy, Nick. What's going on?"

He ignored the question. "So, what's the deal with Vlado Markovic? How will you spin it?"

"To be decided and, thankfully, not by me. Enjoy your time off."

"Enjoy thinking about why I gave in so easily."

He clicked off.

After Nick returned from Langley, he and Annalise took a motorcycle trip down to Hilton Head Island. They went on a dolphin boat, rode into Savannah, and walked the beach every morning. But they spent most of the time in bed in their rented condo. They talked about the Angelo case only once, the first night.

"Case closed," Annalise said. "Petrovic committed suicide in his rented Volvo in the long-term lot at JFK. He had on him the knife he used on Tony Angelo. He had a .25 on him too. Ballistics show it was the gun he used on Tony and Rosa."

Nick acted surprised and pleased. She wasn't buying it.

"I don't know about you, Nick. What's up with the happy act?"

Nick kissed her hard, sliding his tongue into her open mouth. "Up to you, AP. We can talk or we can—"

She answered by climbing on top of him.

———

Three weeks from the last day he had spoken to Joe, Nick, antsy from not being in the shit, called his handler.

"Good morning, Nick. Why don't we meet?"

"Tire shop."

"No. This evening at the Old Homestead. I've reserved a private room for eight o'clock."

The Old Homestead was an Old-World steak restaurant not very far from L'Autobus, the place where the whole bloody mess had begun. A slender blond woman in a tight black dress and stilettos walked Nick up two flights of stairs.

"The entire third floor is reserved for you and your guest. Alfredo will be your waiter and Paul will assist. Enjoy."

His *guest*? That was odd. Despite Joe's recent claims to the contrary, he had always enjoyed throwing his status and ability to arrange for impossible meetings in Nick's face. It was Joe's way of reminding Nick that, as good as he might be at his job, the real power lay elsewhere. The minute he stepped away from the stairs, his confusion vanished.

United States Senator Renata Maduro sat at a large table, sipping a martini. She stood, put the drink down, shook Nick's hand. New York's junior senator was a vision. She kept her black hair cut short on one side and at an angle that matched the line of her jaw on the other. She wore a spaghetti-strapped black dress much like the one worn by the hostess, though it cost several hundred dollars more and showed off all the gym work she had put in. She wore black Louboutin heels, each held to her ankles with six small straps. She was more handsome than beautiful, but incredibly attractive. She smelled like a walk in a dangerous garden.

"Detective Ryan."

"Senator."

"Alfredo, please get Nick a glass of the bourbon I brought with me."

Nick turned to see a stout man dressed in a full white apron. He nodded and disappeared. They sat and waited. A younger man appeared, delivered Nick's drink.

"To success," she said, lifting her glass.

Nick lifted his and drank. "Pappy's."

"Yes, a small token of thanks. After we're done for the evening, I'll have it delivered to your apartment."

"Thanks?"

"By now you know I know about you."

"I figured."

"I was the one who asked your . . . superiors to have you look into Vlado Markovic's murder. I thought it would be helpful to get some face time on the next anniversary of that awful day. I have no love for the senior senator from our state, but he does know how to keep his face in front of the cameras and in the press. Oh, and yes, I've already ordered for us. I think you'll approve."

He drank and listened. "No doubt."

"I'm afraid that the truth of his death will have to remain buried with him. The lie that has been told for the past two decades will live on. I wanted to tell you that in person because I know the truth came at a severe cost."

"A gesture."

"I thought it the right thing to do."

"These days in particular, I'm not fond of gestures, Senator."

"Hear me out; then if you feel you have to go, go."

"I'm listening."

"There will be hearings on how we conducted our intelligence operations in the nineties in Europe so that we don't repeat those mistakes again. Some good will come out of this even if no heads will roll. Most of those involved are retired or dead."

"Senator," Nick said, finishing his drink, "you can have all the hearings you want, but as long as people are greedy and there are long-standing conflicts, those mistakes will happen again. It's always about money and it's all the Jets and the Sharks."

Alfredo placed wedge salads down in front of them.

Maduro seemed not to hear Nick's comment. "Let's eat."

After the wine, the steak, another bourbon, and a martini, the senator said she had to go. Nick stood, thanked her.

She leaned in close to him. "I still have a spot for you on my staff if you want it."

"I'll pass."

"I knew you would. Remember our conversation at Ergo Sum last year. Something you said to me stuck. Alas, you don't like gestures, but you've only yourself to blame for the one awaiting you. Good night."

She turned and left without another word.

On the ride home, Nick pondered what she could have meant. He found the answer when he went to park his rental. In his spot, in front of the Norton, was a new slate-gray Porsche 718 Cayman. A white envelope rested against the windshield. Inside was a computer-generated note.

Nick, I attempted to replace your GTO, but recalled you said you preferred Porsches to thank-yous. This is both. The clear title in your name is in the glovebox, as is the registration and insurance. Enjoy it and remember, there is always a place for you in my world.

The note was unsigned, but Maduro's name might just as well have been written across the car in red paint. Shana had gone through a stage where she tried to bend his will to hers with outrageous gifts. He put a stop to that soon enough. This was different. The car, the Pappy's, and the steak dinner he would accept. The offer, no, not unless he needed cover. Besides, he couldn't stomach spending all his time in that damned Malibu, even if its features had saved his life. The Porsche suited him.

———

Ace never did show at Hometown that night in mid-December. Nick knew it wasn't about the snow but about the job. Ace was done and didn't want to end it with something he could point to, like a gold watch or a goodbye dinner. A boxer like Ace didn't want to look back at that last time he got kayoed by a punch he saw coming but was helpless to defend against. That was okay with Nick. There was little in the world that truly belonged to anyone. He supposed the way a man chose to leave the stage when he was done was one of those few things. So Nick ate some brisket, a few sticky Korean ribs, and a side of beans, drank two beers, and drove home in his slate-gray Cayman.

Stepping out of the car, his radar popped on. Maybe it was the muffling effect of the snow or the beers, but it came on too late. A black Lincoln Navigator screeched to a stop in front of his Porsche and a man's voice came out of the shadows.

"Please come with us, Detective Ryan."

"Is that a request or a demand?"

The echoing sound of more than one slide racking answered the question. A pair of experienced hands removed Nick's off-duty piece and his knife. The same pair of hands held an eye mask out to Nick.

The shadow voice said, "Please put that on, Detective Ryan. No peeking."

Nick did so.

Someone grabbed him by the elbow, but Nick refused to move. "One thing," he said to the man at his elbow. "What time is it?"

"Why?"

"Humor me."

"A few minutes to twelve."

Nick laughed. It was a sad laugh.

"Something funny, Detective?"

"I'm blind to midnight."

"That supposed to mean something?"

"Not to you."

"Okay, let's go."

Someone helped Nick into the back seat. Off he went, blind to midnight and what lay ahead.

ACKNOWLEDGMENTS

I would like to thank my agent, Shane Salerno, and Ryan Coleman at the Story Factory. I am grateful to my editor, Michael Carr, for his keen eye and sage guidance. Much appreciation for the folks at Blackstone Publishing.

But none of this would be worth it or have any meaning without my family. It was Rosanne, Kaitlin, and Dylan who made the sacrifices that allowed me to pursue my dreams. I hope they know they have my eternal love and gratitude.